Gama Generation

Josephine Ronk

First published by Josephine Ronk 2022

Cover design by: Latte Goldstein

ISBN 978-1-7397140-0-0

CONTENTS

The Beginning

Fred Demson

From my Manhattan window, I can see the Statue of Liberty. It is so liberating. Who would have thought I would make it out of the slum and build Overland Investments into a Fortune 500 company and the number one company in the world?

I like what I see in the mirror. At slightly over 6ft in height, I am no longer the skinny boy people used to laugh at, thanks to regular workouts in the gym. Being the last born in a large family of eight, my father worked in a factory, and my mum was a housewife; it was a struggle to eat three decent meals at home. I was constantly bullied in school for my small stature and poor background.

I was intelligent, so I secured a scholarship to one of the best high schools in my area, but I stood out as I was not like the other children. Most came from wealthy homes with the latest cars, and I could barely afford anything; I would walk the hour-long journey from home to school and back every day.

Every time I entered the bedroom that I shared with my three brothers, I told myself I needed to work harder to get out of that rathole and make something of my life. I worked hard. I took all the insults and beatings. I got into Harvard University to study finance on a full scholarship.

Now I am sitting on top of the world. I met my wife, Jane, when I was working at my last job before setting up my own company. She comes from old money; I needed the Brown's name behind me before I could persuade any bank to invest in my business.

I take care of my family in Connecticut, but I rarely see them. I am a busy man, I have many things requiring my attention. In navigating this world, to achieve my aim, I need to be meticulous, have the right image and keep a low profile.

My company is one of the few rated as a trillion-dollar company globally. I have invested billions in Gama Labs and, today, Gamaplugs will be launched after years of disappointment and unexpected problems. This will make my company the most powerful and influential company globally and all my plans will come to fruition.

It has taken eight years of working tirelessly, faced with many failed trials, errors, and disappointments, to get to this stage. It seemed like a crazy idea to buy Gama Labs and invest billions in research on neural sensors when I have already established Overland Investments that is known and respected worldwide.

But I am very ambitious, always looking for ways to improve the world and, finally, our work has paid off; this new artificial intelligence will revolutionise the world and change our way of life more than ever before. We are now in the final stages; it took two years for my company to get the final approval from various government boards worldwide.

The technology is called Gamaplug N24 postnanometer. It is the fastest processor and the smallest and the quickest nanochip ever produced. It is the most advanced AI ever developed. It allows your neural sensory to connect with your brain signals and read your mind. Action will be taken based on your thoughts. It is high quality and super-fast so the response time is instant.

This allowed us to make Gamaplug the smallest, lightest earbuds ever produced. Not only is it beautiful and sophisticated; when worn, it is not immediately visible because of how tiny it is. It is designed for daily use, it is safe and it will not cause any discomfort. People will not know they are wearing it.

It has more processing power than other products and works faster with low energy consumption, and can last forty-eight hours without charging. We introduced fibre 4.0, the fastest communication between Gamaplug and any technology, so any information transmitted will not be lost.

Gamaplug comes in different colours, and customers are able to customise the colour they want. We have made provision for our more affluent customers; they can buy 100% gold, or gold with diamonds, versions. This took an extra year of testing to ensure it didn't add any additional weight to the earbuds.

Gamaplug allows you to communicate with any technology from your mobile phone, television, car, or microwave; the list is endless. We have signed agreements with many technology manufacturers, and the software is pre-installed into their products. Now you can communicate with your car to start the engine before entering your vehicle. The microwave heats up or cooks the meal you placed in it before you even reach home. Your mobile phone can perform any action as instructed; all without you even speaking. In order for Gamaplug to understand how to take action, you must start by saying 'Gama,' and it automatically recognises it is an instruction. Our motto is 'Think it and Make it'.

My greatest desire is to unify the world and make things a little easier by taking control of people's lives. The world we live in is demanding; getting up daily for our jobs and coming home exhausted. We have busy lifestyles.

Now we can live in a more secure environment where criminal minds are read, and their thoughts flagged to the authorities before they take action.

Last month, I had a final meeting with the world leaders, doing live product demonstrations. Gamaplugs were sent to them before the national presentation, which all media houses will cover in two weeks.

The world is excited, and everyone wants to be the first to buy this product; our marketing department has done a fantastic job feeding the public just a snippet of information about what Gamaplug can do. Pre-orders have gone through the roof, and we haven't even launched yet. One thing is for certain; life, across the globe, will never be the same.

My intercom buzzes. 'Mr Demsen, your 10 o'clock appointment is here.'

'Send them in,' I say. 'It's time to conquer the world.'

Chapter One: London

Jude

I am driving my car when I hear a loud booming sound; could it be an explosion? I look around as my car vibrates in the aftermath. What's happening? Suddenly, the vehicle in front of me stops, and I swerve to avoid hitting him, but a car slams into mine from behind. Now, there is white smoke everywhere!

'Help! Help!' I can hear screaming; my head is pounding.

I think I must have blacked out; and I open my eyes slowly; where am I? I try to remember, am I still inside my car? I try to open the door, but it won't budge. I push the door repeatedly, slamming against it with my shoulder, using all my strength, to force it open. Finally, the door opens, and I am free and running, not looking back to see the damage.

I can hear sirens, and people are running, so I follow. I didn't know where I am going. I can see buildings burning, and I start to cough. Smoke! I need to breathe; what is going on? Right now, I need to focus on surviving.

The centre of London is in chaos; people are crying, some are lying on the ground and I'm not even sure whether they are alive. Cars are piled on top of each other; I have never seen this kind of chaos in London.

I am relieved to have got out unscathed. I don't know the state my car is in, but that's the least of my problems. People are stuck in their vehicles, screaming, and some are unconscious. I can't see any ambulances, but firefighters are trying to find a way to put out the fire.

I never thought this could happen. I was on my way to the restaurant when we were told we needed to evacuate the area by a man wearing a mask...

My eyes are burning. I am coughing uncontrollably. Instinct kicks in and I know that I need to get out of here; I can smell gas! *Jesus!* I start running as fast as I am able in my disorientated state. I need to escape from this disaster.

When I finally stop to catch my breath, the air has cleared a little. I can see that the road I am standing on has split in two. Is the world coming to an end?

My phone starts ringing; but my hands are shaking. Why is my Gamaplug not connecting to my phone? I put my index finger in my right ear; it must have dropped out. I'm getting woozy. I start tapping my body. Oh! My phone is in my trouser pocket. I have to try several times before I can finally pick up the ringing mobile. The call is from my restaurant manager, George. 'I just saw the news, Jude. Are you OK?' I know you drive through Chelsea to get to the restaurant.'

'I am fine,' I reply, uncertainly. 'What's happening?'

'They are saying it's a gas explosion; but the information is quite sketchy; the investigation is still ongoing; It's all over the news. Where are you?'

'I'm not quite sure. The whole place is in disarray. I need to get away from here, but the damage is everywhere. I'll have to call you back!'

With shaking hands, I manage to replace my mobile in the pocket of my trousers. My head is pounding and I feel disorientated. I hold my head, groggily, with both hands. I'm getting dizzy. A hand reaches out to try and steady me.

'Sir! Sir! Are you OK? There is blood all over your face, looks like you have a nasty cut. I need to take you to a paramedic to get checked out,' the stranger says.

I touch my face; there is blood on my hands. When did this happen? I must have hit my head, but where? It mostly likely happened during the collision, I must have bumped my head; I didn't even realise. My body is still in shock.

'Thank you,' I say to the stranger.

'You look weak, so I'll have to assist you until we get to the paramedic; they need to have a look at your head as soon as possible.' They are using some of the firetrucks as ambulances.

We walk slowly toward the paramedic. I still can't make sense of what is happening. Today, I had an important meeting to sign the agreement for my cookbook with JPH publishing company. Negotiations have been in the works for over eight months and, today, I was supposed to sign on the dotted line. Then this happened.

I've worked tirelessly to escape the nightmare that was my childhood to achieve this level of success. I am one of the most successful chefs in the country; with sponsorships and television shows. I did all this to make sure that the threat posed by my father can no longer haunt me.

'I feel faint,' I tell the paramedic, when we finally reach her, 'and my head is pounding.'

'You need to sit down,' she says, kindly, helping me onto a chair. 'You have lost a lot of blood; you need to be transported to the hospital, but all the roads are blocked. I will get a doctor to you as soon as I can, and maybe they can stitch you up. You need to sit down,' she repeats. 'Do not move.' I close my eyes.

I will not die today! I think to myself. I still have a lot to achieve. My mother and I suffered too much at the hands of my father. I don't want him laughing at us now, even in death. I just need to rest a little; I am so tired. I close my eyes...

I wake up in hospital with a needle in my vein connected to a tube; it appears to lead to a bag of blood. *How did I get here?* I just closed my eyes for a minute. I look around; the hospital is packed with people, victims of the gas explosion.

A male doctor walks up to me. 'I see you're awake then; how do you feel?' he asks.

'What happened to me?'

'You lost a lot of blood. Looks like you hit your head on a sharp object. We were able to stitch it up. Fortunately, you only had a deep cut and no other damage. You will be discharged soon once the blood transfusion is complete.'

'Thank you very much, doctor.'

I watch the bald doctor walk away; grateful for my life. I'm sure many people have lost theirs today. The news later reports that fifty people died and hundreds were injured, but the investigation is still ongoing as to what caused the gas explosion.

Chapter Two: New York

Martin

He holds a gun to her head. 'She needs to die!' he shouts.

I hold up my hand as my partner and two other police officers call for urgent backup, their guns pointed at the man. We are stretched beyond reason; the governor of New York has declared a state of emergency because the temperature has dropped to -20^C. It's so cold, you would think the crime rate would drop, but I think people's brains have frozen along with the temperature.

'You need to drop the gun, sir!'

'No! No!' he shouts, shaking violently. My greatest fear is that he might accidentally pull the trigger. I look behind me at the rest of the officers; and indicate to them to lower their weapons. I don't want anyone to die today.

'Please, sir, why must she die?'

'She ate the last food in the fridge, the stupid bitch! I must teach her not to be greedy.'

'Sir! I know all the shops are closed because of the extreme cold, but a few centres are open to help feed families and provide shelter for those that cannot take care of themselves during this time. You need to put the gun down!' I say, firmly.

The lady keeps screaming,' Help me! He's crazy.'

The situation is getting out of hand, and I need to calm everyone down.

'I can't. You're going to arrest me. We promised each other we would not eat the remaining pasta until the next day. She was not supposed to touch it but she woke up in the night and ate everything. Don't you think she deserves to die?'

'Nobody needs to lose their life today because of food; we will provide for you.' I understand what is going on; people are getting desperate, and the state is at a standstill.

'Please, sir, just put the gun down!'

A tear rolls down his face. 'I am just hungry; I haven't eaten in days!'

'I understand. Put down the gun and we'll get you some food.'

I watch as he struggles with himself, and, finally, he drops the gun. I dash towards him and pull the woman away from him, handing her over to my partner, Bobby.

The situation is a mess. I walk the now handcuffed man out of his home, and I honestly feel sorry for him. We are in a state of desperation; everybody was instructed to stay indoors a week ago. Cars are drowned in snow, homes are without electricity, and people are dying in their own homes. Calls to 911 are at an all-time high, people are losing their minds, homes are being raided, supermarkets looted, and the city is in crisis. We are only able to move around because my precinct has designated snowploughs. I have not been home in a week; I have not seen my wife and two daughters. I speak to them all the time, but I am worried about not being with them at this critical time.

I hand the offender over to one of the backup officers as a call comes through on my Gamaplug. 'Captain!'

'I need you to get to the mayor's house now!'

'OK, sir!' I respond, sighing heavily.

'Martin, the mayor has personally requested to see you – alone. Tell Bobby I want a full report on this incident on my desk this afternoon.' The phone disconnects abruptly.

I quickly tell Bobby about the strange call. 'Why do you need to go to the mayor's house?' he asks.

'I don't know, but I have to go alone. The captain wants you back at the station.'

Bobby nods. 'Be careful!' he shouts as he walks away.

This is strange; I have never met the mayor; why would he ask for me? I get into the snowplough and ask the driver to take me to the mayor's home. Driving is suicidal; even with some of the cleared roads, they are slippery, and the snow is coming down with a vengeance. Many roads are blocked because of car accidents, and nobody knows when the streets will be cleared. God! Sometimes I hate this thankless job.

I finally arrive at the mayor's house. I am whisked inside, and the door is immediately closed behind me by one of his workers. I am shown into the luxurious living room. *What the hell is going on?* I ask myself.

Standing in front of me is the mayor, Matthew Cleborne. I can see his wife, Stella, crying in the corner of the room where a group of women are trying to comfort her.

'Good afternoon, sir!' I shake the mayor's hand. 'You asked to see me.'

'Yes, we have a problem; I need this case resolved quickly with the utmost discretion. I requested you, Detective Martin Hills, because I have heard great things about you. You get results because of your dedication to the job, and you can be trusted to be discreet. This morning, I found my fifteen-year-old daughter dead in bed with a short note stating, "I am tired of this life". I know you will think this is an open-and-shut case, but my daughter...' he pauses to control his emotions, 'she would never kill herself. No one has touched anything in the room when she was found. I need you to investigate. I know you have daughters, and you could never imagine this happening to them. I know my daughter did not take her own life. So, I want you to help me find the culprit who dared touch my child.' There was great sadness in his voice, and he looked at me intently.'Please!'

I follow a female worker up the stairs to their daughter's room. This was going to be a long day.

Chapter Three: Lagos

Lola

My heart is beating fast and I am sweating profusely. *Am I going to die today?*

My car is stuck in the middle of the road; I can't move forward or reverse. It's raining heavily; I can't see anything. Are the car wiper blades even working? Everywhere is flooded, and my car is in danger of being swept away by the rain. I have never seen this kind of rain before; it is like heaven itself has opened.

The water is rising fast, and my car refuses to move, along with several other vehicles that are also stuck. If we don't find a way to move away from here in the next thirty minutes or so, at the rate the water is rising, I will drown in my car. What am I going to do? I open my car door and attempt to step out; but water rushes in and I lose my balance. I manage to stand up, and the water almost reaches my waist, and it is still raining heavily.

I need to get to higher ground quickly. God help me! I can't swim. I'm completely soaked, trying to shield my eyes as I struggle to move forward. I can hear screaming, people praying, some wailing. It's already 6.00 pm; it will be dark soon, and I am going to drown in Ademola Adetokunbo Street. All the roads are jammed with cars, and no one is moving because of the flood. I need help; I have to get out of the water before I drown.

'Madam! Madam!' I try to wade through the flood. 'Madam!' I hear again. 'You need to move; the sea level is rising at an alarming rate.' I manage to turn in the direction of the voice, straining my eyes and shielding my face from the rain.

I see a someone pointing. 'Can you reach that man over there; he has a canoe.' People are struggling towards him. 'He will want money,' the stranger says. I am soaked; my crossbody bag is wet through. He will have to accept sodden cash.

'Thank you,' I shout. I try to move, but the water has risen even higher. *I am going to die!* I fall forward but, as I am about to go under, the stranger grabs me. 'Madam, are you OK?'

'Yes,' I reply. 'Thank you.'

'We need to hurry. Hold on to me,' he says as I cling to him for dear life. We wade through the water towards the canoe. People push each other out of the way in desperation.

'Sir! Please take us to safety; we can pay.'

The rain continues to fall heavily. 'I don't think we can make it,' says the man with the canoe. 'Everywhere is flooded and the wind is blowing hard. Look!' The man points as the wind tears the roof off a nearby house.

'Oh my God! The world is ending,' I wail.

The man I am holding on to shouts, 'We cannot waste time talking; we need to go.'

I burst into tears. 'The water will soon cover me, and I can't swim.'

'Sir! I'm begging you. Help us get into the canoe; where it takes us doesn't matter,' says my companion. 'We will pay you any amount; just get us out of here.'

We scramble into the canoe, with no idea where we are going but anywhere is better than this place. Many people attempt to get into the canoe with us, but there is not enough room for everyone.

'Get out of here!' yells my companion. 'The canoe will topple over, and we will all drown. Sir! Move!'

The owner of the boat finds it difficult to manoeuvre the canoe because of the many cars and obstacles in the water. We can hear screaming above the noise of the water. It is now dark, and the stranger brings out his phone and switches on the torch. We see a woman and a small boy standing on top of a nearly submerged jeep, waving and yelling.

When the canoe gets close enough to the jeep, the two men jump out and swim towards the woman and another two to try and secure the canoe. Everywhere is now flooded, it is impossible to walk. When they reach the jeep, they call to the woman to clamber down, so they can help her to the canoe. 'I can't swim,' she shouts.

'We will help you and your son,' one of the men yells back.

They managed to scramble down from the jeep, but it is difficult to help someone who has a phobia of water. The boy starts to struggle, and falls into the floodwater. One of men holds on to the mother while the other dives into the water looking for her son.

The mother is shivering and crying. 'Where is my son?'

Between us, we manage to drag her into the canoe. She looks around desperately. 'Help him!' she screams.

Tell me this is a nightmare. Someone needs to wake me up, I murmur to myself.

Her son is lifted out of the water and placed in the canoe; he is unconscious, but one of the men starts to give him mouth-to-mouth resuscitation.

'Wake up, Chidi,' the distraught mother screams. 'Please, wake up.'

The boy opens his eyes, coughing out water.

'Thank God!' says the mother as she holds her son.

We need to get away from here fast. Nobody speaks. We just want to survive this ordeal. After, what seems like hours, we arrive at a motel. Other buildings beside it seem to be flooded or destroyed, but the motel is still standing, though slightly damaged and flooded to the lower level. We rush into the building and see other people sheltering from the rain. This is going to be a long night.

We sit on the floor. There is no electricity; everything is down. I just need to survive this night; then, maybe I will be able to face things tomorrow. I am utterly exhausted, shivering but grateful to the kind stranger. I turn to him, and say, 'Thank you for saving me, my name is Lola.'

Chapter Four: Kabul

Ahmed

I beckon to my two children. 'Hide under the bed,' I say.

I need to escape Kandahar with my family. Our lives are no longer safe. The militants are raiding and destroying homes and they are known for raping young girls, and forcing young men to join them.

'Aisha!' I yell. My wife is almost paralysed with fear. It is getting dark, so we hurriedly pack what we can carry between us. We have to leave now. They must not find us in this house.

The little food we have, we pack into a bag, and we pour water into flasks. We need little clothing; the most important thing is food and water.

I can see a fire burning in the distance. 'We need to go,' I say, urgently. I beckon to the children to come out from under the bed and we all start running, my wife at my side. We need to put some distance between ourselves and the militants; the Ahedan.

The political unrest has been going on for a long time, and no one is safe; we have little or no time left. We thought the opposition group, the Obedian, could stop these militants, but the Ahedan continue to get stronger and stronger. We were told they were fighting for freedom from the oppression of non-Islamic nations, but our homes are being destroyed, our sources of livelihood forcefully taken away from us, and our daughters raped or forced into marriage. Many people have lost their lives; now the question is, what exactly are we fighting for?

'Hurry!' I say, as I encourage my children to keep moving. 'Don't be afraid,' I tell my wife. I reassure my family we will make it to safety, but the militants are getting closer. They must not see us; we will have to hide in the mountains until it gets dark. Then maybe we can find a way to flee while the militants are resting.

We reach Tör Ghar mountain, and see other families also trying to hide. I hope we are safe here. I look at my exhausted children. 'You need to eat, quickly, and drink a little water,' I say. We will have to ration what little we have, but they need their strength because we still have a long way to go.

The sound of screaming reaches our ears, so we move, silently, and hide further down the mountain, secluded by giant rocks. *Please, Allah, don't let them see us,* I pray. I cannot afford to lose my family. I look at my son, Abdul, and daughter, Laila, who are sixteen and fourteen years of age, respectively. Our whole lives have been turned upside down, my daughter is crying, and my son is struggling to remain strong.

I worked in the government army for many years, back when we still had a nation, but I was forced to retire because my children's lives were not safe. The whole system is corrupt, under the guise of freedom; everyone looks out for themselves. We had the latest ammunition. Where that came from, I don't know; we were told never to ask questions.

Now, I need to find a way to get out of this country with my wife and kids; I don't think we can survive the unrest.

It takes four days to walk to Kabul, only stopping briefly to rest. My wife and I have not eaten in two days, which has allowed our children to have the little food. Unfortunately, we lost a lot of families along the way. We got desperate and took water flasks of corpses, or we wouldn't have made it.

The situation in Kabul is worse. What am I going to do? I need to get my family to Pakistan if possible. Presently, we are exhausted, hungry, dirty and sleeping on the street, alongside thousands of other people. The militants are everywhere and they carry the latest guns. I cut my daughter's hair with the knife I carry so that she looks more like a boy. I know this is frowned upon, but I'm desperate; I need to keep my daughter safe at all costs. All I ever wanted was a better life for my family, but now homes are being destroyed and lives lost. As I sit in the street with my family, I put my head on my knees and weep silent tears; I don't want my family to see. I need to be strong for them the journey ahead is still long.

Chapter Five: Sydney

Henry

Driving home, after an exhausting day, listening to Beethoven's Symphony No.5 distracts me from thinking about work or my failure as a husband and father. But my attention is brought abruptly to the road ahead. What's happening? There is a roadblock blocking my way. How do I get home? I can see police officers signalling for me to pull over to the side of the road.

Is that fire? I think as I get out of my car. No! It can't be! That's my apartment block. I bought the flat when my wife decided to take a marriage hiatus. Is my apartment burning? I try to move into the blocked area, but I am stopped by a police officer. 'Please, sir, you cannot go any further.'

'What is happening?' I ask, but the officer does not reply. I can see several buildings razed by fire. 'I live there. Where will I go?' I say, pointing in the direction of my apartment as I watch firefighters trying to put out the blaze. The fire appears to be spreading at a rapid rate. Still, he does not reply.

What's happening in Sydney? Are my wife and son safe? My Gamaplug connects to my wife Mia's phone; it's ringing, but she is not picking up. I need to get to my other house, but the road remains blocked. I jump back into my car, vehicles are parking up everywhere, but I make an abrupt turn and head back in the direction I came. I don't care about breaking the law; the police officers are busy at the moment, and my family is one of the most influential in Australia.

I race towards my former home. I love my family with all my heart; I've tried to make sure we stay together as a close unit. I do this stressful commute between Canberra and Sydney daily to be close to my family. This separation was never what I wanted, but my wife tells me I spend so much time trying to fix Australia I never have enough time to try and fix things at home. This separation is a wake-up call; all I ever wanted to be was a politician; I just want to make the world a better place. My mother is one of the most renowned people in Australia, and I have always been expected to follow in her footsteps.

I need to fix this, I tell myself. I would not be like my parents. My mother gave everything to this country; it came at a price. My parents were separated for a while, which no one knew about, before they reconciled after my mother retired from politics. My phone is connected to my wife, and she is still not picking up. We have decided to see a therapist, and I need to find time from somewhere for those appointments. I cannot afford to lose my son; I don't want him to resent me. But right now, I need to make sure they are OK.

My house is situated in Bellevue Hill; I wanted my family to live a comfortable life, but now I am saddened that my wife is so resentful of me. *Please pick up the phone.* The way the fire is spreading, it might spread to this area. I arrive at the family house and see that everything is peaceful. I press the bell; it takes a while for my wife to open the door.

'Henry! What are you doing here at this time?'

'I just wanted to make sure you are safe? My apartment just got burnt down; the other side of Sydney is on fire.'

'Come inside. Are you OK?' she asks, reluctantly.

'I don't know,' I say, running my hand through my brunette hair. 'Is Carl sleeping?'

'He's in his room; it's 9.00 pm. What are you going to do?'

'I was hoping to sleep in the spare room tonight; tomorrow, I will find out more about what's happened to my apartment.'

She raises her eyebrows. 'I don't know, I don't want to confuse Carl; I don't want him to think we are back together.'

'Mia! Please! I am homeless right now, and this is my house too.'

'Don't you dare say that to me. You lost the right to call this your home when you decided your job was more important than your family. You can go to your mother's house; it's not far from here; I am sure she will welcome her precious son.'

'I don't want to fight, please, just for tonight; I will leave first thing in the morning after saying hello to Carl. I love you, Mia, and I want this marriage to work.'

'Fine! You can stay in the spare room.'

My phone starts ringing, and my wife sighs and walks off.

I watch as she walks away, angrily. How did it get to this?

Chapter Six: Rio de Janeiro

Ana

It will be another long day; and I already have a bad headache. I have been pacing the hospital where my daughter lies sick in bed. I have not had a decent sleep in days; my daughter has been here for six days and seven nights. It is the worst nightmare any parent could ever have; she developed a high temperature in the middle of the night, and I had to rush her to the hospital. Thank God nothing happened along the way.

The worst part is that they do not know what could have caused such a high spike in her temperature; she is caught between life and death. Everything has been done, from a brain scan to taking blood. The tests reveal nothing.

I'm terrified and desperate. My daughter is lying unconscious in ICU, and doctors and nurses are stretched because of the increased number of patients being admitted. What could have caused this? My daughter went to school today and came home without incident. I'm glad I checked on her in the middle of the night and discovered she was so unwell. The doctor told me I was lucky I brought her straight to the hospital because she wouldn't have survived another hour.

As a widow, I have spent all my savings. I have been here for six days now with no update; I can't afford to leave her in the hospital. I'm afraid of losing my job, my only source of livelihood. The company has been forced to restructure in recent months and many of my colleagues have lost their jobs. I fear I will be next. In desperation, I sent a letter from the doctor to the HR department. I also called my boss to explain, he is a kind man, and he promised to do his best to help me keep my job, but he also has to obey direct orders.

I brought my daughter to a private hospital because of the public sector's poor medical facilities, but the cost is substantial. It's bad enough that the medical facilities have gone down the drain; now, we are faced with an unknown disease that causes a very high temperature and puts people into a coma. I don't even know how I will pay the hospital bill. I have sold all my valuables to pay for the deposit for them to treat my child, but if she has to stay here much longer, I don't know what I will do.

The only asset I have left is the house my late husband left to us before he died. We already took out a loan to pay for the huge medical bills incurred during my husband's illness. If I sell the house, we will be homeless, and my daughter and I will likely die of starvation. But I cannot think about this right now; the most important thing is that she gets better.

I approach the doctor. 'Please tell me, do you know what is wrong with my child? It's been six days, and you have given me nothing.' Tears run down my face as I speak.

'My apologies, Mrs Santos, but we don't know. We have carried out several tests, but each came back with inconclusive results. Something strange is happening, and many patients in this hospital are facing the same ailment.'

'What am I supposed to do, doctor, watch my daughter die?'

'We are doing our best, I am sorry.' There is nothing more I can say as he rushes off to tend to his many patients.

I fall on my knees crying. She is unconscious and is being given oxygen, but the hospital management has told me the oxygen will only last her for another three days; after that, they won't be able to provide her with any more. I can't believe this is happening to me; whom can I call for help?

My husband's family turned their backs on my daughter and me after my husband's death. I understood they never liked me, although I tried my best to make peace for my husband's sake, but you can't please them no matter how hard you try.

I used my Gamaplug to connect to my older sister, Maria, trying hard to explain the situation through my tears, and she now is on her way to the hospital. I need to call the office again; one of the few perks of working for Platoon PLC is that we are all given a Gamaplug. I pray I still have my job as I connect to my boss to update him of the situation.

I'm aware that I must smell bad as I've not showered in days, but this is the least of my problems. When my sister arrives, I need to try and source an oxygen tank for my daughter.

Chapter Seven: Hong Kong

Huan

I have been working non-stop with my team to ensure that the next generation telecommunications network will be the best the world has ever seen.

However, I have been restless for the past couple of days, having nightmares and waking up sweating. The nightmares are getting worse; I see myself in the sea, struggling to swim, being beaten by the strong waves, screaming for help until I'm pulled down into the water by an unseen force.

I am suffering from constant migraines. I think it is because of this horrible weather. The heat is killing me. The temperature in Hong Kong has increased to 37^C; I am constantly dehydrated, and I feel faint. We have been advised to find a cool place to reside, but many people can't afford air conditioning. The heatwaves have got so bad that thousands of people are dying every day. To be honest, I am terrified. I am stressed, as there is also mounting pressure to meet my work deadline; my company is working closely with the Chinese government, so the pressure is enormous.

I grew up in the province of Qinghai, and my mother died of breast cancer from a lack of money and care. I wipe my face as the tears start to fall at the memory. I pushed myself because I wanted to make my mother proud. I am now the Chief Technical Officer of Yamson Telecommunications company, the biggest in Asia.

Growing up as an only child, and losing my mother at a young age, was not easy. I never knew my father. My aunt raised me; she managed to smuggle me into the United States of America. I remember being teased for not being able to speak the English language.

I worked hard; I was chosen as the valedictorian in my class when I graduated from the Massachusetts Institute of Technology (MIT) and I have an MBA from Princeton. I worked with many telecommunications companies before moving back to Hong Kong to work at Yamson.

I wanted to make my mother proud. I have won many awards worldwide for being a technical genius, but this new telecommunication must provide a faster and more reliable network. This unprecedented weather has caused many setbacks. Four of our base stations overheated and were damaged; now, we are experiencing mobile outages in several areas of Hong Kong. In this terrible heat, my team is on various sites trying to fix the problem; my phone has been ringing non-stop.

My headache is getting worse; I have a meeting with a government agent in two hours; this problem needs to be solved. We never thought, when developing this technology, that the temperature could rise by such a large degree.

I pick up my desk phone and call the Service Delivery Team Leader, Yichen; I need an update every twenty minutes, a detailed report on what is happening and a way to solve the problem – fast.

Yichen responds: 'We are still working on it; my team has been on-site for the past two days; we are trying to provide a temporary solution with the system backup, then we can work on a more permanent solution.'

'Yichen, I need something now. Unless this problem is solved, I can't go into that meeting, and the clock is ticking. The headquarters of the government of Hong Kong site is down; this is bad. It's been down for two days, and if we don't solve the problem ASAP, we will start to lose customers' trust.'

'We are moving forward; the weather is not helping; a lot of the chips are fried from the heat, we need air conditioning for all our sites, and we need to replace those base stations.

'They have to understand that this heat is also affecting several competitors' networks.'

'They don't care about that; get me a report ASAP!'

'I'm already working on it; it will be on your desk in thirty minutes.'

'Make it twenty; I have little time left before the meeting.'

I drop the phone; I feel ready to faint; the air conditioning is on, but I am still sweating. I massage my head with my fingers. I'll have to take drugs for this headache and drink lots of cold water. This is a nightmare. I only wish I could wake up from it.

Chapter Eight: London

Jude

I can see what looks like a shadow hovering over my head.

Am I dreaming? I wasn't expecting anyone. I open my eyes, startled, when I feel a hand on my head.

'Ella! What are you doing here? Shit!' I gasp. 'Get out of my house! How did you even get in? I had the locks changed.'

'You think you can dump me on national television, and I will just disappear,' she replies.

'Ella, you were caught cheating on me; it was all over the news; I was publicly humiliated,' I reply, struggling to sit up on my couch.

'It's OK, baby,' she says. 'I'm sure we can work this out.'

'What is there to "work out"? Are you crazy? You were dating another man at the same time as me. Gama, start recording! 'I shout.'

'You destroyed my life,' she responds as I watch her fighting back her tears.

'I did not destroy your life; you dug your own grave.'

'I will make you pay for this. I lost all my endorsements, and I couldn't get a decent modelling job afterwards. We have to get back together.'

'What are you going on about? I dated you for a whole year; I never once cheated on you, but you decided to have another man in your life, and then you act all surprised when the press found out? I showed you off to the world as my girlfriend, but you decided to play me for a fool. We are never getting back together. Do you hear me? Never!'

'Baby, I made a mistake; people make mistakes.'

I watch as she smacks her head with her hand; something is clearly wrong with her.

'Ella! Ella! Are you OK? You need to take it easy.' I have to find a way to calm her down. 'OK! OK!' I say. 'We can try and work things out.'

'No!' she yells. 'My name was smeared all over the media; I was called horrible things and portrayed as a scarlet woman. I am sure your public relations team did this. No! No! You do not get to dump me in public.'

She starts smacking her head again. 'You do not get to make yourself a hero. Now everyone wants to be associated with you, and all my brands have deserted me.'

'Ella! You are spiralling. This is just a breakup. These things happen. It's not headline news anymore with the gas explosion in Chelsea; people will not remember. It only lasted so long because you chose to give interviews to the press, portraying me as an uncaring man. That was the reason you felt the need to cheat.'

'You don't care about me; if you did, this breakup wouldn't have been so easy for you.'

I try to stand up, but I feel dizzy again, and I am forced to sit down. Why is this happening to me? I got home from the hospital yesterday, and my mum is arriving this evening from Scotland. I'm weak, I have a headache, and I can't deal with this right now.

'Ella, please, you need to leave my house. I don't feel well. We can talk about this another time.'

'No! No!' she screams. 'You need to fix this. Get your PR team on the phone; they need to do something to improve my reputation.'

'Ella,' I say more gently. 'You are a beautiful woman, a talented model. I gave you the fame you craved, but you destroyed it with your own hands. You became famous because of me, and you got drunk on it. You had lots of men vying for your attention; you thought you could do better than me. What is the name of the guy you cheated on me with? Yes, Marcus. His father is supposed to be a billionaire or something. Why are you not with him? Why are you bothering me?'

'He dumped me. His father doesn't want anything to affect his reputation, and so daddy's boy has to do as he is told.'

I burst out laughing. 'So, I'm the next best thing? You really should leave. Now!'

'Nobody wants to hire me; baby, please, you need to fix this…I did not come here to play with you.'

She runs into my kitchen, where my chef knives are on display. Her hands shake as she pulls one out of the stand. She comes back into the sitting room, wielding the knife at me. I pull myself up; and walk over to the wall, to lean against for support.

'Fix this or I will stab myself and blame you for it.'

'Gama, call 999, I shout.'

'Ella, please stop!' I take a step towards her. 'You need to be reasonable. If this should get out, your reputation will be permanently ruined; there will be no way back, and the doors closed will never be opened again.' I try to reason with her. 'I'll call my PR team; they will help you.' I need to stall her before the police arrive.

'No, I'm going to destroy your career, just like you destroyed mine.' She lifts the knife.

'Ella! Stop!' I reach out to her with my hands, but my vision slides out of focus.

She stabs her right thigh with so much force the blade penetrates her skin. She shrieks, falling to the ground, bleeding profusely.

'Oh, God! What have you done?' I say, as I watch her fall to the floor. I rush towards her forgetting my fatigue. 'Someone help!' I scream.

The door to my house is bust open as the police rush in. 'Help her!' I yell, as I frantically try to stop the bleeding.

She points a finger at me. 'Get him off me. It was him. He stabbed me,' she says.

The police pull me away from her, forcing my hands behind my back. I struggle with them. 'I did not stab her,' I shout. 'I have a hidden camera. I will show you the recording.'

'You are lying,' says Ella. 'There is no camera. I was with you for a year, and I did not know of any camera.'

The paramedics arrive and attempt to stop the bleeding. When Ella's condition has stabilised sufficiently, they place her on a stretcher, and rush out of my house to the ambulance.

I look at the police officers. 'The recording was sent automatically to my phone.' I say, nodding towards my mobile. They release my hands. It is bad enough that police cars are outside my house. I cannot be taken out in handcuffs.

I unlock my phone and show them the recording. After watching it, one of the police officers says, 'You are a fortunate man because it would have been your word against hers.'

'I'd be grateful if you would leave now,' I say.

The officer continues, 'Unfortunately, this is the least of your problems.'

'What does that mean?'

The police officers don't move.

'Gama, call my lawyer.'

'You need to accompany us to the police station. We have a warrant to search your house. Two of your employees have been arrested for operating an illegal cocaine trade in your restaurant, and your name has been mentioned.'

Chapter Nine: New York

Martin

I walk upstairs to their daughter's room; it's a typical teenage room decorated in baby pink with a picture of a pop artist on the wall and a bed stacked high with fluffy pink pillows.

What could make a teenage girl kill herself? The pills are scattered on the table. I pick up the pill bottle, and I can see it's an antidepressant drug prescribed in her name. I look up at the mayor's assistant, who was in the room with me.

'Stefanie? Am I right?'

'Yes, my name is Stefanie.'

'OK, Stefanie, why was the mayor's daughter taking antidepressants? How old was she, fifteen?'

'I am not at liberty to say.'

From what I can tell from the prescription, this should be last her a month, and counting the pills left; she must have overdosed. *Did she take only antidepressants or mix them with other drugs?* I wonder. I look around. I can't see any other pills apart from Ampropaim. I can tell from Stefanie's guarded manner that she's not here to give me any assistance but to monitor me, so I stop asking questions; something strange is going on in the mayor's house.

This is the most excruciating way to die; and the pain must have worsened over time. Why didn't she call for help? Why did no one notice?

I look at Stefanie, who continues to watch me closely. 'Can I have access to her phone and laptop? I need to go through them.'

'I will have to get the mayor's approval, do not touch or take anything without our permission. You need to understand that anything you find must be handled with the highest discretion.'

She walks out of the bedroom, and a young man in his twenties immediately enters. They really don't want me to be alone in here. I discreetly push the pill bottle to the edge of the table, and it falls on the ground, rolling under her bed. I bend down, pretending to pick it up; I want to check under her bed. I lift the duvet on the side and see a stack of books. Quickly going through, I find a little book hidden under the pile. She was obviously trying to keep this secret from her parents. How come they hadn't noticed? This whole room has been staged for my arrival.

How can I take the book without them seeing me? I stand up and approach the young man following me round.

'I need to take notes of what I see and think. Can you get me a notepad?'

'I'm not supposed to leave you here alone.'

'I understand, but the mayor wants this solved as soon as possible; a notebook shouldn't take long to find.'

He hesitates for a few seconds. I can see him thinking. 'I will be back in two minutes,' he says eventually.

As soon as he leaves, I take the little book and slip it into my trousers, held in place by my belt, my shirt is already untucked.

At that moment, Stefanie walks in and looks around. 'Where is Liam?' He is supposed to be assisting you.'

'Oh! He just left to get me a notepad; I need to take notes.'

I can see the displeasure written over her face about me being left alone; what is the mayor hiding? If you are desperate to find your daughter's killer, the police officer investigating should be given access to all resources.

'You can inspect the phone and laptop, but everything must be done here,' she says. 'Nothing can be taken to the station.'

'I can't work like this. I might need an expert to do a thorough check.'

'I appreciate that, Detective, but we have all the experts you need in-house. The mayor doesn't want unnecessary information being leaked to the public; I'm sure you understand.'

I am shown to the digital room where the mobile and laptop have already been opened and, I suspect, much information may have been deleted. I don't think the mayor wants me to find the true culprit, but he is looking for a scapegoat to take the blame. I will play along; I need to find out what this family is hiding.

As I suspected, nothing of interest is found on the mobile or laptop. I walk down to the mayor's home office, where he is waiting for my report.

'From the little I can gather, this looks like suicide, nothing says otherwise.' The mayor looks up at me. 'You best make a statement to the public before the press gets hold of this.'

He nods in agreement. 'We are already preparing a statement, and it will be released in the next thirty minutes.'

'I would advise you to do an autopsy; that is the only way we can indeed find out what truly happened.'

'That will not be necessary. Thank you for coming.'

I shake the mayor's hand, and I am escorted out of the house. What happened to the distressed man I saw an hour ago? He is completely different now; he seems composed and unconcerned.

I get into the snowplough and the driver pulls out of the driveway onto the icy road. Something was fishy, and why was I requested personally? I pull out the book; hopefully, it will shed some light on what they are trying to cover up.

Gamaplug picks up my call from the captain. 'How did it go? The mayor called me and told me you deduced it was suicide.'

'Yes, from the little information I was allowed to gather, it looks that way, but why would the mayor not want an autopsy for his daughter?'

'Some people want peace for their loved one. Let it go! Your shift is over; go home.'

'No problem, captain,' I say, as the phone is disconnected.

Gamaplug is one of the most expensive products I ever bought for myself and my wife. Thank God it was before the cold weather became critical. It was costly but worth it, as it has allowed me to keep in touch with my family during this difficult time.

Something is off with the mayor, I know it is, and I will find out the truth, but whom can I trust? If the mayor wants his daughter to have a peaceful death, why send for me? I am known for being persistent until I get answers. The whole family was in pain when I arrived, the next hour, it was as if no one had died. What happened in that sixty minutes? I need to get home before I open the notebook. I will investigate secretly so as not to draw unnecessary attention. I am not sure whether the captain is involved in what is going on, but I am not going to risk it; I am on my own. I will spend the coming days trying to uncover what led to this poor girl's death; I'm not going to give up.

But for now, the captain has ordered me to go home; my shift is over. I miss my wife and daughters and can't wait to see them. I head for home for the first time in a fortnight.

Chapter Ten: Lagos

Lola

I will never give up. They will not stop me; the truth will be exposed. I will continue to bring attention to those who are missing. People live in constant fear of being kidnapped; bodies are found on the streets of Lagos with parts missing.

I was caught in that terrible storm because I was trying to interview one of the victim's families, but to no avail; they had constantly been on the run, in fear of their lives, because they were being threatened by unknown forces.

This investigation involves secret, buried crimes, with weird happenings and, coupled with the terrible storm from last week, people are living in despair. It took seven days for the water to dry up in Lagos, but some areas are still muddy. Watching NBS News, I don't think Lagos will survive the after-effects. The city is in disarray, and there is footage of cars blown away by the mighty wind, with some being swept into the Atlantic Ocean. People have drowned in their own homes, houses have collapsed, not to mention bridges breaking into two or being swept away by floodwater.

Now people are forced to live in filth; imagine your house being filled with water and poop, and the grief and loss of life is immeasurable. This is the worst disaster to happen in Lagos. Can the city ever recover? I'm fortunate to be alive but still I am traumatised; if it hadn't been for the help of a stranger, I wouldn't be here today. So many people lost their lives unexpectedly; there was no forecast beforehand, so people had no warning.

It has been raining non-stop for days, yet people have to endure great hardship to secure their source of livelihood. My parents have been calling from Abuja; I don't know where my car is, and my phone has been destroyed. I had to use my spare phone to talk to them to put their mind at rest; my house is one of the few houses not damaged by the storm.

I have been pursuing the truth about the missing people for over six months, and I have made no headway, meeting one stumbling block after the other. I went to Maryland last month to interview one of the victim's parents, but they refused to talk. They are so frightened for their lives; they don't want to lose their only surviving son, who had been badly beaten by masked men.

Then I faced a new horror. I saw my best friend's butchered body on the ground with others, their dismembered bodies on display for all to see. Tears clouded my vision; and I vowed that day to avenge her death. It took two days for other severed heads to be identified; over twenty body parts were found that day. Young people between the ages of twenty-five and thirty-five were killed in the prime of their lives.

The night my friend, Chioma, went missing. My friend called me overly excited that she had been invited to a new club that had just opened on Victoria Island. Entry was strictly by invitation only, and she'd instructed to be discreet. She was to be picked up personally by a Rolls-Royce and dropped at the location. I was troubled when she told me and I advised her not to go because she didn't know the organisers, but she wouldn't listen. Chioma told me this was her last hurrah before she got married.

I flew back from Abuja to Lagos, when I didn't hear from her in two days. Her mobile phone was switched off and her worried parents had been calling me. I went with them to the police station to file a report that their daughter had been missing for over forty-eight hours.

I went to see Chioma's fiancé, Emeka, because I was bothered by his nonchalant attitude towards her disappearance, only for him to tell me they had called off the engagement over a month ago. This was strange; Chioma would have told her parents or me. She was excited about the wedding; she wouldn't do anything to jeopardise it. He told me they hadn't spoken in over a month, and he couldn't possibly know where she was.

Emeka was summoned to the police station. I was informed by Chioma's parents that sauntered into the station, unconcerned, and words could not express their pain. Apparently, he remained expressionless throughout the interview, with his lawyer telling him not to answer any more questions.

Then her body was found. Oh my God! Why was everything so fucked up?

We had a heated exchange in front of his house. 'Emeka!' I yelled at him. 'How can you be in a relationship with Chioma for four years and not feel anything when you hear she has disappeared, no matter how it ended?'

'How dare you come into my house and shout at me? You have no right! You don't know anything about our relationship; I don't answer to you,' he bellowed back at me.

'Justice will be served, Emeka! I have never liked you; I only tolerated you because of my friend. I know you have been dating another woman. You are a bastard! How can you move on so fast? You dated my friend for four years.'

'My relationship with Chioma is none of your business.'

'It is my business because she is dead, we have no answers, and here you are sipping wine, without a care in the world. If you loved her, even a little, you will want to find her killers and get justice for her. Look at the horrific way she died?'

He shrugged his shoulders.

I stumbled backwards, away from him.

'You are heartless. I don't know what Chioma saw in you,' I said, before storming out of his compound.

***

I go to interview people disguised as a man, wearing a face cap under my hoodie, trying to hide my identity as much as possible. I know I am in dangerous territory because reporters caught posting such news have been falsely accused and arrested.

I am now the only news platform on the internet bold enough to report on the rampant kidnapping and death of our citizens. I have spent millions of naira hiding my IP address, and I have been undercover reporting for years, and no one knows my identity. I'm the daughter of the former senate president and an entrepreneur who owns my beauty range called Moshébì Cosmetics.

I have been leading a double life; one as a famous socialite, hanging out with celebrities and living luxuriously in Ikoyi, the other as an unknown, undercover reporter who owns a renowned news blog called 'The Report' with over three million subscribers. I have a small office building in Gbagada, where I have been hiding in plain sight. I constantly have to look over my shoulder; I know my life is in danger.

My father must never know.

I lost my best friend; this is very personal. Parents and loved ones appear daily on national television, wailing and begging for answers. Still the police do nothing.

How can bodies be found in abandoned houses, or on the street, with parts of them missing? The story was only deemed worthy of being mentioned in the news because piles of human body parts were found in several abandoned buildings across Lagos.

No one is even talking about it.

Somewhere in Nigeria…

'Find me that journalist who has been running these stories. The police and judges are all in my pocket; who dares to go against me?

'People fear what they do not know, and we do not want them to have detailed updates on these occurrences.

'We need fear and chaos; this is political.'

Chapter Eleven: Kabul

Ahmed

On this cold freezing morning, an icy wind is blowing, and I am shivering uncontrollably in the open air with only my thin, worn clothes to cover me. Everywhere is still pitch black; if we don't die of starvation, we will die from the cold. There is no way to keep warm because we could only carry one small blanket when we fled from Kandahar, and my children are using it.

Sensing movement around me, I am grateful to Allah that I am a light sleeper. I see my wife struggling as a stranger wraps his hand around her mouth to prevent her from screaming. He tries to drag her away as she continues to struggle. My heart is racing in my chest; I can't lose Aisha. The assailant sees me watching him, pushes her to the ground and starts running. I jump on my feet and run after him, carrying the Pesh-kabz dagger I keep beside me every night. I am faster than him; I catch up and wrestle him to the ground. I stab him in the shoulder with my knife and the man screams.

'What were you doing with my wife?'

'Am sorry! Am sorry!' the man says, cowering away from me.

'Were you planning to rape her? Today will be your last day.'

People are awake now, having heard the commotion, and have gathered round. I pull out the knife and I am about to stab him again when I am held back by a group of men. I start struggling, trying to kick the assailant; I am so livid, 'How dare you touch my wife?' I yell.

'Let him go! Everyone is just desperate,' says one of the men. 'Let Allah be the judge.' I watch as the assailant is helped to his feet and taken away, bleeding from his right shoulder.

I run back to my family; Aisha is holding Abdul and Laila tightly; her eyes red and swollen from crying. I have to get us off the street. We need to find shelter; people are being killed daily, and young girls and women are being raped. Nowhere is safe. But why would anyone try to kidnap my wife?

Abdul and Laila sleep in the middle, I sleep beside my daughter, and my wife beside my son. The children sleep on a little mat while Aisha and

I sleep on the hard ground.

It will be daybreak soon. I wipe the knife on my loose trousers to remove the blood and stick it in my bag. I tell my family to try and rest; we will leave this place in the morning. We have been told by the Ahedan Group that all females must wear a niqab, yet my wife is still not safe.

I have not had a good night's sleep in weeks; I have been sleeping with one eye open, and the little money I have is hidden in my undergarments. We slept on the streets for over a week, until the chaos had died down a little, but we couldn't return to Kandahar. Now, we are stuck in Kabul. My children only eat once a day, and Aisha and I eat every other day. I am trying to stretch the little money I have. We can't continue like this; I need a job but from where?

At first light, I roll up the mat and we head out to look for a better place to live than on the streets. So many houses were damaged in the raids; some were burnt down, and others have shattered doors, windows, and bullet holes in the walls.

I've warned Laila not to go anywhere without me; she is also wearing a niqab but nowhere is safe for her. Food is scarce and what little there is sells for exorbitant prices. People are afraid to sell their goods.

I hold my daughter's hand, and Aisha stays close to Abdul as we look for abandoned houses. The Ahedan Group are now in power; they have taken possession of the best places in Kabul, the occupants who couldn't escape have all been killed.

We find a dilapidated house with several holes in the walls. The windows are all broken, the furniture has been destroyed and there is no door. We enter the house and I can see people everywhere; some sleeping on the floor. I look at my wife in despair; I can see the pain in her eyes.

'Aisha,' I whisper. 'You need to stay strong for the children; we will get through this; for the moment, we just need to survive.'

She nods and we find a space on the crowded floor, spread the mat on the hard ground and sit on it. I look around; people are crying, children wailing, couples fighting but, mostly, people sit huddled together, dejected, just hoping to see another day.

'We need food,' Aisha reminds me.

'Have we finished the bread I bought three days ago?'

'The bread only lasted that long because we eat so infrequently.

Ahmed, I'm weak, and I need food.'

'I understand, Aisha. I am sorry. I am trying to stretch the little money we have left; I will go and see what I can buy.' I too am starving. 'Stay safe; I will be back soon. These people have nothing left to lose, so be careful.' I walk out of the building into the gloomy world of grief-stricken people who just want to survive.

I arrive at the market but only a few stalls are open. I approach a fruit seller. 'Do you have any fruit that is about to spoil? The soft fruit, I can't afford fresh fruits.' He points to a basket behind me. 'Just take one melon because people have been begging for food all day.'

I peer into the basket; they are only a few melons left. 'Please,' I say. 'There are four of us. Can I take two?'

He nods.

'Allah will continue to bless you.' I touch one of the melons; it is very soft but manageable; what choice do I have?

I need to see what I can get for free; people are everywhere looking for something to eat. Stealing is prohibited and, if caught, your arm will be cut off.

Ahedan members parade the streets, with their semi-automatic guns, taking any food they deem fit for themselves – hypocrites!

I see a man selling Afghani naan. This bread should not go off for a couple of days; we can't cook, so we need food that will last. I walk up to the man and ask, 'Do you have any stale naan bread? I can't afford a fresh one. How much will you sell it to me for?'

'I have only one left; people are buying stale bread more than fresh bread. You can have it for four afghanis. I would have given it to you for free, but I also need money to provide for my family.'

'Baraka Allahu Fik.'

I look at what I managed to bring back from the market; two almost rotten melons and stale bread – is this what my life has been reduced to?

'Ahmed! Ahmed!' I turn around. Someone is calling my name. I see someone running towards me, waving his hands.

'Yusuf? Yusuf, is that you?' He is an old comrade; Yusuf and I left the army at the same time.

'Yes,' he replies, giving me a hearty slap on the back. 'I have been looking for you; we need to talk.'

'Why?' I ask.

'Not here; what we have to discuss is confidential.'

'I need to get this food to my family.'

Yusuf stares at my dirty, despondent face; I can't remember the last time I took a bath. We just pour little water on a piece of material to swipe our bodies and brush our teeth with twigs.

'What were you able to buy?' he asks

'Two melons and a stale naan.' He takes out some money and visits different stalls. He buys fresh fruits (apples, melons, grapes), fresh bread, and some dried fruit and comes over to give me the bag. 'Give these to your family.'

'My family cannot eat these in front of starving people; they will be assaulted,' I say.

'We need to talk; what I have to say could change your family's life. Follow me.'

We walk for fifteen minutes until we arrive at a mud house on the hillside. He opens the door and we walk in. He tells me to take a seat as he closes the door behind us.

I look around. There is a red U-shaped sofa with an oriental rug in the centre. I sit down.

Yusuf begins to speak. 'I know you have the expertise we are looking for; you were always the best in the field. I have been working for the opposition group, trying to bring down the Ahedan. Just look at the destruction they have caused in mere months; I imagine it will be worse in the years to come; we will be prisoners in our own country. We want to send you as a spy to work for the Ahedan Group leader, Mohammad Pir. We already have people on the ground who will allow you access to the leader. If you agree, I will provide more information, and your family will be taken care of, they will no longer have to go hungry.'

I look at him as if he is crazy.

'But I need you to tell me yes or no; you are not allowed to ask questions until I have your answer.' He looks at his watch. 'And you have just five minutes to decide.'

Chapter Twelve: Sydney

Henry

I watch as my wife strides away.

'What happened to my apartment?' I ask as Gamaplug picks up my phone.

'I'm sorry, sir, the whole building was destroyed, along with those surrounding it. Unfortunately, the fire is still spreading; but firefighters are trying to minimise the damage,' says Rob, my personal assistant.

'What could have caused it? I heard on the news in my car that it is a wildfire.'

'Police don't think it's wildfire.'

'What then?'

'Arson. Police think those areas have been deliberately targeted; they are surrounded by trees but not enough to cause this much damage.'

'Then why is the news claiming it's wildlife?

'We have to say something; we don't want unnecessary panic until the investigation is completed.'

'Keep me updated,' I say, as Gama disconnects the call.

I sigh heavily. I've been given till morning to leave the house that I bought with my money, where I have been relegated to the guest room. I spared no expense in making this house exquisite from the chandelier imported from Italy to the designer kitchen. God! Is this my life?

I walk up the stairs to my son's room. Carl refuses to see me whenever I come to visit. I knock softly on his door, before opening it. He looks up from his books spread all over the table, shakes his head and goes back to reading.

'Hello, son. I know you are angry with me and that I've disappointed you many times. I'm sorry, I know I've messed up. You have given me many chances, but I keep messing up. Please forgive me, I love you very much, and I don't want to lose you.'

My son continues to stare at his books. He won't even talk to me.

'Say something. Yell at me. Anything, so I know how you feel. Please, Carl,' I say as I move closer to him. 'I am so sorry.'

'You don't love me! You are a liar!' he screams, getting up from his chair. He stares at me angrily. 'You have missed every game I played in school after promising me that you would come; you hardly come to the house; you're always too busy. I watch as Mum tries to hide her tears. Your actions prove to me that I am not important to you. You love your work more than your family. I rarely see you now; and it will only get worse when your party nominates you as their candidate to be the next prime minister; we will never see you again.'

'Carl, you are the most important person in my life. You are more important to me than my work; please, I cannot lose you.'

'Leave, Dad! Stop lying,' he shouts. 'Go back to your job that is more important than your family, soon to be prime minister.'

He turns towards his chair, pulling it back with force before sitting down heavily.

'No matter what you think or believe, I love you more than anything. My actions may say otherwise, but I promise you I'm telling you the truth.'

I can do nothing other than walk out of my son's room, feeling dejected. *What am I going to do now?*

***

I get up early to leave the place I used to call home; I am going to stay at my parents' house in Kirribilli Harbour until I sort out another apartment.

Gama automatically informs me that I need to get to the Canberra immediately; there has been a security breach.

Gama, start my car! I need to get to the airport; it's going to be a long day.

I race to the office and, as Rob gives me an update on the incident, I am informed that one of the Government Sector 5 networks has been hacked. This has never happened before; we have the best cyber security team on the ground monitoring every network; this should have been detected immediately. All the security teams are under lockdown; no one can leave the premises until the officials have interrogated them.

'Set up a closed-door meeting with the prime minister, his cabinet members, senators, House of Representatives and Mr Robinson, head of Australian intelligence, immediately!' I instruct Rob. 'Has the prime minister been informed? This is a disaster.'

This should have never happened on my watch. As Minister for Defence, I am supposed to maintain policies on the sea and air, but now we are faced with more attacks within our system than external forces.

The entire building is packed with security intelligence agents and armed police officers. All computers, mobiles and security cameras have been seized, and we have informed the agents that we want this to be done as discreetly as possible, and the press must not get hold of this. This will only cause people to panic if hackers have access to the country's finances, weapons and secret conversations that must never be exposed. If this is not resolved quickly, this information will plunge Australia back into the Dark Ages, and we will have a government at the mercy of the perpetrators. All the security programs have been rewritten, but it may be too late.

'If our conversations are exposed, we are all finished,' I tell the prime minister, the House of Representatives and the Senate. 'This needs to be fixed fast; we can't afford for our private discussions to be leaked.' I speak confidently, but inside I am quaking.

'I want all the IT personnel arrested,' demands Hon. Matthew Cornwell.

'They are all being interrogated as we speak, and no one will be released until the perpetrators are found.'

'We are not safe. They have access to all our personal information; we could be blackmailed at any time. I want to know how this happened? I need answers in the next forty-eight hours, Mr Robinson,' says Jackson Paul, the prime minister. 'You are authorised to use any means necessary. There is a no-holds-barred policy for treatment on the cyber security team, do whatever you have to do to get results.'

'Yes, sir! We believe whoever accessed the network works in this office; to gain access to the network from outside, he or she must have detailed knowledge of your intricate security network to decode each stage; it is almost impossible. All possible suspects are being transported, as we speak, to Cell Site 201 on the outskirts of Sydney, where they will be interrogated.'

***

Cell Site 201 is a three-storey building in the middle of four hectares of land, surrounded by a high wall and electric fence. There is a government warning sign on the iron gate to keep intruders at bay. This is where we take terrorists; and this case is now classified as a terrorist attack. We have about twenty intelligence agents on the ground; some are working on tracing the origins of the hacking while others are going through the suspects' finances. We have ten agents responsible for interrogating the suspects, six men and four women, all dressed in black suits. Armed agents surround the premises to prevent anyone from escaping.

The three main suspects are Shawn, Evelyn and Jason; they are the only ones with the expertise to pull this off. They are hauled into a black sedan with tinted windows and I recognise the fear in their eyes. A foul smell emits from the car; and I look behind me at the three people, looking deathly white, all with their eyes cast down.

'Is there water on the floor?' I ask one of the agents.

'I am sorry.' Jason looks up. 'When I'm nervous, I lose control. I didn't realise that I'd peed myself.'

When we arrive at the site, each of them is strapped to a chair, in separate interrogation rooms. They will be interrogated at the same time by different agents. The rooms have insulated windows with a highly reflective coating that looks like a one-way mirror.

At this moment, their homes are being ransacked. This operation is so clean; all morning, we have been going through everything in their lives and have, so far, come up empty. I have never seen anything like it; not a single trail of data anywhere. The suspects' finances show nothing more than their salaries and the usual living expenses.

'We'll get to the bottom of this,' Mr Robinson tries to assure me. 'We will continue to investigate until we find something.'

I regard him with displeasure; I need answers; we have been given just forty-eight hours to resolve this problem and provide the prime minister with updates.

'Get me something,' I say. 'They must have made a mistake somewhere. Maybe they will crack under pressure.'

I watch as stern-looking agents start interrogating the suspects in the various rooms. 'How can you not know? The system was hacked when you were supposed to be monitoring the system.'

'I don't know how this could happen. The algorithm was used; I have never seen anything like this before.' They all give the same answers.

'Someone must have downloaded it into the system; it can't be done by just anyone. They must be an expert; the data is set to start downloading at 2.24 am on that day,' says one of the agents.

This is strange; why at that time? I wonder.

Shawn has been working in cyber security for five years; he's acting the most nervous. He was working when the computer was hacked, and he was the last to log into the system.

He is shaking, repeatedly stating he knows nothing; he has been set up. 'I am not a criminal,' he protests.

'Who contacted you and told you to hack into the system?' the agent interrogating him asks.

'No one,' he replies nervously. 'I do my job as instructed and, honestly, I wasn't logged into the system at that time, check the camera.'

'We have checked the camera, and we can see you in front of your computer.'

'I worked the night shift yesterday with two of my colleagues. I'm required to work with my computer. I never logged into the mainframe; we are not allowed to do that; our job is to monitor the system.'

'The system was hacked yesterday, and extremely sensitive data was stolen. Did none of you notice?' asked the agent, frowning, as he bangs his hands on the table.

'Honestly, I don't know how it happened. We monitored the systems as we do daily,' Evelyn replies in another room.

'You don't need to worry, Evelyn; we are just crossing every T and dotting every I.'

Just then, some men in suits escort Shawn out of the room, dragging him outside of the main building. Things are about to get rough for him.

One of them has to be involved, but who?

Chapter Thirteen: Rio de Janeiro

Ana

I watch them pull the ventilator tube out of my daughter's mouth.

I can't breathe. I feel lightheaded; everything is spinning around me.

When I open my eyes again, I am told that I fainted. I burst into tears. She is all I have; how can she have died? She was supposed to stay with her mummy. How can I bury my child?

My sister holds me tightly as I weep on her chest. Who do I have left? My husband is dead; now, my only child has died suddenly. What on earth am I doing here?

'I need to die, too!' I said in despair. 'Kill me, Maria! Kill me! I have lost everything that matters to me.'

'You have me; you are not entirely alone,' my sister replies.

'Why? Why?' I say.

How can I move on? I have lost the only thing that mattered to me.

Maria tries to console me, but everything I loved in my life has been taken away. I buried my husband last year; now, I have to bury my daughter. Life is so unfair.

My sister holds me tightly in the car as her husband drives me to their house in Rocinha on the favela hill.

'You need to eat; you have not eaten anything for the past two days.' Maria looks at me warily.

'I'm not hungry.'

'Ana, you must eat. I can't afford to lose you,' Maria says. 'All you do is cry.'

When we reach Maria's home, I am too weak to move. I lie on the floor, curled up in a fetal position.

'I just want to die. I don't deserve to live,' I say.

'I am so sorry, Ana,' says Maria. She lays on the floor beside me. 'You are not alone in your loss. It's all over the news; thousands have lost their lives to this strange disease.'

I don't answer. This does not bring me any comfort.

'I called your office and spoke to your boss and the HR department;

they expressed their deepest condolences. They have given you three months' leave of absence.'

I don't care about my job as I wallow in sorrow.

'I will get you something to eat.' Maria gets up and leaves the room.

I don't care. I feel like my heart has been pierced; the pain has not dulled. *My beautiful wildflower, how could you leave me so soon?* I never got to tell you how much I loved you.

Three months later…

I have been living with Maria and her family for the past few weeks. I have lost so much weight and I have bags under my eyes from crying. I'm a shadow of my former self, but I need to go back to work or I will lose my house. That is the only thing I have that reminds me of my husband and child.

With great effort, I have retained my job. Maria was in constant contact with my boss. I am grateful for his support; he fought to keep me in the company, citing my dedication and excellent results. How he was able to keep my job open for me so long I don't know, but I will be forever grateful. And at a time when the company was making structural changes; so many people have been laid off.

It isn't easy to return to work, but the bills never stop coming. I look pale from exhaustion and lack of sleep, the dark circles under my eyes are the first thing you notice; no amount of makeup can cover them up. I'm skin and bone; I haven't been able to hold down food. I lost my will to live, and I have been admitted to the hospital three times during the past three months.

I enter my office, and my boss does a double-take, walking over to me. 'Are you OK?' he says. 'I am sorry for your loss.'

'Thank you, sir.' I sit at my desk, filled with flowers and condolences cards. I know this pandemic has shaken the whole country, but, this is personal, it was my child.

I move back to my lonely, two-bedroom house after convincing my sister that I will be fine. I work non-stop in an attempt to numb the pain. If I don't stop working, I won't have time to think. Everything in this house reminds me of the family I lost.

I am going through the spreadsheets handled by the temporary accountant. It seems that during my hiatus, my company has been awarded three contracts for mining copper in an Amazon Rainforest. Looking at the figures, there seem to be some discrepancies; the numbers are not adding up. From what I can see, the sum of $60,000,000 is missing from the balance sheet.

I walked up to my boss's office and knock on the door before entering.

'Ana, you said you needed to see me.'

'Yes, sir, I have been going through the spreadsheets for the three major contracts we just received from the government. The numbers do not add up; there seems to be $60,000,000 missing.' I show my boss the figures on my laptop.

'I'm surprised Ms Dias, the temporary accountant, never highlighted this mistake.

'I need to talk to the CEO; this is a great deal of money. HR brought in Ms Dias; so, I'll speak to them and get to the bottom of this'.

I return to my office, looking at the spreadsheet with the project analysis breakdown; something is not right; the figures are all wrong. I have been working for this company for ten years, and this has never happened before.

My office extension starts ringing. 'Hello, sir.'

'Ana, the CEO wants to see you.'

'What! I have been at this company for years. I have never met the CEO before. Will you be coming with me?'

'No, he requested to speak to you, personally. Mr Montes never has the time or patience to talk to subordinates usually, so be very careful.'

'OK, sir,' I say, dropping the phone.

I'm trembling; I have never been to the fifth floor of this building. That is where Mr Montes's office is. I am so nervous, I break out in a sweat. What have I gotten myself into?

The elevator door opens on the fifth floor; and I am met by Mr Montes's personal assistant. He also has assistants working for him. Today, he is alone.

'Follow me, Mrs Santos,' he says.

Walking behind the PA, various thoughts run through my mind. *Are they going to fire me? Am I about to lose everything?*

I enter Mr Montes's office. I have never seen such a display of wealth, from the high gloss wooden director's desk, prominently positioned in the middle of the room, to the plush interior decor. I focus on the 'big boss', that's what I call him, sitting behind the desk.

'Have a seat, Mrs Santos,' he says smoking his pipe.

'Thank you, sir.'

'I heard you just lost your daughter; my condolences.'

'Thank you, sir,' I reply nervously.

'You have been working for this company for ten years; you are very competent, that was why Mr Melo fought hard to keep you here. What I'm going to tell you must not leave these four walls, and you must never tell your boss. Am I understood?'

I nod. 'Yes, sir.'

'Forget all you saw on the spreadsheet; the fact that you noticed the discrepancies in so short a time of returning to work means that Ms Dias is an incompetent fool. I need you to manipulate the numbers so that the missing $60,000,000 will not be accounted for in the spreadsheets during an audit. Can you do that, Mrs Santos?'

I stared at the big boss, speechless. He was wearing a R$20,000 designer suit and expensive horn-rimmed glasses. I could see his receding hair that he was trying to cover with a comb over. Without a doubt, I know this man will not hesitate to destroy me if I refuse to do what he asks; I need to be smart.

'Yes, sir, what do you want me to do?'

He smiles maliciously. I have never felt so afraid for my life.

'Good! I'm glad we have you on our side. My PA will get back to you about the figures; no one must be able to trace them. Do we have an understanding?'

I nod, unable to speak.

'Thank you…and, Mrs Santos, watch your back.'

My legs are shaking as I go to leave; I needed to compose myself. *He mustn't see my fear*, I tell myself. I acknowledge the big boss with a brief smile as he mutters another 'thank you'.

I don't dare breathe until I am safely in the elevator. *What have I got myself into? Who can I trust? How am I going to get out of this?*

Chapter Fourteen: Hong Kong

Huan

Why are there so many police cars in front of my house? I just got home after a long and stressful day working to resolve the outage in the nodes.

My husband is handcuffed and being taken out of the house. I live in a luxurious home overlooking the beach in Stanley. I bought my home for tranquility and peace of mind, only to come home to this horror.

'What is happening?' I ask in a loud voice.

I run over to my husband; he is looking down and crying.

'Can you please tell me what this is about?' I ask one of the officers.

'Your husband is the number one suspect in a murder investigation.'

I watch in misery as he is placed in the back of the police squad car.

'What did you do?' I scream at him.

It's now 8.00 pm. I race into my house, my heart beating fast. I'm confused; what did he do wrong? I need to get to the bottom of this for the sake of my sanity.

'Gama, connect to the family lawyer.'

I wait impatiently as we are connected.

'Zhao, are you at the station?'

'No, I'm on my way; I'll be there before they start questioning him. Do you want to talk to him when I get there?'

'No, I'm coming to the station; he needs to answer some questions from me.'

'They believe your husband is involved in the death of Ms Yang and her two kids,' explained Zhao.

'What are you talking about? Who is Ms Yang?'

'They believe she's your husband's mistress, and he is the father of her two kids.' They were shot multiple times at close range. Her flat was not broken into, and nothing was stolen, which means she knew the person; she let them in, and your husband has a key. The flat is in his name.'

I feel faint; my head spinning; my husband has another family?

My lawyer regards me with a sullen expression, they have damning evidence against him. 'The gun used to kill them was an HK 45; they found out that your husband has that particular gun registered in his name.'

'He owns a security firm, and many of his security personnel carry the same firearm. It doesn't mean it belongs to him,' I say dismissively.

'Your husband is the only one in his company authorised to carry HK 45 pistols. Right now, they can't find your husband's gun, he told the officers his pistol was stolen yesterday morning, and he did not report the missing gun to the police. This is not good!'

I am torn. Should I help him or leave him to sort out his own mess?

He has a family. The news cuts deep. We have been married for ten years and hoping to be blessed with a child. We have done so many tests that we finally resorted to IVF, which we tried twice and failed; it was a painful and traumatising experience.

I stare into space; I do not know how long I have been standing in that position when I finally come back to my senses.

***

I enter the interrogation room, livid, asking for some time to talk to my husband and not listening to our lawyer telling me it is not in his client's best interests. My mind is stuck on one thought: *How long has this bastard been having an affair?* I was surprised I was not thrown out of the room.

I lift my hand and land a heavy slap on his face.

'How could you do this to me? I made you who you are? I gave you money to start your business; and you cheated on me?'

He finally lifts his head, ugly tears coming down his face. 'I would never hurt them,' he says. 'They are the only family I have ever wanted.'

'You bastard! How could you do this to me?'

I watch my husband cry inconsolably; I knew how much he wanted children. He would never want them dead, but I am so angry I can't see straight.

'You bought your mistress a flat? You can go to hell!'

My head is reeling; I rub away my tears with the back of my hand.

I must be dreaming. How could I be so stupid?

'Madam, please, calm down. You need to leave the interrogation room; you can't be in here. This is a murder investigation.'

47

I am escorted out of the interrogation room by one of the police officers. 'Your lawyer will keep you updated,' he says.

I think I just displayed what the police wanted.

I feel numb; I don't know how I'm supposed to feel. How could I be so stupid? I suspected he was cheating when he didn't come home for days stating he was doing his job protecting some politicians or celebrities. He didn't pick up his phone and never called back. I work in a telecommunications company, I had access to his call history, but I decided to ignore the evidence and trust him.

I feel so betrayed, but I know my husband did not kill anyone. I could kill him with my own hands for what he has done to me, but he doesn't deserve to go to jail for a crime he didn't commit.

We had talked about adoption, no wonder he never showed interest.

I sit on one of the chairs in the police station, waiting to hear from our lawyer. Maybe I should just go home; I need to think. I have been on autopilot ever since I got home.

***

The lawyer sits beside me and explains what has happened. The woman was shot ten times in the head, legs and other parts of her body. It looks like a crime of passion; she was wearing an engagement ring on her ring finger.

The two boys, who were five and four years old respectively, were shot immediately after their mother; the crime scene and gunshot splatter show after forensic analysis. The kids were trying to run away when they were killed; blood from one of them was all over the wall; it was a blood bath.

'The problem is,' he says calmly, 'that your husband is not talking to me.'

I don't reply.

'He went to see her yesterday at 6.00 pm, he was seen by a neighbour, and they had a row; their voices were heard in the building. She was killed at precisely 6.45 pm.'

Still, I say nothing, not trusting myself to speak.

'DNA shows he's not the father of those kids.'

I take a deep intake of breath.

'You are also under suspicion, for obvious reasons, but evidence shows you were in the office working on the outage.

'I'm being investigated?'

He nods. 'I'm sure the angle they are pursuing is of the wronged wife. You weren't brought in for questioning because you have the president on speed dial, but you need to be cautious.'

'Did my husband intend to marry this woman?'

'As I said, that's the problem; he is not talking. He just stared at the police officers and me. He's not telling us his whereabouts around the time of the murder, making things complicated. He was seen at the crime scene thirty minutes before the murder took place. Fortunately, a neighbour also saw him get into his car and drive away, so we just need him to confirm timings. The question directed by the police is, what did they argue about? Did he come back to finish the job when he discovered the kids aren't his?'

I look down at my hands.

'The nature of your husband's job allows him to carry firearms; the gun used was registered to him. A silencer must have been used; otherwise, the neighbours would have heard.'

'Thanks for telling me. I am retaining you; I need constant updates; I was played for a fool for far too long. Where is the flat?'

'It is a small flat in Discovery Bay.'

Chapter Fifteen: London

Jude

'I don't sell cocaine in my restaurant,' I say sharply to the police officer.

I can't believe I am in a police station. I wonder what my neighbours will be thinking; they must have seen the ambulance carrying away my crazy ex as I got into a police car and was driven away.

'What evidence do you have against my client apart from the words of some disgruntled workers?' asks my solicitor.

For the past ten minutes, a sergeant, called Roger Smith, has been insisting that I was involved in the illicit selling of cocaine committed by my ex-workers.

'My client is known worldwide as one of the best chefs; people come to his restaurant in droves; he has made substantial amounts of money from endorsements; why would he soil his name by meddling in cocaine?'

'We have seen several greedy rich people who want more money,' replies Sergeant Smith.

'From what I can see, you have no evidence that my client is involved; this case against my client must be dropped.'

'We will do no such thing. He can leave, but be advised that he must not leave the country without letting us know.'

'My client is a celebrity, and he constantly travels on business unless you are charging him; he is free to go anywhere he pleases.'

My solicitor looks at me. 'Let's go!' He then turns to the sergeant. 'Do not contact my client without talking to me first. I'll be having a word with your boss about this; I won't allow anyone to ruin my client's reputation without any just cause.'

We leave the police station and I am left wondering what is happening to me? I need to do damage control before the press gets a hold of this.

'Gama, contact my PR team; this must not be leaked in any way, shape or form to the public that I deal in cocaine; my brand will be destroyed.'

'Be careful! The police are not letting this go, and they will continue to monitor you closely,' my solicitor says.

***

'Sergeant Smith, why did you question Jude Williams? I am told you don't have substantial evidence against him, apart from the words of his workers. Your partner, Mike, told me you insisted on bringing him in.'

'Sir, with respect, we need to find out whether he is involved.'

'You have been investigating this case for six months, and you have not been able to tie anything to him. I just received a call from the Commissioner of Police, and they are calling this police bullying. I'm warning you not to go near or harass Mr Williams unless you have enough evidence; then you come to me first before doing anything stupid.' I am dismissed from the chief inspector's office.

I walk up to my partner's desk. 'You need to be more careful, Roger, Mr Williams is an influential man; I don't want to lose my livelihood.'

'I will not give up. I know he is hiding something; it will come out soon.'

'Listen, Roger, you need to stop; I have never seen you like this? Why do you want to arrest him so badly?'

'I just know he's involved; they have been operating in his restaurant for a year. He can't be so ignorant as not to know. The question is, if he's not gaining anything financially, what else is he gaining?'

'I think you should let this one go; let's concentrate on the two suspects, see if they can tell us anything.'

'OK!' Roger replies. I felt his eyes on me as I walk away.

But I can never let this go, Roger thinks to himself. *My life and that of my family are in danger if I don't indict Jude in this case, one way or the other.*

***

I have not slept in days; why is life upside down? I have called for an urgent meeting at my restaurant tomorrow. How could this be happening in my restaurant for a whole year without my knowledge? Who wants to destroy me?

My mother's flight just landed from Scotland; she will be going to the house soon; I've arranged a pickup.

I have requested the assistance of a private investigation agency to do a thorough check on all my workers because it seems I don't know my

51

employees at all. I place my head on my pillows. I need to try and get some rest; I have spent hours in the police station with that insufferable sergeant. What is his problem with me? I will deal with it all tomorrow. My lawyer has asked whether I wanted to sue my crazy ex, Ella. I don't think it is necessary; I have asked for a restraining order against her.

My mother's arrival in the house, to take care of me, is incredible. I don't want her to worry; I won't tell her my problems; she deserves to live a peaceful life; that is what I want for her.

I look across at the alarm clock on my side table; it's 9.00 pm; why do I have the feeling that something is wrong. I walk out of my room to check on my mother, only to find her in the sitting room tied to a chair with masking tape over her mouth. A man is holding a gun to her head.

'Please! Please! Don't hurt my mother.'

Tears are running down my mother's face.

'I'll give you anything you want, is it money?'

The room is dimly lit, with just one lamp switched on. A man walks out of the shadows, his face obscured. Startled, I jump back. 'What do you want?' I say.

'We will continue to run the cocaine business from your restaurant, and you will not do anything to hinder that.'

'What do you mean to "continue to run"? I was taken to the police station, questioned for hours, and I am still under investigation. If they find out I am involved in cocaine, my restaurant will be closed.'

'They will not find out,' the man replies.

'They arrested you guys today, which shows you are not careful enough,' I reply.

'We knew when they started the investigation. We wanted them to arrest George and William because they became greedy. Anyone that crosses me will be taken out of the way. Jude, we know everything about you, from how you like to take your tea in the morning at precisely 7.30 am, without milk, and your early morning jog for one hour, to your mother's address in Scotland; do you want me to tell you? By the way, are you aware that your mother has a boyfriend? She has been dating him for one year and three months precisely. Oh, and we know you had your father murdered.'

My heart is beating so fast, I think it might come out of my chest.

'We will leave you now, but this is just a warning. The business continues, as usual, ignorance they say, is bliss, so tell the private investigation agency that you are no longer interested.' They laugh maliciously as they walk out of my house.

How did they get in without the alarm going off? Who are these people?

I rush over to untie my terrified mother.

Chapter Sixteen: New York

Martin

It is good to be home. I have missed my family. My wife was my high-school sweetheart. We fell in love, and decided to get married early. That was twenty-one years ago. We have two teenage daughters, who are a mixture of both parents with lovely brunette hair. Emilia, my eldest, is eighteen years old with light blue eyes, like her mother, but she is going to be tall like me; she is already 5ft 10, while Charlotte, my sixteen year old, has green eyes, and, at 5ft 4, is shorter.

The case has me stumped and confused; why won't the mayor investigate the death of his daughter? I urgently need to go through some documents. I look at my lovely wife, Leah. 'Why don't you head up to bed?' I say.

'Didn't they give you two weeks' leave from work,' she asks, raising an eyebrow.

'Yes, sweetheart, but the work doesn't stop; just give me an hour.'

I'm thrilled to be home; I was able to spend the whole day with my family; I have missed being with them.

I watch her head upstairs and then enter the home office. The notebook is in the top drawer of my desk. I have been itching to go through it all day, but I needed to be with my wife and daughters; I can't remember the last time I got to spend time with my grown kids. They are always on their phones, and Emilia is already at New York University. I am grateful for the blizzard; all schools have been closed, and they were forced to be at home.

I take out the notebook; it looks like a journal. I turn to the first page: 'The light is shining brighter every day, and it is drawing me closer... closer to the sun. He loves me too; he whispered it in my ear.'

She was fifteen years old; did she have a boyfriend? I wasn't allowed to ask such questions at the mayor's house.

The next page contains a grotesque image of a sad girl with scars all over her body and blood pouring out. Her face is disfigured by the scars, but you can see the sadness. She is suffering from depression. This drawing depicts a girl in pain who feels ugly and empty.

I go on the internet to search for a picture of the mayor's daughter, Lily. I find one of her standing proudly in her school uniform with her blonde hair in a ponytail, her hazel eyes smiling for the world to see. It was taken last year by the look of the date. What can have happened to her in the past year?

I need to go upstairs to bed, or my wife will come looking for me. Next week, I will go to Lily's school. Hopefully, the road will be clear; I need to learn more about her life, but I need to be careful nobody must know, not even Bobby, my best friend and partner for eight years.

***

I drive to the highly prestigious Red-gate School, a massive red-brick building situated in a prominent position in Manhattan, the school flag swaying in the wind. The school was founded in 1928 only crème de la crème can enrol with the hefty fee of $45,000 annually.

I walk into the school building and am shown the way to the principal's office. The school is relatively empty; it will not be fully open until tomorrow.

The principal is no more than 5 ft 6 or so, with thick glasses, trying very hard to feel important in his expensive suit; he's probably in his late forties.

'What can I do for you, Mr Hills?' he says. 'As you know, the academic staff are the only ones here preparing for the resumption of school tomorrow.'

'I understand, Principal Baker, but I wanted to talk about Lily Cleborne.'

'I don't understand; wasn't the case ruled as suicide by the police? It's all over the news. She was such a lovely girl, may her soul rest in peace,' he says, making the sign of the cross.

'Yes, Mr Baker, I'm here to ask a few questions to understand her better. How was her behaviour in the past year? Did you notice any changes in her?'

'Lily was bubbly, one of the popular girls in school; she was a typical teenager who disrupted the class from time to time, which meant she ended up in the school office. She changed, suddenly, about six months ago and became a shadow of herself, always gloomy, hardly ever talking. She stopped hanging out with her friends and the popular kids to sit by herself. We spoke to her parents about the changes, but we were told she was seeing a therapist.'

'Was she, by any chance, taking any drugs?'

'I beg your pardon, sir, illegal drugs are prohibited in my school. Now, I need to get back to work. Have a good day, Mr Hills.'

I smile sheepishly at the principal. 'Thank you.'

Gama, I need you to start the car!

I know there's more to it than what the principal says; he shut down the minute I questioned him about drugs. I could see fear in his expression before he covered it with anger. I'm sure a school like this will have someone selling pills to these rich kids. I need to find out about her best friend and boyfriend.

I get into my car and start driving home and, suddenly, I feet an impact. My body flies forward but is held in place by my seatbelt. I look at my side mirror; I see a black jeep, with tinted windows, accelerating, preparing to hit my car again. I reach for my gun in the glove compartment and press my leg on the accelerator to prevent another rear collision. I look through the rear-view mirror and see that the jeep has increased its speed. I overtake the car in front of me. The jeep is trying to get behind me, so I continue to overtake several vehicles. I glance at the opposing traffic, there are not too many cars, as I suddenly change lanes.

The jeep follows me for around thirty-five minutes. I slow down to look at the car licence plate when the jeep rams me again. I accelerate away at top speed; I don't know how many people are in the jeep. I hold my gun in my hand as I pressed the accelerator, the jeep moves behind me, trying to overtake my car. The person in the passenger seat opens fire, and I swerve and put my car in reverse. A bullet hits my side-view mirror as I reverse the car, trying to avoid oncoming vehicles honking horns. I do a quick U-turn, the tyres squealing, and the jeep gets caught by traffic. I drive away at speed, checking my mirror constantly, but the jeep is not following. I have lost them, for now. It's lucky the weather has improved this past week, or I may have been trapped.

Who is trying to kill me?

I need to get home. I have to make sure my family are safe?

I can't assess the damage to my car until I get home safely. I park my car in the driveway. I can see Bobby; why is he at my house?

'What happened to the car? Are you OK?' my wife asks, making a quick check of my face and body.

'I'm fine, Leah, it was just an accident; some crazy driver accidentally hit my car from the back, don't worry about it; insurance will take care of it.'

Bobby stands watching me closely without saying a word.

'Hey!' I walked up to my partner, who was leaning on his car. 'What are you doing here?'

'Came to check on you? What are you up to, Martin?'

'Nothing,' I reply.

'Are you sure about that?'

'What is this all about? I'm on leave and have been spending time with my family. I went to get some groceries when some careless idiot hit me.'

Bobby looks at me intently, not saying anything, before getting into his car and driving away.

That's strange, I think. *What's going on?*

Chapter Seventeen: Lagos

Lola

I am terrified for my life. I keep looking back; I have this eerie feeling that someone is following me. I am presently in Ebute Meta based on information I received that more amputated body parts have been found; buried in the grounds of an empty house.

I look behind me as I get into my 1995 Toyota Camry, a big contrast to the latest Range Rover I own at home in Ikoyi. I keep glancing in the rear-view mirror, my heart beating fast. Am I being followed, or am I just scared?

Calm down! I scold myself. *Stop assuming things; no one is following you.*

Gama picks up a call as I arrive back at my office.

'There will be more killings,' I hear on the line. 'You are being monitored, you need to be more careful. All vital information must be hidden *now!* They will be in your office in five minutes.' The call disconnects with a click.

I rush to pick up my office laptop and mobile phone. I have a safe hidden under my wooden floor, and I quickly hide them. I have a spare laptop and mobile on my office desk, used for my cosmetic business; it contains nothing that could link me to investigative journalism.

My locked steel security door opens with ease. I am trying to understand what is happening when a tall, fierce man, with snake tattoos all over his arms, walks into my office. I am almost rigid with fear; afraid that I might be killed at any moment. I tremble as he moves towards me. He pins me to the wall with his hand wrapped around my throat as he snarls at me.

'Are you the owner of 'The Report' news blog?' His hand tightens around my neck. 'Answer me!' he commands, as he releases his hand.

I slide down the wall, coughing profusely, tears running down my eyes. 'I don't know anything about any news blog,' I answer, my vision clouded by tears.

'If you value your life, you will not involve yourself in things that are not your business,' he replies.

'I honestly do not know anything.'

'Where are your computer and mobile phone?'

I point at the laptop and phone on the desk; he picked them up.

'Today is your lucky day, I was instructed not to kill you, but you might not be lucky next time.'

I watch as he casually strolls out of my office. I am hysterical. *Oh my God! Am I going to die?*

I force myself to breathe as I cower in the corner of my office.

When I have calmed down, I open my office door and peep outside; I don't see anyone. I close the door and lock it. I know this won't make a difference, as they had a spare key. But how? I haven't lost any of my keys.

I retrieve my laptop from the hiding place. I try to open my website, but it has been hacked and shut down. I feel like I am losing my mind. What is happening to me? I promised myself that I would find the monster who killed my friend but now I am beginning to doubt myself.

I drive home, feeling dejected, looking behind me constantly, afraid that I might be followed. I arrive at my house, and my friend, Sade, is waiting for me outside my door.

'Where have you been, Lola? I have tried your phone, and it is completely switched off. I have been waiting for you for almost two hours; I'm afraid to go home.'

'What's happened?'

'Someone broke into my house and started asking questions about you and Chioma?'

A chill travels down my spine. 'What does this person look like?' I ask.

'Honestly, I don't know; I was too afraid. All I know is that he is a man, and I don't want to die.'

'What did you tell him?'

'The truth; that you are a socialite who owns a cosmetic company called Moshébì; I told him everything I knew. They kept asking about 'The Report' news blog and whether you run it. I told them it's impossible; you are not a journalist; you are into fashion and beauty and would never be interested in such a thing.'

'Did he hurt you in any way?'

'No, he didn't, but I was afraid; Lola, what are you up to?'

'Nothing, I swear. I don't know what this is all about?'

'You need to tell your parents. Why would someone suspect you of being the one writing those things in that blog?'

'I have no idea. I think I am being set up.'

'I am afraid to go home,' Sade says.

'Come inside.'

As she walks into the house, Gama sets up the security camera.

I need to find out who that man is? I will check the recorded video on my mobile phone from the hidden camera in my office. With every beat of my heart, I am resolute to see this through, I will not give in to their fear tactics.

Somewhere in Nigeria…

'Why didn't you just let me kill her?'

'She is the daughter of the former head of the senate, it will raise too many questions. Continue to watch her and, if she doesn't stop, then I will be left with no choice but to eliminate her.'

Chapter Eighteen: Kabul

Ahmed

I sit quietly watching Yusuf, who keeps checking his watch. My heart feels like it is racing 100 beats per second. *This could be very dangerous*, I think to myself, *but we have been living on the edge ever since we got to Kabul*. There is no guarantee that my family will be safe if we continue to live like this. I lift my long top to wipe the sweat off my brow.

'Yusuf, I am interested; I am going to do this for my family.'

'Good! You answered me in four and a half minutes; I thought you were going to say no. Follow me.'

We leave the house, and I follow him to another similar building but bigger than the previous one. When we enter, there is no furniture inside, but a giant wooden clock is sitting on the wall showing the wrong time. Yusuf walks up to the clock and moves it in a specific direction, and the wall where the clock was situated opens. I can now see a lift; I can't believe it, an elevator in a house.

'What about my family?' I ask. 'I've left them for too long already.'

'Don't worry. Two of our wives were sent to them, and they will be taken to a safe and secure home.'

My wife wouldn't just follow any stranger.'

'We showed her a video of you with me. Try not to worry; my wife can be very persuasive. You will speak to them soon, just follow me for now.'

We get into the lift. Yusuf's retina is scanned, and the elevator closes immediately and starts going down.

'Do you have an underground facility? Where did you get such technology in Kabul?'

Yusuf just smiles without saying anything.

'Who are you? Yusuf, you need to give me something.'

'All questions will be answered in due time; you have nothing to fear.'

The lift door opens to a spacious floor filled with people; some working on computers. I look to my right; there is a glass partition, and some people are in, what looks like, a shooting range.

'Where am I? In a twilight zone?'

'Ahmed, you need to meet my boss, Hussain.'

I follow him through different office divisions; where people are monitoring cameras. We enter a small office, where I see a man I have seen many times on television speaking against the Ahedan. I am facing the most wanted man in Afghanistan!

I greet him by shaking his hand.

'Please take a seat,' he says. 'Ahmed, I have heard so much about you.'

'Thank you, sir,' I respond.

'Yusuf, can you excuse us for the moment?'

Nodding his head, Yusuf walks out of the office.

'I have gone through your military reports; they are very impressive. But, before we commence this discussion, I know you would love to talk to your family so you can put your mind at rest.'

A screen is placed in front of me, and I can see my wife. Her expression changes when she sees my face.

'I was apprehensive when they came to take us away,' Aisha tells me. 'Are you OK?'

I laughed. 'I should be the one asking you that.'

'We are fine; everyone has been so kind, and they are taking good care of us. They prepared a hearty meal for us. Can you believe we took a bath?' My wife laughs happily. 'And the children are sleeping on a bed, Ahmed, a bed.'

I don't know whether to cry or laugh. 'I will see you soon,' I promise.

'Thank you,' I say, as I look back at Hussain.

'Don't thank me, that's our job, taking care of the few selected members because what we do is top secret; even our wives don't know anything about our undertakings.

'Several of our men are working for the Ahedan Group. I will not disclose their identity because we need to be careful; no one can be trusted fully, but your name has been mentioned to Mohammed, and he has done a thorough check on you. He's interested in your military expertise.

'You will go to headquarters tomorrow and introduce yourself; you have an appointment at 3.45 pm, and you need to be there at least an hour earlier; Mohammed hates tardiness but appreciates early comers.'

Hussain opens a massive folder titled 'Mohammed Pir'.

'We have received intel that he has access to nuclear weapons, in a secret location in Afghanistan, and he plans to wreak havoc on humanity. Our men on the ground have not been able to find the location; he keeps it close to his chest; you need to gain his trust. He is one of the most powerful men globally; he has some countries sponsoring him.'

Hussain takes out pictures of the latest artillery, armoured vehicles, trucks and helicopters.

'This is some of the equipment found in various Ahedan compounds. You need to find out which countries are sponsoring him; he is the wealthiest man in Afghanistan, owning the Union Bank of Afghanistan, and he also controls the national bank.

'He needs to be stopped, and that is your assignment. The mission you have taken on might endanger your life, but we promise we will take care of your family. This is for all the unspoken voices of innocent people pleading to live.

'We will talk more tomorrow before you go for your appointment; right now, you need to go, eat something and rest; we need you to be in tip-top shape.'

I shake his hand and am escorted out by another man. 'Please follow me,' he says.

We are walking so fast that I do not have the opportunity to look around. We get into the lift, his retina is scanned, and we are taken back up.

He lets me out of the building and I follow him to a two-storey building. There are

women everywhere with children; some of the children are watching television, and some women are in the kitchen cooking.

The man, who hasn't introduced himself, takes me to one of the women saying that I am the husband of Aisha.

'*Salam!*' I place my right hand on my chest while nodding.

'Please follow me,' the woman says.

I can see several rooms, she knocks on a door, and it is opened by my wife.

I thank the woman and she leaves.

I walk into an en suite with two double beds. Abdul and Laila are sound asleep on one of the beds. Watching them sleep, I have an overwhelming sense of relief; they have not been able to sleep properly in weeks.

'Where have you been? No one seems to be talking.'

'I've been offered a job; I'm going for an interview tomorrow. But I can't tell you much about it. You'll have to trust me.'

'With the people who have taken us in?' Aisha asks.

I nod. 'Through a friend I have known for years. I met him during our military days, and he told me about this place.'

There is a knock on the door; outside is a woman carrying a tray filled with various delicacies. She hands the tray to me and walks away.

I am so hungry I tear into the food.

'Aisha, try to rest,' I say with my mouth full, sensing her fatigue. 'Don't worry about anything; it is my responsibility to care for you.'

After the horrifying weeks we have experienced, I lie down to sleep, grateful but also fearful of the dangerous mission assigned to me. *Will I live long enough to see my children grow up?*

I close my eyes; I can barely keep them open after weeks of sleepless nights.

Chapter Nineteen: Sydney

Henry

'Shawn. No! No!' I shout, approaching slowly.

'How the hell did he get a gun in his room?' I look at the three agents trying to persuade him not to pull the trigger.

'Put the gun down,' one of the agents says, as Shawn holds it up to his head.

'I can't!'

'Why can't you?' I ask. 'Shawn, talk to me. I can help.'

There is a crack as he pulls the trigger. The bullet pierces his skull, and he slumps to the floor.

Looking at all the agents suspiciously, I ask, 'Who gave him a gun?'

'We don't know, that is the problem. We're checking on the other suspects now,' one of them replies.

We rush to the cells and discover their lifeless bodies on the floor.

Fuckin 'ell!

'There is no sign of shooting; how did they die? I need answers now,' I say sharply. 'People don't just die in the most secure facility in Australia.'

I look at Mr Robinson. 'I want all of you guys investigated; someone is involved; one of your men gave Shawn the gun,' I tell the head of Australian intelligence. 'Find out to whom that pistol is registered.'

'That's impossible. My agents are well trained, and they would never break the law.'

'The suspect had no access to a gun; where did he find that pistol, and what killed the others?' I say in response.

As we examine the surveillance videos, there seems to be a glitch. It shows the suspects sleeping for the past hour in their cells; the video has been altered.

I am blinded by confusion and rage; I honestly didn't know whether to scream or punch someone. I need detailed information about what the hell happened, and fast. I storm out of the building.

What should I tell the prime minister? Shit!

The suspects were in isolated rooms with only a tiny bed and toilet;

they were monitored round the clock. How could this happen?

We have been in this shithole for three unproductive days; the suspects have endured severe torture, like sleep deprivation, beating, and even hypnosis but still we have no results. They continued to state they were not involved in the cyber-attack; now this happens.

Gama connects me to the prime minister as I drive to my parents' house.

'Sir, I cannot explain it, the three suspects died mysteriously, a detailed investigation is underway; I expect a report in one hour.'

'That will not be necessary.'

'But, sir! We can't allow this to happen in our facility.'

'I said, do not pursue this.' The prime minister was insistent.

'Sir? We never got any answers from them; we still don't know who can access the database, and we are back to square one.'

The phone disconnects. I am shocked beyond reason; drowning in doubts and questions. Is my mind playing tricks on me? Why would the prime minister give me a direct order not to pursue an enquiry?

Gama connects as a call comes through from Mr Robinson.

'Hello, Mr Graham. We will no longer be investigating what happened to the three suspects at Cell Site 201; all records and investigations will be destroyed; this is a direct order from the prime minister.'

'I don't understand,' I say. 'Can you do me a favour? Tell me what info you gathered before you closed the case.'

'This is a big ask. I am not at liberty to disclose anything.'

'Please! This is between us; no third party will hear.'

There is a long silence, as I wait with bated breath.

I hear a deep sigh. 'I am putting my career at risk, but I will tell you this: Evelyn and Jason died of a lethal injection, and the gun was unregistered. That's all I can say.'

'Thank you,' I reply as the call is disconnected.

I can't think; I need to get to my parents' house; I have not slept properly in three days. Maybe after resting, I will find out what is going on.

***

'Honey! We have been waiting to receive you for days,' says my mum, giving me a warm hug. She is dressed elegantly; the epitome of class and grace. I grew up watching her govern Australia as prime minister; acclaimed as one of the best, I need her guidance.

'Sorry, Mum, something came up; I can't talk about it.'

'Say no more; I understand. You look tired; we have prepared a room for you upstairs. Maybe we can talk later?' she says, tapping my back gently and walking away.

'Thanks, Mum,' I say wearily as I walk upstairs.

I have not been to this home in Kirribilli in months; it's still one of the most beautiful houses I have ever seen. I used the template to decorate my own home, from the stunning wallpaper, imported rug in the dining room in vibrant red, to the walls filled with art.

After a long shower, I get into bed and, eventually, doze off.

I am covered in blood, blood everywhere. 'Help me,' I scream. Somebody, please help me, I am dying. I hear laughter, who is laughing?

I wake up, covered in sweat, my heart beating harder than ever, and check my body, frantically, for blood.

It was just a dream; but it felt so real. Why am I still shaking?

My personal life is in shambles; I technically don't have a home, I'm on the brink of divorce, and my son hates me. My job is the only thing I have going for me; now, I am not so sure.

My mobile pings. I receive a text from an unknown number stating: 'Do not pursue this.'

What the hell is this? Do not pursue what?

Something strange is happening; it is so unlike the prime minister not to be interested in the unexplained death of someone in custody and sensitive information is in the hands of the unknown.

Is the prime minister being blackmailed?

Who sent me this strange text?

So many questions and no answers.

I need to sleep; tomorrow is another day.

Chapter Twenty: Rio de Janeiro

Ana

With a shaky hand, I press the button for the first floor. *You need to control yourself*, I think to myself. Every muscle in my body screams at me to resign and flee. *What am I going to do? I can't talk to anyone; I would be placing their lives in danger.*

I steady my breathing in an attempt to calm the panic. The elevator dings. I need to be careful; my colleagues were informed that I was invited to see the CEO, and they will be watching me.

I walk briskly into my office, trying not to draw any attention to myself, keeping my head down as I pass. I close the door gently and drop to the floor. I use every muscle in my body to stifle a whimper. I place my hand over my mouth to stop myself from screaming, as the tears fall; why did I come back to work?

I hear a knock on my door. I quickly wipe my eyes with the hem of my skirt.

I stand up and hurry to sit on my chair as my boss walks in.

'Ana, are you OK?'

'I am fine, sir.'

'Your eyes are red; is anything wrong?'

'I'm sorry, sir, I was thinking about my daughter.'

'Oh! It will get better with time. I just wanted to know how it went with the CEO. Can you believe I've only met him twice in passing, never one-on-one?'

I wish I'd never met him in person, I think to myself.

'It went well, sir, thank you. He just wanted to commend me on finding the accounting errors and highlighting them.'

'Well done, Ana, for doing an outstanding job; even with all you are going through, I am proud of you.'

'Thank you, sir.'

I watch him leave my office; he is a wonderful and caring boss, I wish I could confide in him, but I need to think clearly about how to get out of this predicament.

My phone rings; it's an unknown number.

'Hello! Who is this?'

'This is Carlos Ribeiro, head personal assistant to Mr Montes.'

I can't speak; I need time to catch my breath.

'Listen carefully; I will be coming to your office with the modified figures for the accounting data; it must be done perfectly so that no one will be able to detect any malpractice, and all documents must be shredded after use.'

***

Carlos looks at his boss after dropping the phone.

'Why keep her, sir?'

'We need her. We hired one of the best accountants to modify the figures, but Ana found discrepancies in just three days after returning to the office; keep in mind that she had just lost her daughter.'

'What do we do next?'

'Get me, Antonio!'

***

If I do the modification, I am implicated in fraud; I quickly move the original spreadsheet onto my flash drive; I need to keep this in a safe place.

I receive an alert on my phone stating that $100,000 has been deposited in an account in my name. My phone slips out of my hands in shock. I have never opened a dollar account; how is this possible?

'Gama call Brazilian City Bank.

'Hello, I just received an alert on my phone stating that an account has been opened in my name; but I haven't opened an account with you.'

'Can I please have the account number?'

I look at my phone and read out the number to customer service.

'Yes, ma'am, you have just received $100,000 in your account.'

'That is the problem; I never opened an account.'

'Can you confirm your name.'

'Ana Santos.'

'And address.'

'2136 Leme.'

'And your date of birth.'

69

'20/07/1986.'

'This is your account, madam.'

'Then who opened it if it wasn't me. And who transferred the money to my account?' 'From what I can see, the transfer was made from an anonymous bank account.'

OK, thanks for your help.'

'Thank you for banking with us.'

The phone disconnects.

Gama asks to connect to an unknown number. I accept the call.

'This is Juliana; we spoke many times after your husband's death regarding the unpaid loan your husband took out on the house. I am delighted to see that you have now repaid the R$54,566.40. Please come to the bank to pick up your house documents at your earliest convenience.'

'Thank you,' I say, stunned, as the call is disconnected.

Terror sucks the breath from my body; what's happening to my life? How can an account be opened and the loan paid off without my knowledge? Who gave me this enormous amount of money?

I need to find a way to close this account and sort out the loan, one way or another; I am not touching that money.

***

A computer is placed in front of Antonio Gomes, which contains all the information on Ana Santos. She is a beautiful woman, but much too thin.

'Last year, she lost her husband, and her daughter died three months ago,' says Carlos.

He moves the mouse to show Antonio pictures of Ana's husband and daughter.

'I need you to find a way to get close to her; her state of mind is very fragile; we have nothing to use against her; we need her to work for us. This needs to be done quickly.'

Mr Montes pads into the room.

'Carlos, has Francisca Dias been taken care of?'

'Yes, sir! According to the police report, she was drunk-driving when her vehicle somersaulted several times before plunging into a ditch.'

'Good! She was an incompetent fool.'

Mr Montes looks at Antonio sternly. 'I was hoping you could use your good looks and charm to find a way to do her work for us; willingly go through all the details provided; you have two days to get this done,' he says, before strolling out of the isolated building in the worst part of Rio with his security agents.

Chapter Twenty-one: Hong Kong

Huan

A week ago, if you had told me I would be walking into a prison, I would have laughed in your face. It would have been unimaginable, but look at my life now. My husband has been remanded in custody until his hearing, which is three months away; he hasn't been granted bail because of the criminal nature of his offence.

I stand in line as a prison officer, with an angry scowl, gives me a pat-down search for security protocol; I feel violated.

What am I doing here? I keep asking myself. I should allow him to rot in jail; that is what he deserves for the humiliation he's putting me through, but something doesn't seem right.

I have received phone calls and visits from family members and friends telling me I'm the dumbest person in the world to retain the best criminal lawyer to defend a cheating husband.

But he is not talking and I want to know why. This is why I am sitting in the visiting room waiting for him. He refuses to speak to our attorney, as well as the police. How can he be defended if he is not ready to cooperate with anyone? I'm supposed to convince the two-timing bastard to confide in his attorney.

I can see sadness in his eyes as he walks up to me; this makes me furious. I don't realise what I am doing, when I raise my voice at him.

A prison officer comes up to me and warns me not to do that again, or I will be forced to leave the premises.

'I'm sorry, I didn't mean to.'

Chun! Look at your life. I was a good wife to you; I never kept my money from you, but how did you repay me; by lying and cheating?

He is sitting with downcast eyes, pleading with me without saying a word, letting his arms fall helplessly by his side.

'Why are you not talking? Say something, damn it!'

He looks up at me and quickly slips a piece of paper into my hand, whispering, 'Look at it when you get home.' He looks back down.

I place the paper in my bag, and stand up angrily. 'If you don't want to talk to me, at least talk to our attorney, which is the only way he can help you,' I say, as I storm out of the room.

The bastard! I weep as I walk away, I wipe away the tears with the back of my hand; I promised myself I would not shed a tear for him.

I get into my car, and the chauffeur drives off.

'Take me home,' I instruct.

My employees whisper and point at me whenever they see me; it's all over the news; the golden couple in a sham marriage. It's humiliating.

I arrive at our beachfront home filled with regrets and unanswered questions. My intuition tells me something is very wrong; I can't explain it, even when I look past my anger and sense of betrayal.

I open the door to my house, to find the living room in disarray. Everything has been ransacked and my furniture is overturned and damaged. I rush to my study; my laptop has been taken, drawers have been pulled out and documents litter the floor.

Who came into my house?

My pulse is racing. *Breathe, Huan. You can t afford to faint right now.*

'Gama call 999.'

The police arrive. The entire house is in a mess. My furniture, art, and chandeliers have all been vandalised, but no money or jewellery were stolen.

***

I stare out at the city from the window of my hotel, and sigh. His mess has become my mess. I can't stay at my house. Chun is not talking; and I don't know what to do. I need answers; I can't continue like this.

Then I remember my husband giving me a piece of paper. I open my bag and take it out. It reads 'everything is not what it seems'.

Chapter Twenty-two: London

Jude

I rush over to untie my mother from the chair she is strapped to. A feeling of dread creeps over me as I look around to see if the intruders are still hiding somewhere. There are tears coursing down my mum's cheeks.

'I'm so sorry, Mum,' I whisper as I remove the tape from her mouth.

'Who are those people?' she asks.

'I don't know them.'

'What do they want from you?'

'I don't know. I had to go to the police station earlier because two of my employees had been arrested for selling cocaine, but I will talk to you tomorrow about what happened to me. Right now, I want you to rest.'

'Are you safe? Jude,' she asks, as I cut the rope tying her hands together. 'Can you at least tell me you will be OK?' She rubs her wrists before taking my face in her hands. 'You have always carried the pain of your father's demise on your shoulders and never allowed yourself to be whole.'

'I am fine; I don't regret setting him up; he was going to kill us eventually.'

'How do they know so much about us?' She clings to my arm.

'Mum, everything will be fine.' I give her a warm hug. 'Don't worry about anything; I'll take care of it.'

'OK, if you say so.'

'So, tell me, Mum, this man in your life, is he worthy of you?' I say, changing the subject.

She smiles and her eyes sparkle. 'He wants to marry me, Jude, but he wants to get to know you before the formal proposal. I am finally happy after years of emotional and physical abuse.'

I walk her to her room. 'Mum, I need you to rest; I know that won't be easy; please try. It would help if you went back to Scotland tomorrow.'

Jude, I'm scared something wrong will happen to you; you're not telling me everything, which makes me worry more.'

'Mum, honestly, I don't have all the answers but believe me, I will get to the bottom of this. I need you to be careful; I don't want anything to happen to you either.'

'Promise me you will be careful,' she says as she closes the bedroom door.

I pick up my phone to view the security video from the hidden camera in my living room, only to find that all recordings have been deleted. How is that possible? Nobody has access to my phone.

I'm going to see a private investigator tomorrow; I need answers. I will not allow anyone to turn my restaurant into a drug house, and I have to keep myself and my mother safe.

How did they know about the death of my father? The case was buried after the trial. It was all over the news about how my father died a gruesome death at the hands of a local gang; he was shot in the head, and his right hand was kept as a souvenir? The judge was sympathetic to the fact that he was an abusive man and I was underage; we were given anonymity, and we had our names changed after the trial. How could anyone have found out I had a hand in his death?

***

Trying to hail a black cab after seeing Charles, the head of a global private investigation company located in Melbourne Road, my phone connects to an incoming call.

'I warned you to cancel the private investigator, Mr Williams, but you refused; I am not playing games with you, the next time you try to be smart I will end you. By the way, you have been followed by a policeman all morning; I'd be careful if I were you, you wouldn't want to end up in jail this time.' The call disconnects.

My heart is racing as I look around frantically, searching for nameless faces; who are these people? I jump into a black cab, giving the address of my restaurant, just as I receive an email from Charles. 'Thank you so much for visiting us today at 'Global Private Investigations' but, after careful consideration, we'll no longer be pursuing your case.'

I throw up my hands up in despair; how do I get out of this?

My restaurant seems like a strange place; everyone is a suspect; who are these people selling drugs in my restaurant? Many of my employees have been working for me for years; some have been with me from the very beginning. I need to be careful; I will install secret cameras, but how can I do that without the nameless knowing?

My agent walks into my office with a big smile. 'Congratulations, Jude!' We've finalised the book deal; you can now share your incredible cooking with the world.'

Finally, light at the end of the tunnel. I shake my agent's hand in excitement and give a silent, big 'up yours' to my father.

***

I have been following him all day, watching him closely; he looks scared and confused, but I can t afford to be sentimental. I look at the fifty grams of cocaine I plan on planting in his office tonight. I wipe the sweat from my brow. How did it get to this? I am a decorated police officer.

I don't have a choice; this is for my family; my son was kidnapped as a warning sign. He's been released, but I can't risk anything happening to him again.

Chapter Twenty-three: New York

Martin

I have been a policeman for eighteen years. I have put my life at risk many times but, in the mayor's case, I have a strange, fearful sense that I'm going to face worse danger than ever before. I was not able to see the faces of the attackers because they were wearing balaclavas and the partial plate number I was able to remember generated no result; I am back to square one.

My partner, Bobby, has been acting strangely after coming to my house unannounced and leaving abruptly. I tried calling him several times, during the week, but my calls have been going straight to voicemail.

I walk into the precinct and see Bobby sitting in his chair.

'What's up, man? I have been calling all week; where have you been?'

'Sorry! I've been busy.'

'Your phone was switched off. Is everything OK?'

'Everything is fine, don't worry about it. My girlfriend Harper and I have problems, so I decided to spend some time with her,' he says, not looking at me.

Hey, why didn't you tell me? I'm sorry to hear that, if you need anything, let me know.'

'Thanks,' says Bobby. 'But right now the captain wants to see you.'

The captain looks up from a document on his desk, 'Martin, come in and close the door.'

I do as he asks.

'I warned you to leave the mayor's case alone, but you didn't. I received a call from the mayor saying that you went to the school to terrorise the principal.'

'Sir…'

'Don't talk; just listen. I will be pulling you off all cases immediately. Bobby will work those cases alone. You have been assigned to desk duty till further notice. I do not want to see you near any investigative matters, or else you will lose your job. Do you understand? Now get out of my office, and send in Bobby.'

I march over to my desk, angrily pushing the papers around. I look at Bobby sitting across from me. 'The captain wants to see you,' I say.

No one is taking me off this case; I will see it to the end, I promise myself.

I glance behind me as Bobby enters the captain's office. He closes the door and pulls down the blinds. What the hell! The captain never pulls down the blinds; something is definitely fishy.

***

I walk into my house. I can tell that my wife is seething with anger.

'Hey, what's going on?'

'Are you cheating on me?' she screams.

'I would never cheat on you; where is this coming from?'

'I received a letter, addressed to me, that contains a flash drive.' She turns her computer screen to face me. I see someone who looks like me, but is not me, kissing a woman.

'That's not me! I would never cheat on you; I love you too much. I am being set up.'

'You're telling me this is not you. Do you think I'm stupid? I have been married to you for twenty-one years. I recognise the shirt I bought you in the picture.'

'I don't know how to explain this, but I promise you that is not me.'

'I called Bobby; he is your best friend and partner, he knows you well. I asked him whether you were cheating on me? Do you know what the funny thing is…?' she wipes away a tear, '…he didn't deny it; he just told me to talk to you. Even your partner can't even lie or defend you.' At that, she races upstairs. I run after her.

'Someone is trying to destroy my marriage and my career; please let me get to the bottom of this. I will fix this.'

'Just get out! I don't want to see your face.'

I walk out of the room in despair. Who is doing this and why? The man looks like me, but it isn't. I have never seen that woman in my life. Somehow, I have to prove that. I need to save my marriage.

Chapter Twenty-four: Lagos

Lola

I am terrified to leave my house. I need a new office; I can't risk going back to my old one. I have to persevere, even in the face of death.

I work through my emails; a link has been sent to me, the subject line reads: 'Important information'. Opening it, I see a video of young men and women, about thirty-seven people in total, I think. They are rounded up and blindfolded; surrounded by men with guns telling them to kneel. I can hear the victims wailing and pleading for their lives. They are forcefully taken, one by one, to another section of the building, where I watch as a grotesque-looking man, with a horrible scar on his left cheek, lifts a steel blade and cuts off their heads, then later chops up their bodies. I start shaking, hyperventilating. I bend over, trying to draw deep breaths.

Oh my God! These people are monsters.

I am upset and angry. So many innocent people are being killed daily, and no one is doing anything about it. Hundreds of youths are dead, and everyone is mute. Why?

People need to see this, but I can only post it anonymously on the web; I need a secure IP address.

'Gama, connect to Frank.'

'Hello, Frank. It's Lola. I need your help.'

'I haven't heard from you in years, what do you need?'

'Can you help me set up an encrypted IP address; I know you are the best.'

'Didn't you have one set up previously. What happened?'

'It didn't work; they got into my system and deleted all my information. I should have used you; you're the best. Please, I need your expertise.'

'Fine, I will have everything set up by tonight, and send you my bill.'

'Thank you,' I say as the call disconnects abruptly.

***

I receive a distress call from my building manager telling me I need to get to my office immediately; my building in Gbagada is on fire. Reluctantly, I return to my office. I don't recognise it as the whole building is engulfed by flames. Firefighters work tirelessly to reduce the damage but to no avail. I didn't feel it was safe to return to my office, at the present time, but I bought that building with my hard-earned money without the help of my parents. Now it's gone; I have lost everything.

I rub my aching forehead, my knees buckle, and I fall to the ground. People rush to try and help me. Someone wants to destroy me.

*****

A figure is watching, from a distance, and records the scene.

He gives an update to his boss. 'It is done. I am sending you the video now. This should break her spirit; she won't want to pursue this anymore.'

*****

How I drive home, I honestly don't know. I'm a shadow of my former self. Maybe I should give up. *What's next?* I think. *Why don't you just kill me? That would be easier.*

The gate of my house is open; where is Musa? Why would my security guard abandon his post? It is 8.00 pm and everywhere is in darkness; why are the security lights not on?

I drive into my compound, my heart beating hard inside my chest, as I alight from my car. I walk over to close the gate, and a tall man; over 6 feet, enters my compound. I can't see his face; it is too dark, but I have an eerie feeling of being in danger.

'Don't be afraid,' he says. 'I am here to help.'

'Help in what way?'

'I was the one who gave you information on the intruder, and I sent you the link.'

'Why do you want to help me?'

'I lost a brother in these killings; I'm looking for justice. We need to work together.'

'Who are you?'

His face is obscured by the dark. 'I can't disclose that.'

'How can I trust you when I don't even know your name?'

'I'm not asking you to trust me; the fact is, you can't trust anyone. We need to find the culprits; I know they are powerful and merciless people. They have eyes on you, so we can't be seen together. I will contact you from time to time,' he says, as he walks away and disappears into the shadows.

The light in my compound suddenly comes on, and Musa runs towards me.

'Where have you been?' I yell.

'Madam! So sorry, I don't know what happened. I went to the toilet and I was locked in; I couldn't open the door.'

'Then how did you get out?'

'I can't explain; the door just opened; please, believe me, I am confused myself.'

I can't deal with this now. I need to think. I open the door to my house and walk in.

Chapter Twenty-five: Kabul

Ahmed

I get up at 6.00 am, having slept soundly; I haven't done that in a while, but my heart is heavy. I have to see Hussain, who is going to prep me for the interview today with Mohammed Pir. As I get ready for the day, I notice my wife watching me uncertainly. I know she has found herself living in a strange house, and I have not given her a good enough explanation to put her mind at rest.

'Aisha! Please don't look at me like that; I don't want you to worry; everything will be taken care of.'

'It is impossible not to worry. What is this place? How long are we going to be here?'

'I don't know. I just have to get through today, then I'll have some answers. The most important thing is for you to remain strong and take care of Abdul and Laila.'

There is a gentle knock on the door. I open it to find Yusuf standing there, waiting for me.

'We need to leave,' he says, matter-of-factly.

'I'm ready.' I hug my wife and children, and whisper into Aisha's ear, 'Be careful.'

I then walk out of the door without looking back. I can't afford to look at my family's concerned expressions.

'You don't have to worry about them; they will be well taken care of. You need to put your head in the game. You can't afford your mind to be wondering; you will make a mistake, and that might cost you your life.'

We walk in the direction of the same building we went to yesterday, Yusuf cautiously looking around to make sure we are not being followed. We enter the building; everything looks just the same, with the clock on the wall.

'When will I be given access to this place?'

'When the time is right, we can't be too careful.'

We go through the same process of scanning Yusuf's retina, and the lift begins to descend. The place is full of is activity, with people working at their different stations. I glance at my watch; it is 6.45 am.

Yusuf points in the direction of Hussain's office. 'He's waiting for you.'

I knock on the door, and someone calls out, 'Come in.'

I enter and, after shaking my hand, Hussain indicates for me to sit.

'We have a lot to go through, and we don't have enough time,' he says.

'Mohammed is trying to find out about your family, but we have falsified documents to show your family were killed during the attack in Kandahar, and you were forced to relocate to Kabul after losing everything. You don't want him to know you have a family; he will use them against you. When he does ask you about your family, you must give the best performance of your life; he needs to believe they are dead. He has all the information about you.' Hussain turns the computer in front of him in my direction, and I can see my face on the screen, with details about my life, my children, even my brothers and family.

I look up at Hussain. 'Why does he want information about my siblings?'

'Don't worry about your siblings; Mohammed likes to play with people's minds, and he uses fear tactics. He enjoys control and the easiest way to control a man is through his family. He takes a sadistic pleasure in tormenting people, so you need to pretend you are intimidated by him. As you will see, he is a short man.'

I am shown a picture of him. He can't be more than 5ft 1inch.

'So, while talking to him, you need to bend forward with your head facing him.'

I nod silently.

'You need to go back to the house and wait for about two hours before leaving for the Ahedan compound. I don't know when you will see your family again.'

He shows me a tiny phone. 'We will find a way to give you this phone once you have settled in the Ahedan compound. Everything will be taken from you, even the clothes you are wearing will be burnt and new ones issued. Mohammed is a paranoid man, and he suspects everyone.

'We have been trying to bring him down for years; we have lost many lives in the process. You need to be careful; getting close to him and gaining his trust will be very difficult; but that is what we need you to do.

We will find a way for you to talk to your family, but I promise you they will never lack anything. All the skills you acquired over the years working in the army, you will need now if you are going to survive this.

'You will be exposed to crime, tyranny, debauchery and luxury you have never seen before, exhibited by him and the people that surround him.' Hussain opens a folder on the computer screen and a video comes up showing drunk men watching scantily dressed women dancing as they try to grope them. 'You need to be like them; you will have to forget you have a wife, children and all your religious beliefs. I hope you are ready.'

Hussain looks at me expectantly.

'I am ready. I will do whatever it takes to ensure my family is safe. I need you to promise, that even if I lose my life, my family will not be discarded and thrown out.'

'By Allah, I will take good care of your family, and they will not lack anything, whatever happens.'

'Thank you,' I say, as my stomach flutters and my heart beats a little faster.

'Look for Yusuf; he will take you back. Spend quality time with your family, but you must not tell them what you are up to under any circumstances. Tell them you are travelling to Khost for training, and you will only be able to call them from time to time. May Allah guide you in this journey.'

I leave Hussain's office. I can't afford to overanalyse this; I will do as he suggests and spend with my family. Yusuf waves at me to follow him. Going through the same process as before, we exit the building. He looks around cautiously.

'You have two hours; you need to get to the Ahedan compound early; I will come and get you when it's time.'

We walk back in the same direction to reach the house where my family is staying. I sigh heavily as I enter the house, greeting the women I meet. I proceed, hesitantly, towards the assigned room. What do I tell my wife? This will be the biggest test of my life; Aisha is deeply sceptical of everything.

I can see the look of relief on Aisha's face when she sees me. I smile at her and wave at Abdul and Laila, who are sitting on the bed. 'We need to talk privately,' I tell her, holding her hand. We enter the toilet, and I close the door behind me; I don't want the children to hear.

Chapter Twenty-six: Sydney

Henry

I wake up feeling drowsy; my head is spinning. I tossed and turned all night, my mind all over the place, there are so many unanswered questions. I didn't know where to begin. What is going on? Have they started blackmailing people now?

I am getting ready for the office when Gama connects a call from Rob. 'Sir, the prime minister wants to see you ASAP!'

'I should be in the office soon; give me forty-five minutes, give or take.'

I race out of the house to try and beat the traffic with a bitter taste in my mouth that I can't seem to get rid of.

I arrive at Parliament House and walk in the direction of the prime minister's suite of rooms. I am called into his office, and I see him sitting behind his executive desk.

'Sir, you want to see me.'

'Yes, we need to increase our dealings with Russia. We produce the world's largest uranium, yet we own no nuclear weapons; I want to change that.'

'Sir, the pride of this nation, is that we possess no nuclear weapons.'

'The world is changing, and it is getting more and more unstable by the day; dangerous countries now own nuclear weapons; how will we protect our people when the time arrives?'

'That is why we have allies,' I respond.

The prime minister got up from his chair and moved towards me. 'I have been talking to the other ministers. Who are these so-called allies? It's who owns the biggest stick; if problems should start today, who do you think they will protect first? Their citizens. We have been blessed to have uranium; the Russians will help build these weapons.'

'Sir, this needs to be approved by the house.'

'Yes, I need you to start the proposal, but I don't think it will be a problem.'

'That won't be a problem, sir; I will start the process,' I say, nodding. 'Sir, could I possibly have your attention for a minute. We have not been able to find the perpetrators who hacked the network.'

'Yes, we did. The three cyber security personnel.' The prime minister sat down and started to review the documents spread on his desk, without looking up.

'But I was with them for three days, they went through excruciating torture, but they still insisted they knew nothing.'

The prime minister pulled down his glasses to the bridge of his nose, and looked up at me. 'Best let sleeping dogs lie. Get back to work, and that will be all.'

I leave his office disgruntled, but I know better than to argue with the prime minister.

This is not the prime minister I voted for and agreed to work for, sweeping a case under the carpet and not bothering to get a solution.

***

Nuclear bomb! I stand in the middle of my office, shocked to the bone.

I walk towards my desk and see a typed note showing the detailed conversation I had with the minister of interior on my stand on immigration. I hold my breath as I read the note, warning that it would be leaked to the press if I didn't do what they tell me. I will be contacted soon.

Breathing heavily, I open the door to my office. 'Did you see anyone come in here?' I ask Rob.

'No sir, I have been here all morning.'

'Then have you been into my office?'

'No, sir.'

'Someone left a note for me on my table.'

'That's impossible! I didn't enter your office today, and I wouldn't allow anyone to go in there.'

I re-enter my office, closing the door, shaking my head in disbelief. I will be ruined; all my dreams of being the next prime minister will be dashed. This phone conversation happened over six months ago; who could have recorded it and why? I recollect that I said some awful things about illegal immigrants, wanting them to be sent back from where they came; but it was just banter between friends; I didn't mean anything by it. This runs deeper than the hacking of our network a week ago, the resources to be able to hear and record our conversations. I'm finished, and I don't know where to turn.

Chapter Twenty-seven: Rio de Janeiro

Ana

I sit on my bed, contemplating my next step. The changes Carlos wants me to implement to the figures will implicate me in fraud. They are stealing a large sum of money from government contracts.

The contract signed is to mine coal for the next five years; from what I can see, they are cutting corners, trying to extort money by destroying the Amazon Rainforest and not following the rules set by the government. The financial transaction shown in the bank statement is different from the money they are making.

I'm edging towards breaking point; fear grips me as I copy all the data given to me onto my private flash drive. I was given strict instructions never to keep a copy. I am doing this at home because I don't know who might be watching me in the office. I need to protect myself; I will open a safety deposit box in a new bank tomorrow for safekeeping.

***

'I did not open this bank account; what don't you understand?' I say to the assistant bank manager I have insisted on seeing.

'The account was opened yesterday and, going through our bank data, it was opened at precisely at 8.45 am.'

'But it wasn't me,' I say loudly.

'That's not possible? We have your passport photograph in our system.' He turns the computer screen towards me. 'This is you, right?'

I look at the picture in the system. I am staring at myself; this is crazy. I pinch myself. *Is this really happening?*

'I have requested the security video; it will be here in five minutes. We are a reputable bank; are you saying you are being impersonated?'

I was stunned, and I became speechless, as I stare in wonder at the picture.

'Ms! Ms! Are you OK?'

'I'm fine.'

A smartly dressed woman enters and whispers something in the assistant manager's ear, before walking out.

The assistant manager clears his throat, nervously, before he begins to speak. 'Ms Ana, it seems you are a little confused; from our records, it shows you were the one that opened the account.'

'Please can I see the security video?'

He clicks on his computer, and shows me the video just sent to him. I see an image of myself entering the banking hall.

'Thank you,' I say, uneasily, as I stand up to leave the assistant manager's office.

I need to get out of this bank. As I rush out, I have a strange feeling that I am being watched. Looking up, I see the same woman that whispered to the assistant bank manager staring at me from a wall-to-ceiling window as I walk out of the banking hall.

When I am clear of the bank, I bend over and draw in heavy gulps of air. What am I going to do? The resemblance is uncanny; how is that possible? I won't bother going to Juliana to talk about the loan, I am sure the same thing will happen.

It will all be fine, I think, with false bravado. I need to open a safety deposit box, and fast; this is getting out of hand.

***

'She came to tell us that she didn't open the account; it seems she is not swayed by $100,000.' The woman looks at Carlos.

'That account must not be closed under any circumstances; it must appear she's running the account.'

'Don't worry about that; we have taken care of that; she can't prove she did not open the account.'

'Good. Keep me updated.'

***

I place the flash drive and the hard copies of all the transactions in safety deposit box 0107, which I begged my sister to open in her name. I don't want Maria to be in danger, but I don't know what else to do.

89

I return to the office and I hear my name being called as I pass in front of my boss's door. 'Ana! I have been to your office several times; Mr Montes wants to see you, he says it is urgent.'

My heart sinks when I hear those words. I curse myself for ever meeting that monster.

'I will go and see him immediately,' I say, as I turned around with heavy steps and walk towards the elevator.

***

'He is waiting for you, just go in,' his PA says.

I knock and enter Mr Montes's office.

'Ana! I asked to see you over thirty minutes ago.'

'I'm sorry, sir, I worked long hours last night to send the requested figures to Mr Ribeiro.'

'Yes, he told me; he said you sent the final figures to him at 2.36 am. Do you ever sleep, Mrs Santos?'

'I try, sir.'

'Anyway, I did not call you here to scold you; please take a seat; we have a lot to discuss.'

Chapter Twenty-eight: Hong Kong

Huan

Being able to go through my husband's call history for the past three months is one of the perks of working for a telecommunications company. I notice that he received a call at the same time Ms Yang was murdered. According to the report from the police, she was killed at 6.45 pm. I highlight the mobile number and time; going through all the numbers on the list. I noticed this number also came up a month before the incident.

I try pinging the number location, and noticed that the number is no longer active. Luckily, the sim card is registered to the company, bringing up the subscriber's details. The sim is registered to a woman called Ju Liáng who lives in Fujian. Who is this woman, and why was my husband talking to her for an extended period? The longest call lasted for forty-five minutes.

I honestly don't know who my husband is right now. I need to find out who this woman is? What is the meaning of paper Chun slipped to me when I went to see him? 'Everything is not what it seems'?

'Gama, find me the best private investigation agency.'

Three top options were detailed on my mobile screen. I am going to see the one rated five stars; Top Hong Kong Detectives. I need them to find out what is going on. Firstly, I need to concentrate on work and then go to Chun's office; I haven't been there since his arrest.

***

I walk into my husband's security agency unchallenged using his access card; all of his employees deserted him after his arrest because of the uncertainty of his release. A separate agency operates the building. I enter his office. Everything is in disarray, drawers pulled out on the floor, office cabinets opened, and files everywhere. What were they looking for? Where is his laptop?

Gama requests to connect the incoming call from a number I don't recognise.

'Hello?'

'Mrs Li, your husband, took something from us, and I want it back.'

I steady my breath; trying to stop the panic.

'Who is this?'

'Just return our property.'

'What did he take?'

'Talk to your husband, I want it back, or you are next.'

The phone disconnects.

I sit on the floor trying to calm my nerves. I need help; I'm way over my head. I don't want to lose my life. I need to see my husband, but I can only see him in the morning. I will be the first thing he sees tomorrow.

I get up, close the door to his office, and lock it. I speak to the guard manning the building and ask if he has seen anyone strange entering the building?

'We have different shifts, but no one is allowed into the building without an access card.'

***

'I need your help,' I say. I am speaking to the owner of the Top Hong Kong Detectives agency, wondering how they can afford to rent a sky-high building in the centre of Hong Kong.

'Good evening, Mrs Li, unfortunately, your family have been all over the news.'

'Yes, that is why I am here. I don't think my husband killed his mistress and kids; he is being set up.'

'Where was he at the time of the murder?'

'I don't know; he is not talking. He gave me this piece of paper when I went to see him in prison.' I show him the note.

'What do you understand from this?'

'I don't know, that's why I am here.'

'We will need access to your husband's computer and files.'

'That is the problem, our laptops have been stolen, his office was ransacked, files scattered everywhere.'

'OK, Mrs Li, is it possible to visit his office tomorrow? I need to go through the remaining files in your presence.'

'That's fine. I won't be able to go with you, but I will assign one of my employees to accompany you. Give me a call tomorrow when you're ready to go; I will send someone. Thank you very much,' I say, shaking his hand.

As I walk out of the building, a hand closes over my mouth, and I am dragged into a dark corner. I feel the blade of a knife press against my neck. 'If you shout, I'll kill you.'

My life flashes before my eyes. 'Please! Please!' I murmur.

'Where is the document?'

'What document?' I whimper, as he removes his hand from my mouth.

'I want that document; too many parties are interested.'

'I don't know what you are talking about.'

'Then I suggest you talk to your husband, and fast!'

He removes the knife and races away.

Chapter Twenty-nine: London

Roger

I sneak into the building at 2.00 am. I glance around the deserted room, moving cautiously; you can never be too careful. I need to get to his office, which, from my detailed investigation, I believe is located upstairs. Looking at a sign that reads 'Employees Only', I bring out the master key we use during raids, a painful doubt filling my soul. I look at the bag of cocaine held in my gloved hands. *This is for my family*, I tell myself repeatedly.

I feel the end of a gun barrel on my head, precisely on the back of my head.

'You move, you die. I can see you're thinking about trying to reach for your gun; I promise you, you'll be dead before any attempt. Why do you work for the English Syndicate, Roger?'

'I don't know who they are; they threatened my family. I'm a police officer, I tried bringing them down, but they kidnapped my son as a warning, they released him but I don't have a choice if I want to keep him safe.'

'You always have a choice. They are trying to take over the cocaine business in the UK. You're just a pawn in their hands; they're going to kill you as soon as you get the job done.'

'So, what would you have me do? What choice do I have?'

'Roger, I know everything about you, including the little affair you had four years ago; I promise you I am more dangerous than the English Syndicate. I will not only destroy you; I will wipe out your family and your relatives just for fun. Don't worry, I'll take care of the English Syndicate. I'll contact you when the time is right. Now, run along.'

I turn around, I can no longer feel the gun on my head. Everywhere is silent; the only sound is that of my heavy breathing.

***

Jude

I receive a call from my solicitor that the case on my former employees, that is supposed to start the next day, has been dismissed.

Gama switches on my television; just in time for the headlines. The breaking story is that Judge Noah Clark has been found dead at his house. Jesus! That is the judge who is supposed to be presiding over the case.

The police are still investigating, but his wife is the prime suspect at the moment, as it was surprising she did not notice her husband was dead until this morning. He was lying beside her, shot in the head at point-blank range. The police are also looking at several trials he was overseeing, trying to narrow down possible suspects.

'Gama, switch off the television.' I can't deal with this right now; these people are dangerous, and they have no problem eliminating anyone who stands in their way.

My phone connects immediately, without me accepting the call. How is that possible? I'm using Gamaplug.

'Jude,' I hear a strange voice, 'remember me? I'm your phone companion. This is the instruction: you will re-employ your ex-employees, George and William.'

'That's impossible! They were held for the illegal distribution of cocaine; this will destroy my business if word gets out that I took them back.'

'The case has been dismissed, the evidence has disappeared without a trace. Now a statement is being released to the press, how the police manipulated the whole scenario to favour them, trying to smear your name. You are looking good right now.'

'I don't understand, you told me that they are being punished, what changed?'

'I am a gracious man; I forgive when someone learns the error of their ways. Listen and listen well; this is not a discussion; it's mandatory; you have twenty-four hours to do what the needs to be done.'

The phone disconnects.

What am I going to do? These people want to control me; I must not let that happen.

My PR agent Brenda's call is connected; I can hear her excitement as she speaks. 'Jude, you are being hailed a hero for standing by your former employees; I wasn't aware of that?' she says in surprise.

'I'm surprised as well,' I say dryly.

'What do you mean?'

'Never mind.'

'The news is about what a great employer you are for backing your employees and not cutting ties with them, knowing this could destroy your business. I have received endless calls from different companies wanting to work with your brand. You will be rich beyond your wildest dreams; this is unbelievable.' She pauses. 'You don't sound excited.'

'I am just shocked; the excitement will come later.' I feel only deep sadness. *How can I be excited when I know I am being manipulated?* I think.

'My God! You have the most prominent sports brand in the world calling to sign; we are looking at a minimum of a five-year contract for nine figures, you have mobile phone companies calling, just to mention a few. Anyway, I will get back to you later today,' she says excitedly.

This was supposed to be the happiest day of my life. I have worked hard not to be like my father, but I am slowly turning into him; this is the worst day ever. I'm being forced to re-employ those despicable characters. What will they demand from me next?

Chapter Thirty: New York

Martin

I open my closet and take out the distinct multicoloured shirt. I remember when Leah bought me this shirt; I laughed out loud, telling her there were just too many colours for my liking. I wore it that very day just to please her and never wore it again. That was three years ago. I look at the picture on my computer again, the image looks so much like me that I begin to doubt my sanity. I would never wear a rainbow-coloured shirt outside of home, no matter how much my wife told me it was on-trend. And I have never seen the woman in the photo before in my life.

The shirt was worn intentionally for Leah to recognise, so it would be impossible for me to deny it. I will do face recognition in the precinct tomorrow; I need to find out who this woman is. I have to try and convince my wife of my innocence.

I walk back upstairs and knocked on the door to our room. I can't remember the last time I fought with my wife, and I ended up being thrown out of the room; we have been together for such a long time.

Hearing no response, I stand behind the door to talk to her.

'I can't explain this, but I need you to believe me when I tell you that I am not the one in that picture. I fell in love with you the day I met you; I have not stopped; you and the kids are the most important thing to me; I would never mess that up. I promise you; I'll get to the bottom of this.'

I hear the sound of whimpering from behind the door.

'I am sorry I hurt you, but I would never cheat on you.' I walk away.

***

I rub my stiff neck, moving it from side to side; that couch was uncomfortable. I am determined to find out what is going on as I drive to the precinct. My wife refused to look at me this morning; I was fortunate to kiss Charlotte as she rushed to school. I had to get out of the house; I have never felt so uneasy in my own home.

I park my car and get out when I catch sight of Bobby. I decide to confront him, as I am seething with anger and resentment. He is my friend, why won't he defend me? I walk up to him as he alights from his car. I punch him in the face and he falls backwards, hitting his vehicle.

'You are a bastard! Do you know that? Why didn't you defend me?' I say. I am held back by a group of cops, as he wipes the blood from his lips. 'Don't touch me!' I tell the other cops. 'Leah called you in a vulnerable state; you made it worse by not saying anything; silence is consent. You have known me for years; I would never cheat on Leah.'

I storm into the precinct. I am livid; Bobby has been acting differently for a while now, and I don't recognise him anymore.

'Martin! Come into my office now!' the captain yells. 'How dare you fight your partner? Do you want to terminate your friendship by indulging in rancour? What happened out there?'

'Nothing, sir. It's personal.'

'Then do not bring your personal shit to my precinct, do you understand me? The next time this happens, you can kiss your job goodnight. Now, get the hell out of my office!'

I honestly don't know who to trust anymore. First, I need to find out who that woman is. I sit behind my desk and stare at my partner. I am still angry. 'How could you do this to me?' I ask him.

'I did nothing that you did not cause yourself; stop blaming others for your mistakes. I'll not apologise to you for this.' He went back to looking at a document on his desk.

'I don't know you anymore,' I say.

'Ditto!' he responds.

I take out the flash drive sent to my wife and upload the picture into my computer. I run facial recognition. I hope she is in the system because that is the only way I can get information on her. Nothing comes up. I walk out to the car park to make a private call to my friend, computer hacker, Edward. 'I need your help,' I tell him.

'No hello? What going on?'

'Sorry, I can't talk for long; I need you to help me find someone.'

Sounds serious, send me their picture.'

'I'm sending it now; whatever you find, send it to my private email, OK? Thanks!'

As I return to my desk, I can see Booby talking on the phone, but he disconnects the call as soon as I get to my chair. I have an uneasy feeling that my best friend is trying to set me up. *No, that can't be possible*, I tell myself. But if I don't get any answers, I will tail him, just to be sure.

***

There is a message on my phone from Edward. 'I need to talk to you now.'

I rush outside to call him. 'Who the hell are those people you asked me to trace?' he says. 'They tried to hack into my system. I've set up five layers of protection, but they were able to hack three layers of security before I sent a virus into my system to bring it down.'

'I don't know who they are, Edward, that's why I called for your expertise.'

'These are dangerous people; they have the best team working for them. I thought I was the best in this game, but they come close. I couldn't get much on the lady you asked me to trace before they tried to access my system. Check your email, and good luck; you'll need it.'

An alert pings on my phone. I open the email, and I see a picture of a brunette with blue eyes, but in the photo sent to my wife, she was a blonde with green eyes. The notes show 100% face recognition. She is operating under the alias Vanessa Allen; she lives on 13th Street, Brooklyn.

I jump into my car and drive to that address. I have been watching the house for ten minutes now, to see if there is any activity inside the house. I can't see any movement, so I get out of my car, walk to the front door and press the bell. To my surprise, the woman in the picture opens the door and hugs me, holding me tightly. I try to remove her hands from my body, but she tightens her grip. 'Release me now, or I'll use force,' I say.

***

A car is parked across the street, from where a man is watching the whole thing, recording it. 'This should make his wife happy,' he laughs maliciously.

99

Chapter Thirty-one: Lagos

Lola

I sit on my bed in tears after the adrenaline rush has faded, trembling with fear. My tears blur my vision. Rocking back and forth on my bed, I gradually lose my sense of reasoning. *What has come over me? Did I really think I could do this?*

The stranger said I'm going up against a powerful opponent; I am just one person. I have not been able to concentrate on my business, Moshébì Cosmetics. Thank God I have an efficient team to handle it in my absence.

I open the video sent to me. These innocent people were killed for no just cause; who will fight for them? There is a big cover up; this issue is being swept under the carpet, and no one is allowed to talk about it. I need to be honest with myself, can I do this? I just lost the only thing I bought with my own money. I look at the luxurious sofa in the bedroom, with the smell of genuine leather, the 100% silk bedding I am lying on, all these were bought by my parents. *Can I carry on?* If I don't do anything, then Chioma will have died for nothing. I remember the hopeless despair I felt when I left her parents, and Emeka appearing smug and unremorseful after her death.

I received a call a short while ago to say that the new IP address is now secured. I will release it on the internet; it must not be traced back to me. I created a new blog #slaughter #innocent lives lost #Lagos killings and upload the video. I know they will try to take it down, so I send copies to news agencies worldwide.

Do I want to work with a stranger? He's assisting me for the moment; and I need his help.

Gama requests to connect a call from Frank. Why is he calling me?

'Hello, Frank!'

'No, this is not Frank, I warned you repeatedly to stop pursuing this, but you refused. Congratulations! You just got your friend killed. Now I'm coming for you.'

The phone disconnects.

Oh my God! Frank is dead. I am so frightened that my legs go weak, and my knees knock together. I don't know what to do.

An alert pings on my phone. 'Hide now!'

I pull myself out of the crippling shock, rooting me to the same spot, race downstairs to the guest room and crawl under the bed. I lift the large hatch cut into the floorboards, and try to fit myself into the opening without moving the bed. I place my leg on the wooden staircase leading to the tiny lower floor no one knows about. I hear the door of my house open; it's impossible to get through the steel security door, but who am I kidding? They walked into my office the same way. I hear someone say, 'Look for her,' as I creep down the stairs, closing the hatch quietly. *Please, God, don't let them find me*, I think as I switch off my phone.

I can hear movement all over the house, as I sit on the floor with my head on my knees.

'We can't find her, sir; she is somewhere in the house.'

'She must be. Find her! Her phone is switched off, so I can't trace it; the last location shows she's in this house.'

'Sir, what do you want to do with her? The big boss has not given us an instruction to harm her.'

'She is a nuisance, but I don't want to kill her. Maybe break her arm, or a leg, give her face a battering as well; she needs to be in the hospital for a little while. Then I won't have the displeasure of having to follow her around town.'

They enter the guest room; I can hear them clearly.

'Check everywhere, one of the men commanded.' I cover my mouth to prevent me from shrieking.

In less than twenty minutes, the whole house has been combed and turned upside down. 'We still can't find her, sir.'

'OK, let's go! I want a car parked outside her house. I want her followed the minute she leaves the house; I know she is here somewhere, but she is more intelligent than I thought.'

'The boss wants to talk to you.'

'I thought I told you to break her spirit; why is she still posting online?'

'Sir, I burnt her office yesterday, and I sent you a video of her lying on the ground wailing. I never imagined she would have the willpower to upload that video today.'

'The video is all over the internet; we couldn't shut it down before millions of people viewed it, it's being discussed all over the world. The government was forced to release a statement that it was all a hoax and a figment of someone's imagination, the people in the video are actors, and the whole thing was staged.'

'What do you want to do with her? She is becoming more dangerous.'

'I don't want her killed yet; her father is too important in my long-term plan.'

'We can make it look like an accident.'

'Not yet. I want you to send her a message that we will start eliminating her friends one after the other if she doesn't stop.'

'OK, sir.'

The call hangs up.

'Let's get out of here. She lives to see another day.'

I try to stretch my aching limbs in the cramped space. I am exhausted and my head aches. I can't remember the last time I slept properly. I have been in this position, looking at my wristwatch for two hours. Should I continue to stay down here? I can't hear any sound, but I can't be too sure.

Calm down, Lola, you will get through this, I repeat to myself.

Chapter Thirty-two: Kabul

Ahmed

I hold both of Aisha's hands, looking at her directly. 'What I'm about to say to you is going to be very difficult, but I want you to understand that everything I do is for you and our children, you are my number one priority.'

'Ahmed, you are scaring me.'

'There is nothing to be afraid of. I am going to Khost to train for my new job.'

'What job?'

'The only people recruiting now are the Ahedan Group; I will be working in one of their compounds as a security guard.'

'The Ahedan Group,' she cries.

'You need to lower your voice, Aisha. What I am telling you is confidential. I am not a bodyguard or military personnel; I'm just a security guard protecting the compound.'

'Then why do you need to go for training in Khost?'

'Mohammed is very meticulous; it's part of the training. I need to know his security protocol, and it is based in Khost.'

'You are not telling me everything. I know, whatever it is, it is to protect us. You carry so much weight on your shoulders; I'm afraid this burden might get too heavy for you to carry alone.'

'Don't worry about me; I will call you from time to time. What I want from you is to protect Abdul and Laila while I am away. Yusuf's boss has promised to house you until I get back, so you have nothing to worry about.'

Aisha nods but continues to look troubled.

'I need to rest; I have less than two hours before leaving, and I want to spend as much time as I can with you and the kids.'

***

I hear a knock on the door. I hold my children tightly in my arms, telling them not to cry but to be strong. I finally hug my wife goodbye and walk out of the door to start a new chapter in my life.

I follow Yusuf out of the house 'Don't worry about them,' he says. 'I promise you they will be fine; Hussain is a man of his word.'

I need to compose myself; I've to become a different person. I will need to keep my wits about me if I am going to survive this.

We walk for about an hour, and Yusuf points to a building surrounded by a massive wall. 'This is the primary location for the Ahedan Group. I can't go any further; they might spot me. You are the best man to do this; think about how many lives you will be saving.'

I walk the short distance along a tarred road, heading for the side gate. The gate is open before I can knock, and I see a security camera above the entrance. I enter the compound. I have never seen anything like this before; a mansion sitting in several hectares of land. I can see the latest pickup trucks and bulletproof jeeps. A man appears in front of me. 'Follow me!' he says.

I enter a reception area with marble floors. The man points at a black three-seater sofa. 'Sit down! They will come and get you soon,' he says, walking out of the building. I notice three hidden cameras. I know I am being watched; this is a test. I know if I fail this interview, I am never leaving here alive.

I sit upright on the sofa waiting to be called. Another man is sitting on my right; I can tell he is nervous. He constantly fidgets with his fingers, trying but failing to pull himself together. Eventually, I hear my name being called from a speaker to go to the door on the right. I have now been waiting for close to two hours, and I was told to arrive early.

I open the door and am faced with six of Mohammed's right-hand men. Mohammed is sitting on, what looks like a throne. *A symbol of his vanity*, is the thought that runs through my mind. I bow deeply and do not lift my head as he gets down from his throne and stands in front of me. Yusuf was right; he is indeed a short man.

'Ahmed, I have carried out an extensive investigation on you. I understand that you lost your family when running from Kandahar to Kabul.'

'Yes, sir,' I answer without changing my posture.

'How did they die?'

'On our attempt to leave, they were hit by stray bullets.'

'I find that hard to believe. I don't like people without immediate families working for me; how do I keep them in line?'

I hear a burst of particularly nasty laughter from some of his men.

'But we located their bodies; you buried them in haste. I am glad you told me the truth, you lie to me, you die. You are an excellent soldier; I could use you, and you know how to show respect. You can now stand upright. I already have all the information I need on you; you'll be one of my bodyguards.'

The man who had been sitting beside me in the reception area was dragged into the room.

'We found a recording tape on him,' one of the men says.

They kick his legs out from under him, and he falls to the ground.

'Who sent you here?' Mohammed demands angrily.

The man bows his head, pleading for his life to be spared.

'I said, who sent you?'

'No one, I'm just a reporter.' His voice quivers.

'A stupid one,' another man yells. Everyone laughs.

Mohammed stretches out his hand, and a gun is placed in it.

'Please! Please! Don't kill me; I have a wife and children.'

Mohammed places the gun in my palm. 'Kill him!'

Chapter Thirty-three: Sydney

Henry

I'm feeling so frustrated and confused. I was hailed as one of the youngest ever to be nominated by my party for the position of the prime minister at thirty-eight years old. I know it is because of the legacy my family left behind. Everything I have done in my life is for this singular purpose; all this will be destroyed because I misspoke?

I receive a text from an unknown number on my phone. 'Are you ready to accept?'

I respond, 'What do you want from me?'

'Everything!'

'I don't understand.'

'When the time is right, you will.'

There is a knock on my door, and Rob enters my office.

'Sir, we have a problem. We have been investigating the fire that ravaged your home and several other houses in Sydney. The fire started in your apartment building.' 'What! Are you saying my house was targeted?'

'In the report I just received from the fire investigator, the fire started from your building and spread to the other buildings to make it look like wildfire. They think specific houses are being targeted. Today, the home of the opposition leader, Jason Atkinson Jnr., was burnt down.'

'Did anybody die?'

'Surprisingly, no one lost their life but the whole house was reduced to ashes. They can't find the culprits; this crime is conducted so perfectly, no evidence is left behind. What are we going to tell the public, sir?'

'We can't tell them a psycho is going around burning houses; that will cause unnecessary panic. Leave it as it is; they already believe wildfire is the cause.'

Gama connects me to Mia.

'Hello, Mia.'

'You have to come home. Carl got into trouble in school, and he's behaving strangely. He is always on his mobile phone not talking to anyone. He's just so angry; this is all your fault.'

'How is this my fault?'

'Really? You want to have this argument; I need you to leave the office right now because your son just got expelled from school.'

'Why didn't you tell me he has been getting into trouble?'

Her voice becomes unsteady; I know she is crying. 'Just get here.'

The phone disconnects.

I drive home with a sense of guilt. I have neglected my family in the pursuit of being prime minister, and I am about to lose everything.

'I don't want to talk to any of you,' shouts Carl.

'Carl, please!' Mia says. 'You need to talk to someone. I recommended therapy; you said no. You often come home with a bruised face. The school told me you have been fighting everyone and are extremely rude to the teachers. This is not you.'

'Carl, talk to me; I am your father.'

'Now you're my father,' says Carl, laughing bitterly. 'Where have you been then? Sometimes I don't see you in weeks; you only come when mum threatens you. I don't have a father,' he says, as he races upstairs to his room.

'Do something!' Mia yells at me. 'I'm losing my son.'

I hug my wife as she sobs. We need to think of something together; talking to him will not work.

***

Carl unlocks his mobile phone, chatting to his only friend.

'Well done for getting expelled from school; I told you that would get his attention. He loves his work more than he loves you; to get more of his attention, you need to be more destructive. You know what to do next.'

'Yes, I do!'

Chapter Thirty-four: Rio de Janeiro

Ana

I sit down, trembling and afraid; and my life flashes before my eyes, as I timidly wait to hear what Mr Montes has to say.

'I'm going to change your job title. You'll no longer be working for your boss, you'll now be working directly for me. You're going to be moved from the second to the fourth floor.'

'That's not necessary, sir. I can still work for you without moving office.'

'I want you on the fourth floor; your office has been set up for you, that is non-negotiable. Along with a promotion, I'll also increase your salary to compensate you for all your work.'

Fear runs through my veins, as I nod. 'OK, sir!'

'This needs to be done today. Thank you very much, Mrs Santos.'

I leave his office, my eyes watering, shaking my head, as I walk quickly to the elevator. I keep my head lowered, trying to prevent his many assistants from seeing my bloodshot eye.

I feel someone bump my shoulder and, as I stumble backwards about to fall, I am held steady.

'I'm so sorry, I didn't mean to bump into you.'

'That's OK,' I say, trying to steady myself without looking up.

'I am Antonio Gomes, I believe I will be working closely with you.'

'Thank you,' I say, straightening up and rushing inside the elevator as it arrives, just in time.

***

This will be harder than I thought; she won't even look at me; my job is to be an integral part of her life, and she needs to trust me. I've been given a limited time to spark her interest. I'm a good-looking man at 185 cm, brunette with hazel eyes, and I never have to work hard to get a woman. I have to get this done, or Carlos will destroy my face or kill me out of spite.

***

I arrive back on my floor. I have to move office, where I am 100% certain I'm going to be monitored. I close the door and survey my puffy eyes with my compact mirror. *You can do this,* I think to myself. I just need to get through the day, then I can think of what to do next.

My current boss walks into my office. 'Ana! I just got a call from Mr Montes; he said you will be working directly for him from now on. Congratulations! You have been working for this company for ten years; you have not received any recognition for your dedication and handwork. I know it is a significant loss for the accounting department, but I am proud of you.'

'Thank you, sir.'

'What will you be doing for him?'

'I don't know, I am sure it's something to do with accounting. I have to pack up my things; I'll be moving to the fourth floor.'

'Wow! Ana, all the directors are on the fourth floor, only the CEO is on the fifth. Are you now a director and my boss?'

I smile in spite of everything. 'I don't know, sir.' My voice quivers. 'I'll always see you as my boss; that will never change.'

'You don't seem pleased, are you OK?' he asks worriedly.

'It's just a lot to take in. Of course, I am happy. Thank you for everything, you're the best boss.'

Some strange men walk into my office carrying cardboard boxes. 'We have been instructed to move your stuff to the fourth floor.'

'That's not necessary. I don't have much and I can move everything myself.'

'Mrs, we have to follow instructions; you don't have to lift a finger,' says one of the men. He raises his voice to the other men following behind him. 'Start packing.'

I pick up my laptop and the picture of my husband and daughter; I don't care about anything else, as I leave the office with my former boss.

Back on the fourth floor, I am shown to my executive office. I have never occupied an office so extensive, it's three times the size of my old office. All the furniture and the paintings on the wall are so elegant. What

109

am I doing here?

I hear a voice behind me, 'I am sure you will soon settle,' he says. I turn to see a handsome man standing by my office door with his hands in his pockets.

I am baffled at his arrogance as he struts into my office uninvited.

'I am Antonio Gomes, but you can call me Antonio. I bumped into you earlier today, and I came to apologise again for that.'

'Nice to meet you, but that won't be necessary. I'm sorry, who are you again?'

'I'm the new temporary project director, I will only be here for a couple of months, but I hope to extend it; it depends on my performance.'

Carlos saunters into my office. *Can people just walk into an office without knocking?* I wonder.

'Ha! I am glad you have met Antonio; you will be working closely with him. We are coming to the end of the fiscal year, and the final documents will be presented to the board of directors. We need you to work together to make sure everything corresponds. I'm sure you understand what I mean; we don't want any surprises,' he says, as he walks out.

Antonio looks up and smiles. I dismiss the uneasy instinct I am feeling. I just need to get him to leave my office. 'Thank you, Mr Gomes. As you can see, I've only just moved in. Can you give me some time to sort myself out?'

Disappointment is written on his face as he leaves.

***

'I can see she is not charmed by your good looks. Tick tock, time is running out. Get it done, or you won't like me, Antonio.' I watch Carlos walk out of my office.

A cold sweat breaks out on my forehead and I mop it away with my forearm, I am in deep shit!

Chapter Thirty-five: Hong Kong

Huan

I'm currently hiding in a hotel, afraid to go to my own home that I paid loads of money for because my house has been broken into. My life is in danger because of this nincompoop I call my husband.

I am at the prison, waiting for him to show his ugly face, the bastard! Eventually, he is escorted in, helped by the prison warden, his face is bruised and his eyes are swollen. There is a cast on his right arm, and he's limping. Dear God! What happened to you?

'I was beaten to a bloody pulp; I was saved in the nick of time.'

'I know it is a stupid question, but are you OK? Are these offenders being held accountable?'

'This is a prison; people turn a blind eye to certain things.'

'Chun, I need you to come clean for me, the house was vandalised, your office was broken into, I'm receiving strange calls to say that you took something from these people, and they want it returned. I am living in fear; someone placed a knife on my neck, damn it.'

'I don't have the answers,' he says, holding my hand as he slips another piece of paper into my palm. 'You need to be careful. I don't know how much time I have.'

'Chun, please talk to me,' I say, tears rolling down my cheeks. 'What do I do? I'm in over my head.'

'I'm sorry I got you into this. I don't think you should come here again until the trial because your life will also be in danger.' He tries to stand up; and is assisted by the prison warden back to his cell.

I get into my car. I have already sent my personal assistant to go with the private investigator to my husband's office to see if he could find anything; they should be arriving there now.

'Gama, connect to Ling. Ling, are you in there?'

'Yes, I'm with Qiang Lin, the private investigator. He wants to talk to you.'

'Why?'

'I think he can explain better.'

'Mrs Li, you told me everything had been tossed around in your husband's office when you came yesterday, and his laptop was missing, right?'

'Yes! That is correct.'

'We opened the door to his office and everything is immaculate; nothing is out of place, and his laptop is on his desk. I spoke to the security men downstairs, but they seemed to be oblivious to what was happening. I've taken some pictures of the office; all his folders have been arranged, but we can't tell if anything is missing.'

'If you need anything from me let me know. I'll see you in the office, Ling! Bye, Qiang.'

I can't wait to get to the office; I need to open the piece of paper Chun slipped to me; I was able to chuck it into my purse without anyone seeing me.

I have been battling with sleepless nights; I hate not having answers. Hopefully, Qiang will be able to shed some light on what's happening.

A call comes through on my phone. I don't pick up, but Gama connects the call anyway – strange!

'Mrs Li, I see you went to see your husband today? Did he tell you where he keeps what he took from us?'

'Please, I am innocent! He didn't tell me anything, I swear.'

'You saw how he looked, right? If you don't want to receive his corpse, you better advise him to speak; better yet, maybe you don't care about him, then I'll have to hurt you.'

'Please! Don't hurt me for a crime I know nothing about.'

'We don't want to hurt you; we just want what he took from us. You have a short period to get answers from your husband, or we will be forced to eliminate you.'

I am shaking so badly, I am finding it hard to breathe.

'Mrs Li, are you OK?' my chauffeur asks.

'I am fine.'

'I got worried when I opened your door, and you didn't come out.'

I get out of the car, and take the VIP elevator to my floor. *You have limited time, or we will be forced to eliminate you.* The words keep ringing in my head.

'I don't want to be disturbed for the next hour, move all appointments,' I tell my secretary. 'Something important has come up.' I close the door to my office and open my bag, in a panic, trying to find the piece of paper.

All that is written on the paper is a name and number. I can see a drop of blood on the paper; Chun must have written it after he was hurt.

'Feng - 024929964 Gama, connect to this number.'

The phone rings for a while before someone finally picks up the phone.

'Who is this?'

'Is this Feng?'

'Who is asking?'

'I'm Chun Li's wife; he told me to call you.'

'Drop the phone right now; you are being traced. I'll call you another time.'

The call is disconnected.

I try the number again, but the phone has been switched off.

What just happened? My head is spinning.

Chapter Thirty-six: London

Roger

'How could you have done such a sloppy job? I just had to stand in front of the press to explain how Jude Williams was implicated in a cocaine scandal he knew nothing about? I gave you a simple task; catch the perpetrators, who you identified as George Harris and William Carter, and then the pieces of evidence against them just magically disappeared. To make matters worse, the press was able to prove that the actual criminals were the English Syndicate before the policemen I hired to do the job. Do you know how bad I looked?' shouted the chief inspector.

'You made me look like a fool. I warned you repeatedly, Roger, to stay away from Jude Williams, but you refused and insisted he was involved. Now the chief of police wants heads to roll. Sadly, Roger, and you, Mike, are two of my best policemen in the field, but you're both going on three months' suspension. You need to keep your heads down until this case is resolved.'

'But sir, we had strong evidence that George and William were selling cocaine. How it disappeared, we don't know; it was kept in the evidence storage area waiting for the tribunal; that can't be our fault,' said Mike.

'The chief of police was livid; he had to answer questions from Members of Parliament and the prime minister. The press is having a field day tarnishing the police image; we are lucky that Jude Williams is not suing us for slander.

'How could you have missed the English Syndicate? Six of them were arrested today with overwhelming evidence that they are the prime supplier of cocaine in the United Kingdom. Thanks to the press for releasing that evidence on national television.

'Go home! I don't want to see your faces for a while.'

I am too shocked to speak. How were they able to destroy the English Syndicate in one day? I walk to my desk, ignoring Mike rambling on about our unfair treatment.

My phone starts to ring at the precise time I reach my desk and, on answering, I hear, 'Roger, we have killed the Goliath in your life; now you owe us.'

'Who is this?'

'Your good Samaritan! Now, you saw how easily we destroyed the English Syndicate; that's how easily we can destroy you.

'Listen well, anytime I call and tell you to do anything; you must not hesitate to do it. Like I told you yesterday, I'm worse than the English Syndicate; I'll not hesitate to kill your family while you watch them die in front of you.'

The phone disconnects and fear clutches my heart. I'm in trouble.

Jude

I have not been able to sleep; I have tossed and turned all night, my phone has been ringing off the hook since yesterday, and friends, well-wishers and celebrities have been calling to show their support for me.

The press has been talking about the police force all night, how they tried to tarnish my image and destroy my brand. The prime minister has issued an apology to me on his Twitter account. My head is spinning. These people are too powerful.

I am in an impossible position; I've to re-employ George and William. My public relations team have released a statement to the press thanking the public for their outpouring of love and support, stating how I'm a proud citizen of this country. I have no bad feelings towards the police and I am glad that the truth has come to light.

I'm being called for interviews; celebrities are flooding to my restaurant, and I have been offered endorsements from different companies that want to associate with my brand. My life is upside down, everything that I desired in my life is happening, but it is coming at a high cost.

***

My employees, George and William, are starting work today, and the press are outside waiting to interview us.

My Gama connects as I get up from my desk. There are just ten minutes before the interview is due to start.

115

'Jude, you've become a famous man in the past couple of days; I think congratulations are in order. As you go out now, we are watching you; you must show your excitement that your workers are back at work. I made all this happen, the interviews, the offers. You're going to be influential and wealthy beyond your wildest dreams, but I can also destroy you. The same people clamouring to get your attention will not want to be associated with you. I will take everything away; your freedom, your reputation, and the worst part, make your mother watch. I will make sure she dies of heartbreak and despair. So, don't mess with me.'

The call disconnects.

I scroll down the list of the recent numbers that have called me; I see nothing; am I dreaming? At that moment, there is a knock on my door and Brenda appears.

'It's time!' she says.

'Thank you.'

I take a moment to compose myself, then walk out of my office to the waiting crowd and press that have gathered outside; I need to give the best performance of my life.

Chapter Thirty-seven: New York

Martin

'Get your hands off me now!' I repeat.

'Hello, darling, why don't you come in?' she says, and then let's go.

'Who are you?' I demand.

'What is all this about, Martin?'

'How do you know my name?'

'I don't understand. Is this some sort of game?'

'I have no idea who you are.'

'Please don't joke with me; I'll not have this conversation outside my door for my neighbours to hear.' She strolls into her house, leaving the door open for me to follow.

I hesitate and look around to see if I am being followed. I don't see anyone, so I follow her inside the house.

'Please close the door,' she says.

'I'd prefer to leave it open.'

'This is my house. I don't know what has come over you; you'll show me the respect I deserve by closing my door.'

I do as she says. If I am going to get answers, I need to play along. I follow her to the living room and she starts taking off her clothes.

'What are you doing?'

'You have seen me naked many times; I was about to take a shower when I heard the doorbell.'

'Stop! I've never even seen you before, let alone naked. I don't understand what is going on, and I need an explanation now!' I show her my badge.

She starts to laugh as she strips to her underwear, walks into another room and comes back wrapped in a bathrobe.

'Martin! Did you bump your head or something? I know you are a cop; look around,' she says, indicating with her hands.

I look around; I see loving pictures of myself with this strange woman positioned around the living room.'

'This is not me. I've never seen you before.'

She laughs again. 'What do you mean, this is not you?'

'When did we start dating?' I ask.

'Dating? We are married; we have been married for three years.'

I feel a sudden rush of blood to my head as I move towards her, hold her arms and shake her. Do you think I'm joking with you? You better tell me the truth now!'

'You're hurting me. And I am not joking; we have been married for three years.'

'That's impossible! I am a married man with children; having more than one wife is bigamy and a crime.'

'I have the marriage certificate if you want to see it. I am the victim here; you have been lying to me for years.'

I release her, and follow behind as she opens her home office. There are two desks, and my picture is on top of one of them, I'm wearing my favourite colour shirt; my wife is always making jokes about the number of navy-blue shirts I have. She opens one of the drawers, brings out a file, takes out a document and hands it to me. I can see my full name 'Martin Osborne Hills' and 'Mary Ashley Cox' written on the certificate. How is this possible?

'From my investigation, your name is Vanessa Allen.'

'I don't know what you are talking about. Now I'd like you to leave my house before I call the real cops.'

'Fine, but I'm taking this with me.' I grab the certificate.

'No! You don't get to take the certificate. If you want to verify this marriage, you can search the marriage records, you are a cop, so you say. Get out of my house and give me back my certificate before I get you arrested for trespassing, since you insist you are not my husband.'

I take a picture of the certificate on my phone, before dropping it on the floor as I race out. What just happened? I could get up to three years in prison for bigamy, and how will I explain this to my wife? First of all, I need to verify what my fake wife has told me.

I get into my car. I can't call anybody for help because I don't want anyone to know about this. I drive to the county recorder's office, my heart beating fast. What if I am married to this woman? How do I explain this to my wife? Can someone be this identical to me?

I search the county clerk's website, using the marriage date, after requesting information on my supposed marriage. I am shocked to see that I am married; it's impossible to get married in the same state using the same name. How can this happen? I need to think and I need to fix this. Firstly, I need to find out who that imposter is?

Gama connects me to the captain as his call comes in.

'Where the hell are you?' he yells.

'I'm sorry, sir, I had to leave the office.'

To do what? You've not done any work today. You've been placed on desk duty; why are you not at your desk? Are you tired of being a cop?'

'I'm sorry, sir, please give me an hour; then I'll be back in the precinct.'

'I don't know what is going on with you, but I haven't fired you because you have been a great cop for years.'

'Thank you, sir.'

'Don't thank me; I need you back at the precinct ASAP!'

***

I need to talk to my wife. I drive home, praying, 'God! I need her to understand and trust me.' I park my car. Then I see suitcases outside the house; what is going on? I run inside the house. 'Leah! Leah!'

'I need you to leave now.' Leah's eyes are red from crying.

'Sweetheart! Please talk to me, what is going on?'

'Get out of this house. I have packed your clothes, go and live with your mistress.'

'I don't have a mistress,' I shout.

'I am tired of your lies. You went to see her today, hugged her and watched as she got naked in front of you, yet you tell me you don't know her.' Her voice quivers.

'Sweetheart, I can explain.'

'I don't want to hear any more lies. If you love me, you will leave this house; I don't want to see your deceiving face. Get out!' she screams, as she tries to push me out of the door, tears rolling her face.

'OK! I'll go but believe me, Leah, I'm being set up. I love you and would never do this. I intend to prove it.'

I go outside, pick up the two suitcases and place them in the car's trunk. I get into my car and look at my home one last time before driving to God knows where.

Chapter Thirty-eight: Lagos

Lola

My muscles are stiff; I've been sitting in this uncomfortable position for hours. Everywhere is silent, and I'm in total darkness. I have not eaten or drunk any water; I feel weak.

I move from the tiny space, walk up the stairs, push up the hatch and peep out. Everywhere is dark. I crawl out from under the bed and creep out of the guest room, my heart pounding. Am I going to die today? I fumble my way as my eyes become accustomed to moving in the dark.

I reach the living room; it is a mess. My beautiful white seats have been slashed with a knife and my glass dining table is broken. Oh, God! I force myself to breathe steadily as I enter my kitchen; all my plates, glasses and cups are broken on the floor, and my kitchen appliances have been smashed. I run, silently, to my bedroom. My closet is open. My designer clothes and bags have all been shredded, and are lying all over the floor. I sit on the floor of my room; unable to control my emotions any longer. I weep silently and bitterly. The only sound in the house are cries of pain and hopelessness.

I switch on my phone; there is a text from an unknown number: 'Are you OK?' It was sent over five hours ago. Is this from 'my helper'? I look at the time; it is 12.45 am; I have been hiding for over eight hours. I need to eat, but everything in my house has been destroyed. They even took the food out of my fridge and threw it on the floor. It all looks so dirty and disgusting, as if it has been stepped on. They want to break me, and they are winning.

Gama connects an incoming call. What is happening? I don't want to speak to anyone.

'Lola, I can see you have decided to switch on your phone. I've been very patient with you. You are not taking me seriously; you have been warned not to get involved in the investigation of those deaths, but you chose to ignore me. So, this is what will happen; for every story published story on the web about the cold-blooded massacre of youths in Lagos, I will kill one of your friends. If you publish twenty stories, I will kill twenty of your friends. You went after this story because of a friend; now you will get to lose more. You decide their fate.'

The call disconnects.

I am just one person; I can't do this anymore. I have lost so much pursuing this story; but they always seem to be one step ahead of me. Maybe I need to see my parents in Abuja, then I can think properly.

I climb on to my torn mattress in my bedroom. I don't care anymore; I am so tired. I fall asleep as soon as I rest my head on the destroyed pillows. Tomorrow will take care of itself.

***

I wake up to the reality of my life; I need to book a flight to Abuja; a break would do me good. I can't put my friends in danger for the sake of this story; how will I live with myself. I get up and place Gamaplug in my ears. Immediately, Gama connects me to a call.

'Are you OK?'

'Who is this?'

'Your friendly helper,' he replies.

'I don't think I can do this anymore.'

'There is so much to do. You can't afford to give up now.'

'They've threatened to kill my friends; how can I live with that?'

'I won't let that happen.'

'Really! Can you promise me that?'

'I can't; you will lose some friends, but it is for the greater good.'

I laugh bitterly. 'I didn't want any of my friends to die because of me.'

'We'll devise a new strategy; no more posting online. Going to Abuja for a week is a good idea; we want them to think you have given up. When you get back to Lagos, you need to start going to parties again; then, we can devise another way for you to post the stories.'

'Why don't you do it yourself and leave me out of it? You don't need me to post videos.'

'But I do need you. If I didn't, I would have done it myself.'

'I don't want to lose more of my friends.'

'Life is dangerous. Don't you want to know who these people are? You need to confront this problem head-on.'

'I honestly don't know. The price is too high for me.'

'I can't do this alone. Go to Abuja, rest; we'll talk when you get back.'

Chapter Thirty-nine: Kabul

Ahmed

I examine the pistol in my hand, lift it and point it at the weeping journalist's forehead, as he pleads for me to spare his life. I can hear Mohammed's men cheering me, as Mohammed quietly watches me closely. I know it's a test; if I don't kill this man, I'll never leave this place alive. I pull the trigger, and the man falls backwards on the ground.

'Well done!' Mohammed starts clapping. 'You will be very useful to me,' he says, taking the gun from my hand and walking away. I watch as they drag the dead man out of the room.

'Follow me,' one of the men says. 'I'll show you to your quarters; you need to give me your old clothes, new ones have been placed on your bed.'

'Thank you,' I say, as we walk out of the building, turning right to one adjacent. 'You don't have to thank me; I am just doing my job. Understand this, no one is your friend here; we are all doing what is necessary to survive.' I nod and follow behind him.

The building looks like a hotel; every door has a number. We get into an elevator that takes me to the third floor and I am shown to room 309.

'If you don't want to take the lift there is a staircase that takes you to all the floors.'

I look around, there are cameras everywhere. I enter my room, followed closely by the stranger.

'Please, what is your name?' I ask.

'It's Abdul-Ali. I am here to collect your clothes and underwear. That is the restroom.' He points to a door beside the entrance.

I walk into the restroom, take a deep breath, remove my clothes and wrap myself in a towel I find in the bathroom. I open the door and give them to Abdul-Ali. He then enters the restroom and conducts a thorough inspection before leaving with the clothes.

What have I done? I just shot an innocent man. *How am I going to survive living here?* I think. I turn up the shower's water pressure. From what I can see, this place is designed like a hotel; where did the money come from? I wash my body vigorously in an attempt to remove the guilt. My new clothes lay on the bed. I check the closet and perahan tunbans, our traditional dress for men, line the closet.

I hear banging at the door as I finish dressing. On opening it, I find another stranger.

'Follow me,' he says. 'Make sure you lock your door and keep your keys safe. Let me give you a piece of advice; it's a dog-eat-dog world here and people will do anything to be the right-hand man to Mohammed himself. You will be one of his bodyguards; he has about five men around him at all times. The head of security is Ghani; his job is to train you for the next five days. It will be intense.'

We leave the building and I follow him round the back to an open field. There are fierce-looking men walking the perimeter with submachine guns. As we walk, I see men participating in combat training, some of them learning to shoot. It is very organised. So much is going on. *Are they preparing for a war?* I wonder.

'This is Ahmed.' The stranger introduces me to a sinister-looking man, a third of his face knotted with horrible scars. 'Ahmed, meet Ghani.'

'I was told you were an excellent soldier before, show me what you can do,' he says. Without warning, a large rifle is given to me with a paper target 100 yards away. 'Aim for the centre.'

I inspect the rifle, place it on a sandbag, calculate the adjustments I need to make and shoot the target three times. The paper is brought to Ghani to examine. All three shots are at the centre of the target.

As they look at the paper target, I hear some of the men say that the only person capable of doing this is Ghani. 'You have a rival,' one of the men chuckles.

Ghani directs his angry scowl at me. 'I don't like a show-off,' he says. 'Follow me! There is more to be done.'

One of the men whispers in my ear as I follow him, 'Be careful; Ghani doesn't like to be the beaten at anything. The last guy who disgraced him was found dead in his room.' We enter a room set up as a wrestling ring. 'You fight me now,' says Ghana, getting into the ring, as several people gather to watch.

I climb into the ring. I've been fighting since I was five years old, before going into the army. My opponent is around 5ft 8 inches tall and weighs about 83kg; I can take him down easily, but I have to allow him to beat me. I need to be smart if am going to win these people over.

He swings his fist, I move back and stagger a little. I watch him rush towards me to punch me; this guy is an amateur fighter. I block his second punch, but the third hit lands hard on my face. I fall to the ground and hear the sound of people applauding. The side of my eye becomes swollen. Some men hold me up and assist me out of the ring. I hear one of them say, 'Ghani just wanted to prove he was the best; he became envious after you showed him your impeccable shooting skills.'

I am placed on a bench and given an icepack to hold over my eye.

'I don't think he can do any more training today,' one of the men cackles. 'Next time, he will not challenge the master.'

I have a serious headache; why did I let that arsehole hit me so hard? *It would be best if you endure the pain,* I tell myself.

A man sits down beside me.

'My name is Jabar,' he whispers. 'Hussain sent me to make contact. I saw what you did there; that was a smart move allowing Ghani to beat you, remember, you are constantly being monitored, even in your room; the only place you are not being watched is in your private restroom; we will talk soon.'

He gets up and walks away.

'Go to your room!' one of the men shouts. 'It's getting late, entertainment will be sent to your room.' I force myself to get up. I can't see out of one eye; I need help, but no one seems to care. I trace my way back to my room and lay down on the bed. I am exhausted and starving.

I don't know how long I have been lying here before there is a knock on my door. A young girl, not more than eighteen years, is standing outside my room, holding a tray of food.

'Thank you,' I say, trying to take the tray.

'No,' she says, looking down. 'I am part of the entertainment.'

'I don't understand?'

'I come with the food,' she answers timidly.

Then I realise. 'Come in,' I say, closing the door. 'Have you eaten?'

She nods. I watch as she stands in the corner, frightened. I need to eat.

'Sit down,' I say, but she shakes her head. This girl is just a little older than my daughter.

'What is your name?

'My name is Moska, she replied timidly.'

How am I going to get out of this situation when I'm being watched? This place is hell!

Chapter Forty: Sydney

Henry

I hold my wife in my arms as she weeps bitterly, beating herself up for not paying enough attention. 'You can't continue to blame yourself; that won't solve anything,' I say wearily.

'I blame you for not being around for your son,' she says, moving away from me and wiping her tears.

'I blame myself, too, but this is not the time to apportion blame; we need to find a way to fix the problem. I'll go to Carl's school tomorrow and see whether I can get them to reinstate him.'

'I don't think that will be possible; he caused so much trouble in school that all his friends have deserted him.'

'Nothing is impossible; we need to try. Can I stay in the guest room? I don't think I should leave this house; our separation is causing too much damage to our son.'

'Are you blaming me now?' she says, raising her tone.

'Please, try to understand me; I'm not blaming you; this is about our son and what's best for him.'

'You can stay for a week; let's see how that goes.'

'Thank you, let me see whether I can talk to him.'

I walk up the stairs to Carl's room and knock on the door; there is no answer.

'Carl! Can I talk to you?'

'Go away!' he screams.

'Carl, you've to talk to me at some point; what is going on with you? We are worried.'

'What do you care? Leave me alone! I don't want to talk to anyone.'

I go back downstairs and text Rob, asking him to contact me if any critical issues come up. I won't be returning to the office until further notice.

***

In the darkness, Carl lies in bed, chatting on his phone to the stranger that calls herself Lucy.

'My dad is concerned about me.'

'He is lying to you; he is just concerned about his image.'

'I don't know; he came here straight away when he heard that I got expelled, and his car is still parked outside.'

'What did I tell you, Carl? Do not believe what you see or hear; remember that the only reason your father is still in the house is the trouble you are in, not that he is worried about you.'

'OK, what do you want me to do?'

'We stick to the plan, don't be afraid; the only way to get back at your father is to make him suffer for all the years of neglect.'

'I'll do it,' he says, resolute in his determination.

'Remember, I am the only one who loves you.'

***

Gama switches on the television; the proposal for nuclear weapons is being discussed in the House. It is all over the news, and the country is divided. Some people believe it is about time we become a world power, in our own right, rather than rely on other countries for defence. Others want to stick to the status quo; if it's not broken don't fix it, we have survived many years without nuclear weapons. I hope the House will not pass the motion, but it's not looking good for me. The prime minister also wants to scrap public healthcare stating the government can no longer afford it unless taxes are increased. This is not the prime minister I know and respect.

Right now, I need to fix the problems at home; my son will not leave his room, Mia has tried many times to persuade him. What am I going to do? I fix policies, talk to world leaders, command an audience, and yet, my son will not even speak to me.

Earlier, I went to visit his school; the headteacher almost didn't change his mind even with the donations I promised to the school.

'He has become someone else,' the headteacher lamented. 'The teachers are afraid of him; he threatened to kill Mr Young, his science teacher; he held an army knife to his teacher's neck. We cannot condone

129

such an act in this school; the only reason he was not reported to the authorities is because of who you are.'

'This is one of the best schools in Sydney. I came to this school, and my mother graduated from this school; this is the school I want my son to graduate from, too. Please give me a month to fix this. He will go to therapy, and then you can reassess him. If you still don't want him, I'll not push the matter and I'll still donate to the school as promised.'

I've been coming home early; maybe this will change Carl's mind. I'm also trying to mend my relationship with my wife. God! I run my hands through my hair in frustration; this is a mess.

I have been back in the house for two days now; but I'm yet to see my son. I am done. I've given him enough time; if he's angry with me, he needs to express it. I am tired of the silent treatment. I march up the stairs to Carl's room and knock on the door. When there's no response, I try to open the door, but it is locked.

'Carl!' I shout. 'You need to open this door right now.'

'Go away!'

'Open this door, or I'll break it down.'

'You have no right to break down my door.'

'I paid for this house, and everything in it belongs to me. I have given you two days to get over yourself. Enough already!'

Mia runs upstairs. 'Stop!' she begs me.

'No! We have been trying to handle the situation with kid gloves because we don't want to hurt his feelings. I am done. He needs to talk to us. Carl, open the door, or I break it down.'

'You can't do this,' says Mia.

'Watch me.' I start kicking the door with my leg.

'Henry, I said stop, or you'll have to leave this house and never come back,' Mia shouts.

'Your son placed a knife to a teacher's neck, and you think you're safe with him?'

***

Inside his room, Carl is in a rage. He gets up from his bed, pulls open the desk drawer, takes out his trusted army knife, unlocks the bedroom door, holding the knife firmly behind his back, walks up to his father and stabs him in the stomach.

***

I fall to the floor, blood seeping through my shirt. Mia is shaking. 'Carl! What have you done?' she screams. 'Gama call 000.'

I watch as my son re-enters his room, without looking back, and slams the door. Mia kneels beside me, crying. 'Henry! Please don't die!'

'Don't tell the police anything,' I say, as darkness takes over.

***

Chapter Forty-one: Rio de Janeiro

Ana

I sit down and place my head on my executive desk. *Dear God! How can I get out of this?* My former colleagues watched with envy as the movers carried my boxes. I'm sure they have many questions, but I have kept to myself ever since I lost my daughter. How I wish things could have stayed the same. I don't want this life; the price is too high for me to pay.

I have work to do. I open my computer. The new contract, extending the mining of copper from the Amazon Rainforest from three years to five years, pops up on screen. Looking at the estimates from the project and sales management team, I don't think this is visible, but why am I surprised?

Antonio knocks and enters the office.

'I gave you one hour to settle in, but we have a deadline to meet.'

'I'm just going through the figures and projections; I'm looking at the numbers from when the project started six months ago.'

Antonio smiles. 'I was told you are very thorough. We believe we can make more profit than before, we are changing the expatriates to local contractors.'

'Do you think they will have the expertise to do the job?'

'They have been doing this kind of work for years.'

'OK, please, give me more time; I'll be able to get it done by tomorrow.'

'Wow! They told me you're a hard worker; you don't have to get everything done by tomorrow; you've got till the end of this week to complete it, which is three days away.'

'You'll have figures tomorrow,' I reply.

Antonio approaches my desk, and leans towards me. He gives me a seductive smile and then whispers in my ear.

'I like you, Ana; I can't seem to get you out of my mind. I noticed you a while ago. You always sit by yourself in the canteen. I was told you lost your family; I am sorry. I think you could use a friend and I would like to be one.'

The realisation of what he just said makes my laughter short and humourless.

'I'm sorry. I don't need a friend.'

His eyes flash with anger for a split second before his smile returns.

'I'm just offering friendship, Ana, nothing more. We are forced to work closely together, at least let's make it a friendly environment.'

'Thank you, Mr Gomes. I'll send you the figures tomorrow,' I say, trying to concentrate on my laptop.

I don't lift my head until I hear the door close. Was he flirting with me? I don't trust anyone from this company, apart from my old boss. I hope he got the message. I can't deal with this right now.

Antonio

I pace up and down my office in frustration; this woman wants to get me killed. I have less than twenty-four hours to gain her interest. Everything I do is not working, and she has a heart of stone. I know I am being unfair; she's going through a lot, it will take time for her to heal, but I don't have time.

Gama connects a call from Carlos.

'Seeing how you stomped out of Ana's office, and the way you are now pacing, I take it she's still not interested. Don't make me inform Mr Montes of how incompetent you are; you know what will happen. We need her to trust you; her only living relative is her older sister. We don't think that is enough to manipulate her; after all, she has suffered more losses than anyone could cope with in such a short time. I'll not be calling you next time, Antonio; I'll take pleasure in rearranging your handsome face. Get it done!'

I look around my office, filled with fear. We are being watched; what am I going to do? I was given this assignment without an option, take it or die. That is the simple rule Mr Montes lives by. I need to think what to do next.

I remove the Gamaplug from my ears for charging.

Ana

I'm inputting the numbers Carlos has given me. They are hiring local contractors, but they cost more than expatriates. I look at the prices of the types of machinery needed. Dear God! These are crazy figures; they are making millions without even trying. I note all the changes and store them on my new flash drive; I'm glad I am working from home.

The bell rings. I look at the time; 8.00 pm, and close my computer, before hiding the flash drive in my bedroom drawer. I don't have visitors and Maria won't come without calling first. I look through the peephole and see Antonio. What is he doing at my house? I open the door.

'What do you want?'

'Please, we need to talk, we can't do it in the office.'

Reluctantly, I let him in. 'What do you want from me?'

He enters the living room and turns to face me. 'I need your help.'

I take a step back and regard him quizzically.

'Listen! I'm in trouble, and you are the only one that can save me.'

'I don't understand.'

'Telling you this might get us both killed, but I'm left with no option. I was hired by Mr Montes and supervised by Carlos to ensure your trust. If that doesn't happen,' he looks at his watch, 'in less than ten hours, I'll be dead.'

'What!'

'Please, I need you to pretend that you like me; you are also in this predicament; they are monitoring you, too, and we could help each other. Mr Montes is ruthless; he will not hesitate to kill you if he finds out.'

My breathing has become shallow and ragged. 'How do I know you are not setting me up?'

'Mr Montes uses people to get results; once he gets what he wants, he will have you eliminated and leave no trace. You'll not live long enough to enjoy whatever he gives you. You have no choice but to work with me; we're in it together.'

***

'Mr Ribeiro, Antonio is in Ana's house; he has been there for over thirty minutes.'

'Are you able to hear what they are saying?'

'Not yet, sir. From what I can see, they are talking, but Mrs Santos looks upset, and Antonio seems anxious.'

'I want that house bugged by tomorrow; I want to know what is being discussed; I hope it's not; what am I thinking? Bring him to me when he leaves the house.'

Chapter Forty-two: Hong Kong

Huan

I try the number again. 'The number you have dialled is currently switched off; please try again later.' I spoke to someone a few minutes ago. Why did he switch his phone off? What do I do now? I heard a buzz on my intercom; I told my secretary that I didn't want to be disturbed.

'Come in,' I say.

Ling enters. 'I'm sorry to disturb you, but I know you will want to hear this. Your husband, Chun Li, worked closely with one of his employees, Feng Zhao? He was reported missing by his family, having disappeared at the same time your husband got arrested. Do you know him?'

I shake my head. 'No! Chun had three permanent security agents working with him for years, and the others were temporary, brought in depending on the available jobs.'

'Thank you, Ling; I'll talk to the private detective, Qiang Lin. later today.'

She leaves my office; could this be the same Feng that I just called? What are they hiding? I try tracing the call, but the phone is off, and it is not communicating with any mobile tower. I ping the last location, which shows Fujian province. I can't think. But I need to get back to work; I have bills to pay.

***

I enter the hotel elevator and press the button to the seventh floor. A woman enters and stands right behind me as the elevator door closes. I feel something pressing into my back.

'Don't scream,' she says. 'I need you to stay calm. We have been waiting patiently for you and your husband to return what he took from us, but it seems you are not taking us seriously.'

'Please, I don't know what my husband took from you; if you would tell me, maybe I can find it more quickly,' I say, shaking badly, trying not to cry.

'If you think we are playing with you, then you will be made a scapegoat; nobody is going to save you.' She presses the emergency stop button and removes the gun from my head. I feel a blow and then nothing. I blackout immediately.

When I open my eyes, I find myself in my hotel room. My hands and legs are bound to a chair.

'I'm glad you are awake,' says the woman. 'The boss would like to talk to you.' She puts the phone on speaker and holds it in front of me.

A voice comes over the line. 'I'm sorry, you have to suffer for your husband's sins, but he is refusing to speak, and he needs to be persuaded.'

'Please,' I beg, 'killing me will not solve anything. You know he had a mistress; I don't think I'm important to him.'

I hear laughter on the other end of the line. 'Oh! You're important to him. We sent a picture to him of you like this. He was devastated. You think we are lying? After all, he's in jail; why would he worry about you?'

The woman presses her phone, and shows me a video of my battered husband begging for them to spare my life, saying he would give them what they needed.

'As you can see, you are still important to him. I tell you this: if your husband is lying to us, you will be dead the next time.'

The woman hangs up the phone and unties me. She points the gun at me, telling me to close my eyes and count to a hundred.

1, 2, 3, 4…20…

I open my eyes and I fall to the floor, as my grief pours out in a flood of uncontrollable tears. How do I get out of this?

I lose track of how long I am lying on the floor before I manage to control my emotions. First of all, I need protection.

'Gama, connect me to Cheung, my husband's trusted employee.'

'Hello, Mrs Li. To what do I owe the pleasure of your call?'

'I want to hire you.'

'Why?'

'My life is in danger, and you are my husband's trusted friend and employee.'

'I'm surprised to hear you say that; when Chun was arrested, nobody reassured us and we didn't know whether we still had our jobs. There was complete silence from your end. I understand that a lot was happening around you; but a phone call would have gone a long way.'

'Like you said, a lot happened, and a lot is still happening; I don't know what to do. Are you willing to help me? I would pay you handsomely.'

'Chun is my friend. I wouldn't want anything to happen to you, so, yes, I will protect you.'

'Thank you.'

Gama disconnects the call.

Is my husband OK? I question myself. He looked badly beaten in that video; but he told me not to visit him until the trial.

I am finding it difficult to relax. I have to force myself to eat. I have not been able to concentrate on work with everything going on around me. We are moving to the next generation of wireless communication; but I can't think straight.

I lie down on the bed and sigh heavily. The good news is that, from tomorrow, Cheung Wu will be protecting me.

***

'She called me to be to ask if I will be her bodyguard.'

'That's good news. That is what we want; she's afraid and doesn't know who to turn to. Have the private detective followed; maybe he will lead us to Feng. I told you to take care of him, but you failed me; you allowed him to escape.'

'I was Chun's trusted friend. I don't believe he gave those documents to Feng instead of me.'

'He had his doubts about you, but the good thing is he never conveyed that to his wife. So, learn as much as you can while working for her. We have too many parties interested in those documents, and we need to get them before they do. Once Feng is found, we will kill him and the private investigator. No one else must have access to those documents.'

'She was manhandled today by the Kung Group; they are chasing after the same thing; I need them taken care of today. Get to work! Chun will never talk; he knows if he does, he will die, so he is buying time. And,

if his wife is killed, we'll have no leverage against him.'

The call disconnects.

I'll make Chun Li pay; he thinks he is better than me, but he is in jail now for a crime he never committed. I advised him not to cross these people; he thought he was smart, now he will be squashed.

Chapter Forty-three: London

'His mother called him; she is worried about him, and she encouraged him to speak to the police about the threats and manipulations. What should we do with to her?'

'Nothing yet, Jude knows the price it will cost him if he defies me, but I want to put her in her place. She is dating this man called Robert; I want him in our pocket.'

'I'll get it done, boss.'

'I will turn her happiness to sorrow,' he says, laughing maliciously. 'I'll break her into pieces so she won't have time to interfere in my business. Get me the prime minister.'

Jude

I hear a buzzer. I go to my door and check my peephole. It's Sergeant Smith; what does he want? I open the door.

'Are you here to arrest me?'

'No! I am here to applaud you for a job well done. You made me look like a fool; I have been placed on a three-month suspension.'

'You come into my house to make unnecessary allegations against me without facts. I didn't make you look like a fool; you are a fool.'

'I'll make you pay for this. I don't care who is helping you; I have not slept in days thinking about how my life has turned upside down.'

'I don't know what problem you have with me, but that's on you, you will have to deal with that. Get out of my house, or I'll have you arrested, and then you will lose your job altogether.'

Sergeant Smith paces along the hallway. He comes up to me, holds my shirt, and glares at my face. 'You think you have won but believe me; this is just the beginning.'

He storms out of the open door.

What just happened? What's his problem?

Roger

I'm losing my mind. My wife and son are worried about me. I have been manipulated for too long, first by the English Syndicate, and now this new group who seem to be even more powerful. I searched for months to find a way to bring down the English Syndicate, but found nothing, and this new group has swept in and destroyed this gang in a day. Now they want me to sit tight and wait for their instructions. I know the link to them is Jude Williams; I'm sure he is working for them. I'll follow him since I am jobless for three months.

There is a knock on the side window of my car, as I sit watching Jude's house. A stranger hand-signals for me to wind down the car window.

I try to identify the person but he is wearing a hoodie and sunglasses – even though it's not sunny. I shake my head, and the next thing I know, the car door is opened and another man slips in beside me.

'What the hell!' A gun is pointing in my face.

'Roger! You are a fool. It seems you are tired of living; that is why you are messing with us.'

'Who are you? I don't know you? I'm a police officer trained to uphold the law, not subvert it.'

'Look at me,' says the man. 'You're a police officer; so, memorise my face. You will find nothing. I know you had an affair three years ago when you were having marital problems. Are you aware the affair resulted in a beautiful little girl called Katy?'

'You're lying.'

The door to the driver's seat is opened, and I am shown a photograph of a little angel with my blue eyes and blonde hair. Jesus Christ!

'She looks like you, doesn't she? It won't be a bad thing if your wife happens to find out about it.'

'Please! Don't tell my wife.'

'Roger, I can destroy you with a snap of a finger and turn your life upside down. Stop following Jude Williams. We have a new assignment for you; we want you to follow Paul Appleby. As you know, he is the newly appointed Secretary of State for the Environment, Food and Rural Affairs after his predecessor was unceremoniously fired.

'What do you want me to do?' I say, resigned to my fate.

'Just follow him and report back to this number everything you see.' A piece of paper is placed in my hands. 'Don't bother to run fingerprints; nothing will come up. You double-cross me and I'll inform your wife about your torrid affair, destroy your marriage and then go after your family, one by one, just for fun.'

He gets out of the car, closes the door behind him, and waits while I drive off, waving me goodbye.

In all my years as a police officer, I've never seen anything like this in my life. The resources they must have; how do they know about a daughter even I never knew I had?

Jude

'Mum, why are you crying? Is everything OK?' I'm surprised to be receiving a call from my mum at 10.00 pm. 'Mum! Say something; you are scaring me.'

'Robert broke up with me; he wants us to take a break from each other; I don't know what I did wrong?'

I sigh, relieved she is not physically hurt. 'You did nothing wrong, Mum, you're kind and loving, you just fell for the wrong man. Do I need to come to Scotland to break his legs? Did he touch you?'

'No! No! Robert is not like that, everything was fine yesterday, we were planning to come to London so that you can formally meet him, then today, he suddenly wants to break up, I don't understand.'

'I'm so sorry, Mum, please try and sleep; I'll call you in the morning.'

Chapter Forty-four: New York

Mayor Cleborne takes out a bottle of his 1953 vintage wine, 'Jaiora', that he drinks on special occasions. He pours a sizeable amount into his wine glass and picks up his registered gun, that he removed from his home office safe, with his right hand.

Shame engulfs him. How did I get myself involved with these horrible people? He thinks to himself. I have lost the most meaningful thing in my life just because I disobeyed them.

He remembers the call he received from them.

'You lost your daughter because you wanted to do the right thing, your wife is suffering from depression, and your son hasn't been home since the death of his sister. I warned you, but you refused to listen.'

'You intentionally requested Detective Martin Hills.'

'I needed a respected cop to rule it as suicide.'

'No! You knew the kind of cop Martin Hills is; you knew he wasn't going to let go of a case he finds suspicious until he gets to the bottom of it. Luckily, we've kept him busy; he will not have time to investigate anything. So, I'm warning you, for the last time, if you don't want your son to be sent to jail and your wife to lose her sanity as she watches her only living child smeared all over the news for a crime he never committed, don't test me again.'

Mayor Cleborne wipes away a stray tear, regret written all over his face.

I killed my daughter. How can I live with myself?

He points his gun at his head and pulls the trigger.

Martin

I'm homeless. I need to look for a cheap motel to stay in for the night, but first I have to go back to the precinct, or I'll lose my job.

I am grateful that Bobby is not at his desk and I don't have to deal with him. I can see cops whispering around me.

'What is going on?' I ask one of the detectives.

'You don't know?' He replies in surprise.

'Know what?'

'The mayor is dead. He shot himself in the head in his office, about forty-five minutes ago. I think your partner and the captain went to investigate; I am surprised you haven't been told.

'Thanks,' I say, turning away from him, looking at the ton of paperwork on my desk. I can't think about this now, or I'll go crazy.

***

Later, I drive to Brooklyn; I need answers from Mary or is it Vanessa, whatever her name is. I was set up; they knew I was coming to that house. How were they able to get those pictures to my wife?

I sigh heavily as I pull up outside. It's dark and there's no outside light. I knock on the door repeatedly, but no one answers. I enter the house by picking the lock; the house is empty. I was here in this house, earlier today, it was furnished entirely with framed pictures on the wall of Mary and me. Now I can't see a single piece of furniture as I use my flashlight to navigate the house. What am I going to do now?

***

'He just left the house, boss.'

'Was the house completely cleared, and nothing was left behind?'

Yes, the house was wiped clean; he found nothing.'

'Good!   I want him followed; he is a good cop; he can't be controlled easily.'

'We can use his daughters to our benefit.'

'No, I know his kind; he would rather lose everything than be manipulated, so we will get him incarcerated, but to make it fun, let's use his wife. Send her the marriage certificate.'

Martin

I'm sleeping in the most uncomfortable bed; how did my life turn out like this?

'Gama, call Leah.'

'I don't want to talk to you,' she responds.

144

'Please, I need you to hear me out.'

'No, you will speak to my attorney; I will get full custody of Charlotte; Emilia is an adult, she gets to choose, but right now, neither of them wants to talk to you.'

'You are not listening; I'm being set up.'

'I'm a fool for trusting you for twenty-one years. I received an email five minutes ago that shows you are married to another woman.'

'I'm telling you the truth, I'm being set up,' I say again, angrily.

'Really! In the same way you said you did not know that whore, but you went to see her the next day.'

'I'm a cop; I wanted answers.'

'I'm tired of crying over you; you don't deserve it. I will show the marriage certificate to my attorney then we'll go from there. Maybe you got too cocky; you thought no one would find out. Goodbye, Martin.'

The call disconnects.

If I don't resolve this problem, and fast, I could end up in jail tomorrow.

'Gama, connect me to Edward.'

'I don't want to have anything to do with you, Martin.'

'Please, I am desperate; I've no one to turn to but you. I am being set up; there's a record of me being married to a woman I do not know. I need you to help me remove the record.'

'I don't know how you have gotten yourself involved with this mess, but these people are dangerous; you put my life in danger the last time I tried to help you.'

'I'm begging you. Please? I'll send you a copy of the marriage certificate.'

There's a pause at the end of the line and I hold my breath.

'OK, I'll see what I can do, but this is the last favour I am doing for you; I'll no longer be picking up your calls.'

'Do this, and you will never hear from me again, I promise.'

Gama disconnects the call.

Who are these people? I think hard. My problems all started when I began investigating the death of the mayor's daughter. I was placed on desk duty; and then the captain and Bobby became much more chummy than usual. I pick up my notebook, trying to tie in the facts. I need to find the person impersonating me. That is the only way to find Mary Ashley Cox or Vanessa Allen, whatever name she is using. The only person who can help me now is Edward, but that's impossible. And why did the mayor kill himself? I put three question marks in front of his name. I need my life back; the only way to do that is to get answers. Whoever you are, I'll not give up; you have taken everything away from me.

Chapter Forty-five: Lagos

Lola

It's been two days since I arrived at my parents' home in Asokoro; a fourteen-room mansion with a swimming pool. My two younger brothers just happen to be home from university on a school break. I feel safe; I haven't had that in a long time.

Reflecting on recent events, I felt like I failed in bringing justice to those who killed Chioma, but what can I do? I called her parents yesterday; they are distraught by the failure of the police even to investigate this case. The whole situation is appalling. I'm afraid for my life and my friends. I have lost so much because of this case. I know they are material things, but I worked hard for them.

I hear my name being called. 'Lola! Where are you?' Why is my dad in the house at this time of the day? Chief Adeyemo is home at 2.00 pm; not at the office working on his government contracts supplying armoured cars to the Nigerian army. He enters my room.

'Lola! I received a strange call today; I have had to leave work. What have you been doing in Lagos?'

'I don't understand.'

'When did you become a journalist? I sent you to a prestigious university to study law. You returned to the country, went to law school, and completed your call to bar ceremony. But you never practised law, not even for one day, and decided you wanted to start your own business. So I gave you the capital for your cosmetics business. Now I receive a call saying my daughter manages the controversial blog called 'The Report'. What do you have to say for yourself?'

'I'm, I'm…' I cough to clear my throat. 'That's not true.'

'That's not true,' repeats my father, laughing sarcastically. 'Do you love your life? Do you care about your family? You are poking your nose into the strange deaths happening in Lagos. Do you think it is just Lagos? It is happening everywhere in the country; people are being massacred, and something is going on for sure. Even the president chooses to ignore it, but my daughter has decided to get involved and be the country's saviour.'

'They killed Chioma,' I say.

'I'm sorry your friend died, I liked her, but I can't afford to lose you. Did you buy a building in Gbagada that got burnt down, and was the house you live in vandalised?'

'Dad, who is telling you these things?'

'You should be the one telling me these things. I should not be receiving calls from a stranger telling me what is happening to my daughter, that my daughter has a death wish. You're not going back to Lagos; it seems you don't care about those who love you or wouldn't be doing this; this is madness.'

'I promise you that I came to Abuja because I have stopped journalism; I need a break from everything.'

'Lola, when things like this happen, and people turn a blind to it, it means that powerful people are behind it. You know the election is coming soon, chaos and fear are used to manipulate. You need to be careful; I didn't get to this position in politics by not keeping my ears close to the ground. Strange things are happening that I can't explain; for the past month, two of my friends who are political juggernauts have lost their lives mysteriously. This is bigger than you, don't get involved. Do you understand?' He walks out of the room angrily.

I can tell my father is afraid. What have I done? Who are these people? Whoever they may be, surely, we can't be cowards and allow them free rein over our country.

Chapter Forty-six: Kabul

Ahmed

'What do you mean "entertainment"?' I pull the girl forcefully into the bathroom, the only area that's not being monitored. 'I need you to listen to me carefully.' I notice that she is shaking badly. 'Listen!' I lift both my hands. 'I'm not going to touch you; I did all that for the hidden camera. We will stay here for thirty minutes or so, pretending we are doing something. Get into the shower and pull the curtain across; I promise you, I'll not touch you, but we need them to believe that I did. How long have you been subjected to this?'

'My mother sold me because she couldn't afford to care for me. I've been in this compound with several other girls for about three months.'

'I'm sorry! I need you to understand what transpires between us; you must never tell a third party. No one!'

She gets into the shower cubicle fully clothed, pulls the curtain across and then takes off her clothes. How can I save her from being abused by these crazy men? She is just a small girl who has found herself in an impossible situation.

I step into the shower, after she gets out wearing a long towel to cover herself; we need them to believe that I slept with her. A little later, she watches me nervously as I get dressed into my tunban.

'I need you to cry. Can you do that?' She shakes her head. 'They need to believe that I've been abusive to you.' I lift my hand and slap her face hard; she starts sobbing. I whisper, 'I am sorry,' as I push her out of the bathroom. She falls to the floor. 'Get up,' I shout. 'Get into bed.' I whisper to her, 'Do not take off the towel, I'm not going to touch you.'

We get into bed and I pull the blanket to cover us completely. 'Sleep!' I say. 'But you must tell everyone that I was horrible to you, OK! What is your name that I may request you again? If I can't save the other girls, maybe I can at least help you.'

'Moska,' she whispers quietly.

***

I've been training for five days now. Today is the final day. Ghani has been particularly aggressive towards me. Mohammed came to watch me shoot. Apparently, he has heard how good I am at shooting and self-defence. He has heard that I can bring down my opponents with ease. The only person I allow to beat me is Ghani, not because he's better than me, but because I don't want to make my life here more difficult. I want Mohammed to request that I be his number one bodyguard as that is the only way I can get close to him. I have never seen anything like this place. The compound has a massive cinema, and the men go to watch the latest movies from different parts of the world. Their disregard for human lives as they rape and kill innocent girls in the compound is beyond belief.

'Ahmed, Mohammed wants to see you in his office,' one of his right-hand men, called Jamil, shouts.

He regards me menacingly as we walk together to Mohammed's office. 'I've been working closely with Mohammed for over eight years; I'm very close to him,' he says. 'My intuition tells me that you are hiding something, and it's never wrong. I'll be watching you closely; you come here from nowhere, you have this incredible résumé, your wife and kids are all dead, that is fishy.'

'Why would you think that?' I demand. 'After retiring from being a soldier, I became a simple farmer in Kandahar; I lost everything that meant anything to me in one day; there is nothing fishy about me; I am just unfortunate. I would give everything to have my family with me.'

'We'll see!' He points at Mohammed's door and walks away.

I knock and wait until I hear, 'Come in!'

I bend down to greet him, not lifting the top of my head until he tells me to. He is sitting behind a magnificent executive desk. One wall of his office is covered by a large bookcase. The Mohammed that I studied doesn't have time to read, so that wall must lead somewhere.

'Sit!'

'Thank you, sir.'

'I have been looking for a man called Hussain Atta, he is my number one competitor. He is a dangerous man who needs to be brought down, but we can't find him. You are very good at your job; you came highly recommended. I need you to find him. You are new here, nobody knows you are working for us, it will be easier for you to get information from people. If you can get me, Hussain, I'm a generous man; not only will I make you my right-hand man, I'll give you more money than you have ever seen in your life, and I'll help your extended family. From my research, it seems they are struggling to eat. If nothing is done soon, they will die of starvation.'

'I'll try my best, sir; I won't disappoint you.'

'You can go now.'

My heart is beating fast; what am I going to do? I need to pass information to Jabar that I have been assigned to find Hussain. I am supposed to be with the other bodyguards, but, honestly, I have to find him. I have not spoken to my family in days, and I'm sure my wife will be panicking. I walk out of the main building, and someone taps me on the shoulder from behind. It is the very man I am looking for.

'Follow me,' he says, 'but maintain a small distance from me; they must not know we are walking together.'

I do as he says, keeping some distance behind. Eventually, we arrive at a secluded building used as a morgue.

'I was just thinking about you, and how I could find you,' I say.

'We don't have time. This is the encrypted phone; so you can call your family and the boss, Hussain. I would advise you to be very careful; nobody must see you use it. It is safer for you to text rather than call; the numbers are programmed into the phone, but be cautious,' he says as he walks swiftly out of the building.

I place the phone in my inner garment as I leave and walk back to my building. I have to talk to my family and Hussain.

'Ahmed! Ahmed!' I turn swiftly. 'We have been looking for you.'

'I'm sorry, I didn't know what I was supposed to do; I just finished my training today.'

'I understand, but you are supposed to meet the five bodyguards formally. I am Latif, the head bodyguard; let me introduce you to the others. As the senior bodyguard, I give instructions on what needs to be done directly; I have been in this position for three years. This job is very dangerous, and you could lose your life at any time; we need to work as a team to protect ourselves and Mohammed. I hope you understand?'

'Yes,' I reply as I follow him, wishing I could talk to and hold my family.

Chapter Forty-seven: Sydney

Henry

I wake up in hospital with my wife's head on my bed; she is sleeping. I am in so much pain as I try to move. My wife lifts her head and wipes her sleepy eyes. 'Thank God you have woken up.'

'How long have I been out?'

'A day. You were rushed to the hospital; thank God the knife did not hit any vital organs.'

'Are the police asking questions? What did you tell them?'

'Nothing, but the strangest thing is that the police got a tip that someone broke into the house and stabbed you. They are looking for the assailant; no one suspects Carl.'

'Where is Carl?'

'In his room, he didn't even come out when the ambulance and the police arrived. It was all over the news that minister Henry Graham was stabbed in his own house. Is Australia safe anymore? The prime minister made a statement about your stabbing, telling citizens it's high time everyone protects their homes and nation from intruders. The police will come to interview you soon, a police officer is manning the door.'

A doctor enters with a nurse. 'Mr Graham; how are you feeling?'

'I'm in pain.'

'Let me check your stitches; you will be given painkillers until the pain subsides.'

I feel so weak; I can't think straight, but the most important thing is that Carl is safe and not indicted for his crime.

Two police officers come into the room. 'I hope you can talk now, Mr Graham; we want to catch the assailant as soon as possible and your description will go a long way in identifying them. My name is Angela and this is my partner, Steve.'

The doctor and nurse leave the room after telling me I don't need to worry; I'll heal nicely.

'I don't remember much; I got home and went upstairs. I was about to knock on my son's door when a stranger wearing a balaclava opened the door and stabbed me; I don't remember anything after that.'

'Where was your son when this happened?' asks Angela.

'I don't know, I collapsed on the floor, and the assailant fled.'

'Where is your son right now?' says Steve.

Mia answers, 'He's at home. There's a stationed police car monitoring the house.

'He wasn't at home when the incident happened. I was in the kitchen when I heard someone running down the stairs. I thought it was my son; I didn't think anything of it until I saw the front door was open. I closed the door before going upstairs and finding my husband on the ground bleeding; I called 000.'

'Why didn't you tell us all this when we arrived at the scene yesterday, Mrs Graham?' enquired Angela.

'My husband was lying on the floor. I wasn't sure how badly he was injured, or whether he would survive. I wasn't thinking at the time; all I wanted was for him to be OK.'

'Aren't you and your husband having marital problems? From our investigation, he's no longer living in the house?'

I look at Angela, livid. I raise my tone. 'What kind of question is that? What has that got to do with anything?'

'I'm sorry, Mr Graham, it's our job to ask uncomfortable questions, to cross every T and dot every I.'

'I came back home to be with my family. Is that hard for you to understand?'

'When did you return home, sir?'

'A week ago, what has that got to do with anything?'

'Nothing! Just asking questions. Surprisingly, we received an anonymous call yesterday, and a video was sent to us of someone running out of your house at the estimated time the incident happened. Do you have a security camera installed in your home?'

I look at Mia; I can see fear written all over her face.

'No! We don't have a camera in our house.'

'That's strange. I wonder how we could have been sent that video then. You don't have any neighbours close enough to your property. As I said before, we will continue the investigation, and we would like to talk to your son also; since he is seventeen, I would like to do it in your presence.'

'Why do you want to interrogate my son?'

'We are not interrogating your son; we just want to know what he saw. You say the assailant came out of his room, wearing a balaclava, so that could be anyone, and from my report, you don't seem to have a good relationship with your son.'

'Get out! I will have a word with your supervisor. Do not go near my son until you have substantial evidence to back that up.'

'My apologies, Mr Graham, I am not here to offend you; I'm just doing my job.'

'Then do "your job" elsewhere and leave my family alone.'

I watch them leave the hospital room, closing the door gently behind them.

'What are we going to do?' asks Mia.

'Don't worry; I'll find a way to take care of it. But they must not interview Carl; I don't know what is going on with him now.'

'I am afraid. I don't want my son in jail.'

'He won't go to jail.'

'Where did they get a video from Henry?'

'I don't know anything about a video, but that is a good thing; I think Carl went back to his room; he didn't leave the house, did he?'

'I don't know; he could have climbed out of the window.'

'Don't worry about it now, everything will be fine,' I say, more confidently than I feel.

***

I was discharged two days ago, and I am resting in the guest room. I'll be going back to work next week. I've received endless phone calls from friends, family and well-wishers. I have been told that my popularity vote has gone up. I grace the front of newspapers and magazines, stating how extraordinary talented I am.

Gama connects a call.

'Henry, I'm glad you are home safely. I asked whether you are ready to accept in my previous text. I don't remember you giving me an answer.

154

I know your son stabbed you, and I've evidence of him doing so. Check your phone; you will have a picture of your son confessing to someone that he just stabbed his father. What do you think will happen when the police find out?'

'What do you want from me?'

'I don't want anything from you right now, but you will likely take over from Jackson Paul to be the next prime minister in the next two years. Everything I tell you to do, you will do without question, and that will start soon because we need to test your loyalty. You mess up; not only will your son go to jail for a long time, I will also destroy your reputation and your family. You can kiss your political aspirations goodbye.'

The phone disconnects.

My heart is racing and I am sweating heavily. How do I get out of this?

Chapter Forty-eight: Rio de Janeiro

Antonio

'Get in the car! Carlos wants to talk to you.'

The door of the Mercedes Benz G-Wagon opens. I get in. Inside the car is Carlos.

'I have been waiting for you for twenty minutes to leave Ana's house. You have been there for over an hour. What have you been telling her?'

'Nothing, I swear. I'm not so stupid as to tell her anything.'

'You better not be stupid, Antonio, because it will be a shame for you to have your face restructured; that is your prize possession.' He laughs menacingly.

I touch the side of my face with both hands. 'I didn't say anything,' I repeat.

'Antonio, she doesn't look like a woman that has fallen under your spell. She is apprehensive about you. What did you say to her?'

'I told her how much I liked her. She said she had just lost her daughter, so she was not open to dating, but she could be my friend.'

'Antonio! Are you lying to me?'

'I would never lie. She agreed to be my friend and nothing more, but it's something, right?'

Carlos watches me intently, not saying anything. 'I don't trust you, and if I find out you have lied to me, I will kill you. Do you understand what Mr Montes can do to your father and mother? Think about that next time you try anything stupid. Get out of my car.'

I do as he says and stand watching as the car drives away, breathing heavily. I look behind me, and I see another vehicle watching Ana's house. I need to get away from here; I have been able to escape death, at least for today.

Ana

I try to sleep, but all I can think about are the words that came out of Antonio's mouth; these people are so dangerous that the only way out is death itself. I have to play along with Antonio, or we both die. What do they want from me? I am just an ordinary accountant, anyone can do my job; they don't need me.

I have to do everything they ask of me without question, and I will be rewarded accordingly. So they were the ones that paid my outstanding loan and the anonymous hundred thousand dollars.

I don't want to be manipulated by anyone, but there is no escape, according to Antonio. I have agreed to pretend to like him; but how can I trust him? Maybe he is playing me? I honestly don't know what to do. I open my curtain slightly. He told me I am likely being watched. There are so many cars parked outside, and it is dark, so I can't see anything. I close my eyes, and try to stop myself from thinking. After a while, I drift off to sleep.

***

I get out of my 2006 Ford, one of my price possessions because it was paid for in full. I hear my name being called. I turn around. It is Carlos, and my heart sinks. What does he want now?

'Ana, you're our new director of accounting; you shouldn't be driving such an old car; it doesn't reflect well on the company.'

'I am OK with the car; it is one of the things my husband left me, and it's sentimental.'

'Nevertheless, follow me.'

I follow him. I am shown several jeeps ranging from Mercedes to Range Rover. 'Choose one of the cars, and it is yours.'

'I can't! I couldn't drive this car to my house; the vehicle won't be safe.'

'I was going to talk to you about that; our directors are given apartments in Gávea, we would love for you to move there.'

'I'm a simple person, don't get me wrong, I'm grateful for all that you are offering, but it's unnecessary. The boss has already promised me a salary increase, based on my new position, which is enough for me.'

'Ana, this is not about you; it's about the image of this company. You are a director, and everything will change according to your new status, and that includes a clothing allowance.' He looks at my skirt and blouse with distaste. 'No one should be caught dead wearing such hideous clothes.'

'This is too much. Please can I think about it?'

'There is nothing to think about; you have twenty-four hours to change everything about yourself; we have a luncheon with other directors and board members on Friday, and we can't have you looking like an unsophisticated person.'

I feel like crying, but I am not going to give Carlos the satisfaction.

'I don't care, choose any car for me, and I will drive it.'

'I have booked an exclusive appointment for you with the best stylist in Rio de Janeiro. She deals with luxury clothing, and you have an appointment at 6.00 pm today; you will be driven there and then back to your new apartment. I already know where you live. Do you need any of your old furniture?'

'I don't want anything moved from my house,' I say with a heavy sigh. 'Everything in that house reminds me of my family; please, they are very important to me, leave everything the way it is.'

'As you wish, Ana, we want the best for you, but you seem reluctant. Don't you want to work with us?'

'I am delighted. It's just a lot to take in.'

He walks away and I wipe my eyes quickly as tears threaten to fall. I'm in deep trouble.

I take the elevator to my floor and rush to the toilet to wipe my face; no one must know I was crying; like Antonio said, they are always watching. I must allow them to think they are winning. I must find a way to get out of this.

I walk into my office and send the updated accounting figures to Antonio for review.

***

'Can she be trusted?'

'I don't think so; she doesn't care about money; she looked uncomfortable when I offered the car and the new apartment.'

'What about Antonio?'

'He told me he has convinced her to be his friend, and he would work his way into her affections from there, but I doubt it.'

'His father owns an automobile repair shop, right?'

'Yes, He's been running it for twenty-five years.'

'Burn it down, and take the building away from him. That should be a warning to him that I'm not joking.'

OK, sir, what about Ana?'

'She has an older sister called Maria; I want her on our side. She lives in a slum with her husband and four kids; they are desperate. Lure her with what she wants the most, money.'

Chapter Forty-nine: Hong Kong

Huan

It feels good coming back home after hiding in a hotel for days. The house had been cleaned, and every piece of furniture broken has been repaired or replaced. I look around my home; it will never be the same again. I have worked hard for many years and, at forty-five years old, I should be home with my husband and children. Instead, I have a husband in jail and no child to call my own.

I enter my spacious white room; the only splash of colour comes from the paintings that I sourced from different parts of the world. On my bed is a big brown envelope; who placed that there? I tell Ling to monitor the activities happening in my house.

I open the envelope only to see pictures of my husband in a compromising position with his mistress, about ten pictures of him laughing, kissing her and playing with her kids. The photos drop from my hand in shock; Chun told me not to believe everything I see. I decided to believe him when he says he did not have an affair with that woman, but these pictures prove me wrong. Did he want children so badly that he accepted someone else's as his own? DNA proved he didn't father those children.

I sit on my bed; I feel a heavy weight on my shoulder. I have been a fool for too long; maybe I should divorce him. All my problems started because of him. Someone knocks on my door, and I quickly hide the envelope containing the pictures.

'Come in!'

Cheung walks in. 'I'm sorry to disturb you, but it's 8.00 pm, can I leave? I have assigned someone else to protect you in my absence; she is downstairs. Huan! Are you listening?'

'Sorry! What did you say?'

'I said I am leaving now, and I want to introduce you to my replacement for the night. Are you OK?'

'Did Chun have a girlfriend? You are his close friend, you should know.'

'Huan, you are a good woman. I don't think you deserve what Chun is doing to you, but it is not my place to say anything.'

'I need to know for a fact.'

'Ms Yang came to the office regularly; I have met her many times. Chun never openly told us that she was his mistress, but it was easy to put two and two together.'

'How long?' I ask, tears blurring my eyes.

'I shouldn't be telling you this, Chun is my friend, but I would say he has always wanted children for years.'

'Thank you.' I get up from the bed. 'Let's meet your replacement.'

I follow him down the stairs where a young woman, not more than thirty years old, is waiting for us.

'Did you get me a female bodyguard?'

'I feel you'll be safer with a woman in your house at night. Don't let her pint-size fool you; she is a lethal force. Huan, I would like you to meet Chyou. I've known her for three years, and I've seen her work; you have nothing to be worried about.'

'Nice to meet you,' I say, shaking her hand.

'Don't worry, Mrs Li; I have checked the whole house, installed new security alarms and made sure that the doors are locked.'

'Thank you,' I say, turning to Cheung. 'See you tomorrow.' I walk back upstairs; I am mentally exhausted and I need sleep.

***

I watch her walk back upstairs looking despondent. I feel sorry for her, but her husband is to blame for messing up. He meddled in what was not his business, and those closest to him had to suffer with him.

I turn to Chyou and whisper, 'Watch her closely; we need to know everything she is up to. Did you put the hidden cameras in her room and across the house?'

'Yes, everything is done as requested.'

'I want to know whom she calls and what they talk about; we have limited time to get a result. I know she is trailing Feng, and I think he has the information we are looking for. This document must not get into the wrong hands, the boss is anxious, and you know what that means? If we don't produce results soon, we might lose our lives.'

***

I have to find a way out of this mess. I need to find that document; that is the only way I can distance myself from my husband and the troubles that comes with him. I've been waiting for information from Qiang, I have called him multiple times today, and his phone has gone to voicemail. This is unlike him; he is very professional and he usually gives me daily updates on his progress. I will call his business partner Xiuying.

'Gama, connect me to Xiuying.'

'Xiuying, I'm sorry to bother you this late, but I wonder if you have heard from Qiang since you work closely together in the same agency?'

'There is something wrong; I've not heard from him since he left this morning to travel to Fujian province. He never switches off his phone, only if required, and then he puts it back on immediately; I am a bit worried,' he replies.

'What do you want to do?'

'Let's wait till tomorrow; I'm sure he'll call.'

'Thank you, please keep me updated.'

Gama disconnects the call.

***

'What happened to Qiang Lin?'

'He has been shot,' Xiuying replies angrily.

'By whom?'

'We don't know; he was rushed to hospital. I received a call from a stranger using his phone who told me he was found in the middle of the road, having been shot. He later died in the hospital.

'I'm sorry, Mrs Li, but we will no longer be handling your case at our agency. Whatever Qiang found out led to his death; I'll not put my other agents in danger. The worst part is that nothing was found on him apart from his phone, and it had been wiped clean with no information apart from my number in his contacts. I know for a fact that he carries his security ID with him everywhere and he packed a little suitcase to travel.'

'I'm sorry about the death of Qiang, but what am I supposed to do?'

'Whatever your husband got himself involved with is more dangerous

162

than we can handle in this agency. I'm sorry.'

The call disconnects.

What do I do now?

Chapter Fifty: London

Jude

I just got home from the restaurant. I have a guilty conscience about George and William, and I'm tempted to fire them. I was told to look the other way; I know they stay in the building after we close for the day, but to do what I don't know. They are very efficient in their jobs, George as my manager and William as a waiter. I am just not comfortable knowing that they use my restaurant for cocaine. There are reports in the news that several young people, between the ages of sixteen and thirty, have overdosed using a drug called 'demalon', that is made to look like sweets but it is 100% cocaine. It is the new party drug, and the government doesn't seem to know where it is coming from. How can I sleep at night knowing that I am responsible for the death of tens of thousands of people?

'Gama, switch on the light,' I repeat multiple times but, strangely, the light does not come on. I walk over to try and switch it on manually when I hear my name.

'Jude, why are you upset? I've given you your greatest heart's desires, and I'm capable of doing more.'

I look around frantically, but can see nothing in the dark. 'Who are you? What do you want from me?'

'Nothing! All I ask is for you to look the other way and not grow a conscience.'

'You told me to take them back. I did. You said my restaurant would continue to be used as a drug house; I did not complain. What more do you want from me?'

'You seem not to understand. I don't need you, but you need me. I can close down your restaurant today and send you to jail; all I have to do is leak it to the police that you're the one running the drug operation that is killing tens of thousands in the UK.'

'That's the problem; people are dying. I feel so guilty. Why my restaurant? You could use any other place.'

'Jude, I like you, that is why I am using your restaurant. But, listen to me, to prove to you that I'm not joking, you will receive a distressed call from your mum to say her boyfriend, Robert, who just broke up, has died in a car accident. He was drunk-driving and killed a woman and her three-month-old son.

'Oh, God! Why kill them? They are innocent people.'

'They are not as innocent as you think. Robert was in debt, his business ran down, he filed for bankruptcy about a year ago, and he lost all of his possessions because of it. He met your mum at the right time, a lonely woman living in a big house bought by her wealthy son; he saw an opportunity and decided to date her. He has been collecting large sums of money from your mother to take care of his younger girlfriend and three-month-old son. Being the good man I am, I took care of them. So, you see, Jude, they are not innocent; I saved your mum from a gold-digger.'

I sigh deeply. I need to sit down, and I try to navigate around in the dark.

'I'm not worried about the money; they didn't need to die.'

'Oh, he needed to die; he was going to have your mother killed after marrying her to allow him to take all her possessions. He would play the role of a loving husband; knowing you were going to take good care of your mum, probably buy them a bigger house and putting more money in her bank account.'

I hear the sound of movement.

'Jude, this is the last time I'll be coming for a friendly conversation; all I want is your loyalty. There are many more things you will be doing for us in the future with no questions asked. I need you to concentrate on the fact that I own you, and I can dispose of you at any time.'

The light comes on, and I am standing alone in my living room.

Roger

I knock on the door of my ex. I have not seen her in years, but I need to confirm whether I have a daughter I know nothing about.

I hear movement in the house before the front door is opened.

'What the hell are you doing here?'

'Hello, Michelle.'

'I repeat, what are you doing here?'

'I just, hmm, please, I don't know how to say this but do I have a daughter?'

'What do you mean do you have a daughter?'

I take out the picture and show it to her.

'Where did you get this?'

'Where I got the picture is not the problem, it's that I have a daughter, and you never told me.'

She laughs bitterly. 'I never told you because I don't want anything to do with you. You dumped me without looking back. I kept you warm when your wife wasn't there, but you ran back to her when she decided it was fit for her.'

'I have got a right to know.'

'No! You have no rights here because you don't have a daughter.'

'Please! You know I'm not a bad person. I'm sorry I hurt you. You can't prevent me from seeing my child.'

'What are you going to do? Sue me? We all know you can't do that; your precious wife must not know you fathered another child apart from hers. Leave and never come back.' She slams the door in my face.

She's right! There is nothing I can do, if my wife found out, she would divorce me, and I would never see my son again. I turn towards my car, disgruntled and angry with myself; my life is a big mess.

'Gama, connect me to Danger.' I saved the number given to me as 'Danger'.

'Hello, Roger, what do you have to report on Paul Appleby?'

'I have been watching him for two days; he has a close bond with the prime minister, and he's had several meetings with farmers from what I can gather from his workers. We will be facing major food scarcity in Europe, due to tax increases imposed on the farmers, and many farmers have stopped farming and are being forced to sell their lands. For the ones willing to farm, the unpredictable weather is killing the crops.'

'OK, good. We tend to reward our workers for their loyalty. What do you want? Promotion to the position of chief of police? Do you want your daughter in your life? Or do you want to be a wealthy man? We can do all that very easily.'

'I'm good. I don't need anything.'

'You'll get a call tomorrow to come back to work; only you, not your partner, Mike. You'll be promoted to inspector but, in the next two months, you will be promoted to superintendent.'

'How will I be able to explain coming back to work without my partner and being promoted at the same time?'

'You don't have to explain to anyone; I just told you what is going to happen. Your ex will also allow you visiting rights to see your daughter and you will be able to do that without your wife knowing. Your wife spends all your money on designer clothes and shoes, she refuses to work, she depends on you entirely, and you have not been able to tell her that you are suspended from work. What choice do you have but to return to work with the salary increase that comes with your promotion? In the next two months, if you have shown us, without a doubt, that you are loyal, not only will you be a superintendent, but you will be moved to a luxurious house in Mayfair. Think about that,' he says, as the call disconnects.

Shit! I'm going out of the frying pan and into the fire!

Chapter Fifty-one: New York

Martin

I park my car a few houses back so that I can watch Bobby's house in the still of the night. I have a gut feeling he is hiding something. I check my watch; it is 10.00 pm.

I have been watching this house for about thirty minutes when he enters his house. I am determined to find out what's going on, even if I have to trail him for days. My wife spoke to him at her lowest point, and he wasn't there for me. We have been partners for eleven years. I know his children; I was there for him during his divorce from his wife Martha, losing his house in the process. He slept on my sofa for four months before he could rent a small apartment; shortly after he met Harper. I suspect he must have been dating her before his divorce.

I watch as he gets into his car and follow behind him carefully, so as not to raise suspicion. We drive for an hour until we get to Madison Avenue and he enters the underground parking lot. What is Bobby doing here? I find a parking space in the street; I need to sneak into the building without alerting security. I sneak into the parking lot, where there are all sorts of cars from Ferraris and Jaguars to Rolls-Royces, the list goes on. I spot my partner's unmarked vehicle parked amongst them. I know that Andrew Lawrence owns this building; he is the CEO of Largas Corporation, the biggest broadcasting network in North America. I can't get into the main building, but I need to find out what is going on.

I hide behind a white Rolls-Royce with gold alloy wheels. I must have been here for over an hour before Bobby comes down with my captain Marcus, talking and laughing. Bobby gets into his car; and my captain Marcus gets into a silver Rolls-Royce Phantom. Where did my boss get the money to own such a vehicle? I race back to my car, without being noticed, and I follow my captain. He drives to 15 Central West and parks the car in front of the building. One of the security men collects the car keys to park the car in the building's underground car park. The captain is greeted at the door and it opens for him. I lose visual when he enters the building. When did my boss become so rich to live in such an area?

He drives his unmarked car to the precinct every day; nobody is aware of his new life. So many unanswered questions. I need to go back to my rented motel; it's already 2.00 am.

***

'What do we do about Martin Hills?'

'You said he couldn't be easily manipulated, Bobby. The hacker he works with, do you know him?'

'No, he is very secretive about his contacts; the bastard hacker was able to remove all records of his marriage to Vanessa Allen from the government system.'

'Were you able to trace him?'

'Not yet, but we are close; the next time he enters his system, we'll catch him. Do you want me to put the records back into the system and have him arrested?'

'No, Bobby. I want his hacker; he needs to work for us. I want to make life miserable for Martin. I want him fired tomorrow and make sure his wife takes everything from him. Speak to Judge Jackson. I want him eating from hand to mouth. We'll see whether he can uphold his morals. Also, get close to his wife, make sure there is no chance for reconciliation, and have his children followed, send the necessary people into their life; I want them to hate their father. Send them the compromising pictures you sent his wife.'

The phone disconnects.

Bobby laughs heartily. Martin will not know what hit him. I am so glad I can repay him; he did nothing to help when my wife Martha left me. Martha always held Martin in high esteem; I'm sure she would listen if he told her to give me another chance. Now, he will feel what I felt sleeping on his uncomfortable sofa, miserable without my family.

Martin

I arrive at the precinct early; I have many questions that I need answers to.

My name is called by the captain.

'Martin, come into my office now!'

169

I do as I am asked. What does he want this time?

'Martin, sit down! I'm sorry, I will have to let you go. I received a letter from Mayor Cleborne's lawyer that you are the reason for his suicide. I told you not to follow up on the investigation, but you refused to listen. They threatened to sue the precinct for over 100 million dollars unless you are fired and never allowed to work as a cop again.'

'Sir, that's not true; I didn't follow up with the case after you told me not to.'

'I have always liked your dedication to the force and sense of integrity, but unfortunately, my hands are tied. This is coming from the top. Pack your things and leave this premises immediately. You will be watched closely by your former partner, Bobby, to make sure you don't take anything that doesn't belong to you. Take care! I wish you nothing but the best.'

I am confused; what just happened? I've lost my job, my home, I have no income coming in and my wife is divorcing me. How can I afford a lawyer?

I stand in front of my desk where a brown cardboard box had been placed. All the paperwork I had on my desk had been taken away. I remove the pictures of my family from the desk, placing them into the cardboard box.

My former partner smiles widely as he watches me. 'I have taken the liberty of going through your drawers,' he says. 'All files and stationery have been taken away.'

I look around; I see the other cops looking at me. I've worked in this precinct for eleven years; why am I being treated like a criminal?

After packing my personal belongings, I pick up the box and walk out of the precinct into the world of the unknown.

My phone connects as I drive away with a heavy heart.

'Martin, where are you living now?' my wife asks.

'Why would you ask me that? I don't have a home, remember, you chased me out of the house, without allowing me to explain.'

'What is there to explain? I have seen the evidence.'

We have been married for twenty-one years. Does that not count for anything?'

'I just got a call from Bobby to say that you have been fired from work.'

'Why is Bobby calling you? Do not talk to Bobby under any circumstances; do you hear me?'

'You no longer have any say about who I talk to; if I want to talk to Bobby, I'll speak to him.'

'This is for your own good,' I shout.

'Anyway, I am calling to serve you the divorce papers, but nobody seems to know where you live.'

'I don't know you anymore, how can you be so cold?'

'I am tired of being played for a fool after you decided to marry a younger woman.'

'I did not marry her!'

So, you say, are you giving me your new address or not?'

I disconnect the phone out of anger.

What the hell is happening to me as? I hit my hand on the steering wheel.

Chapter Fifty-two: Lagos

Lola

I finally convince my father to allow me to return to Lagos, after spending two weeks and four days in Abuja. I needed the mental reset. I was able to assess my life, and I have realised that I cannot not put my life, family and friends in danger. I mourn the death of Chioma. She was my best friend; she had my back and was my number one cheerleader. It is just unfortunate that her life was cut short by callous and vengeful people who hide in the shadows and destroy lives.

I pay the taxi driver and arrive at my gate, but the security guard is not here; where could he be? The side gate is open, so I wheel my suitcase to my door only for the strange man to appear in front of me. He has the same silhouette as before, but he wears dark glasses and a hoodie. How do you always manage to enter my house, and my security guard is never around?

'I have limited time to talk here. This is a new sim card; you need to change your number; it is being traced.'

'By who? I am done. I honestly don't want to do this anymore.'

'I am afraid you have no choice, your friend Chioma's fiancé Emeka was killed yesterday in his house. It was a brutal murder; he was tortured for several hours before his neck was sliced open. You would have been the police's number one suspect, but, luckily for you, you were away in Abuja, and no one will interrogate you without concrete evidence because of who your father is.

'Oh my God! Why was he killed?'

'I have been watching him for a while; it was strange when he said he broke up with your friend that she never mentioned it to you? I think the same people were manipulating him to look the other way because, shortly after her death, he changed his car and bought a house in Lekki. He must have done something wrong for them to have him killed. Your friend went to a private party; that was how she was killed, but she is a party planner; I think she was at the wrong place at the wrong time. She was killed somewhere else, and her body was moved and added to mass killing to make it look that way.'

'I am not sad about the death of Emeka; he who sups with the devil should have a long spoon; he deserves it.'

'Nobody deserves to be murdered. You are being followed, you can't afford to post those videos anymore, but you can go to parties. I think some strange and powerful people are recruiting others to their organisation. I need to find out who they are.'

'Like I said before, I can't do this anymore; I promised my father that I'd no longer be involved in this.'

'I can't do this by myself; I need your help. Don't you want to know who killed your friend? Do you think these people can be trusted to keep their words and not kill your father? Like I said before, use the sim I just gave you; don't use your old sims anymore. I'll talk to you another time.'

The stranger slip away. I am trying to open the front door to my house when my Musa appears.

'Madam! I've been waiting for you to come back.'

'Why have you not been locking the gate?'

'Since you left, strange things have been happening; men came and entered your home. I hid under my bed when I saw them holding guns. I don't know what they did inside your house, but I have to tell you I'll no longer be working here anymore; this place is not safe. I'm sorry, madam!' With that, he runs out of my compound.

'I've just got back, and all this has happened. I go to my gate and lock it. My heart is beating fast as I open the door to my house.

Inside, everything is in place. How strange! My house was trashed when I left over two weeks ago; now everything has been replaced as before using the same furniture. My head is spinning. I rush to the kitchen, and it's the same, everything has been cleared and replaced. I'm trembling as I walk upstairs to my bedroom. Oh my God! I can't sleep on that bed. What is happening to me? Are they trying to drive me crazy? Because it's working. Musa said they were carrying guns. Why didn't he tell me they had removed the trashed furniture and replaced it with brand new, exactly the same?

What am I going to do? I can't go back to Abuja; my father will never allow me to return to Lagos. It took much pleading to convince him that a twenty-seven-year-old woman can take of herself. I have depended on him for a long time; and the only asset I own has been burnt down now.

I look around my bedroom. I am terrified of living in this house. What do they want from me? The stranger said I'm being followed; maybe I'm also being watched.

***

'I followed her in Abuja for over two weeks; she only received calls from her friends, not a single call from the helper.'

'Does she have another phone?'

'We have been monitoring her calls for weeks now, we collected her other phone a few weeks back, but I'm not aware of another phone.'

'Have security cameras been installed in her house?'

'Yes, but we experienced a glitch in the camera facing her front door when she arrived, it was out for about fifteen minutes, then everything started working again.'

'Listen, I don't want any more mistakes; if she should post another video, without you knowing, I'll kill your family one by one. Get me the one who is helping her. I have a strong feeling he is getting closer and that has never happened before. Go to her, beat her up a bit but don't kill her; find out from her who the helper is? Your face must not be seen.'

The phone disconnects.

I turn to the enforcers working for the boss. 'He wants her beaten, but our faces must not be seen. He needs answers about the person helping her.'

'What is she doing right now?'

I glance at the security camera; she is sitting on the floor with her head between her legs.

'Should we go now?' one of the enforcers asks.

I shake my head. 'No! We'll go late at night when she least expects it. Go and get ready. I need answers; this is for my family.'

Chapter Fifty-three: Kabul

Ahmed

I listen as Mohammed Pir stands in front of the camera to address the country on the new structure of the nation:

'I want Afghanistan to be one of the world leaders, but we have been sidelined for too long. People are afraid of what they don't understand. Change takes time and patience. It will take time for the economy to come back up but, as a country, we can do that together if you sign your allegiance to me, not the opposition party that likes to attack without actually doing anything.

'I am ready to invest millions of dollars in schools and agriculture. Most importantly, I'm willing to give a million dollars to anyone who can provide me with intel on where to find Hussain Atta. This man has deceived you into believing that he can get Afghanistan out of poverty by trying to eliminate me. You are being misled; he is just telling you what you want to hear. I am a man of integrity; I keep my word. For anyone who can give accurate intel, their lives will change for the better, and they will receive the money instantly.'

I've been following Mohammed Pir for the past two days, walking behind him, looking around for any sign of danger. The other bodyguards surround him as he walks; we are given prior instructions on his movements for the day, and our job is to secure the parameter before his arrival.

He gets down from his seat, the TV crews shaking with fear as he addresses them.' I want this sent out to the public immediately.'

'It is airing as you speak,' one of them assures him, bowing deeply.

The owner of Afghan TV is dragged to him. The man kneels in front of him.

'Listen to me, Ibrahim, the reason you are still alive is that I need my reputation cleaned up, and I can't do that without the press.'

'I didn't say anything at all about you?'

'That is the problem; you talk about how bad the economy is, which is a reflection on me. Tell them the good things we are doing, even if you have to fabricate them. Do you understand me, or do I need to find your replacement?'

'I understand, sir.'

'I'll be watching the news you broadcast. Do not disappoint me, or I'll kill you and all that you hold dear. You know what I am capable of.'

Ibrahim nods. 'I'll do as you say.'

Getting a moment to myself is one of the hardest things in this compound; we are constantly being watched. I managed to send a text to Hussain telling him that Mohammed's new assignment for me is to find him, but I haven't spoken to my wife yet. Yusuf has sent a picture to my phone. I can see that my kids have started school, but I cannot read the expression on Aisha's face; even though she is smiling, it doesn't reach her eyes. I am warned to delete the picture immediately.

As we drive into the compound, we notice a man standing by the gate. One of the security men walks up to Khan, one of Mohammed's right-hand men and whispers to him. He signals for the man to be brought to him. Mohammed is standing far off and watching.

'I understand you have information about Hussain.'

'Yes,' the man replies.

'What do you know?'

He is hiding in one of the houses in the city; I can take you there.'

'Search him,' Khan commands.

Three men walk up to him to carry out a body search. The man moves back. I run towards them, screaming,' He is wearing a bomb!' There is an explosion and I am lifted off the floor, my back is slammed onto a car.

There is commotion everywhere and smoke; I can't see. Bodies lie on the floor. Allah! I look around. I see that Mohammed has been whisked away into the house. My body aches; this place is more dangerous than being outside. I later find out that ten men died, including the bomber and Khan.

I get to my room, my head still pounding. I have cuts all over my body. After cleaning myself, I sit on the toilet seat lid. I have five minutes; I need to call Aisha quickly. The phone rings and I am happy to hear her voice.

'I don't have time to talk for long,' I say, 'but I just want to ask after you and the children.'

'How are you, Ahmed? Please tell me you are OK?'

'I am fine, don't worry about me. I need to know how you are doing?'

'We are well; they are taking care of us, and Abdul and Laila have gone back to school.'

'That's good.'

'When are you coming home?'

'I don't know, just take care of the children, do not attempt to call me on this number. I can only contact you; do you understand?'

'Ahmed, what is this all about?'

Nothing you need worry about. Stay strong! I will speak to you again soon.'

The phone disconnects just as there is a knock on my door. It's Jabar. 'Follow me quickly!' he says.

I follow behind him, trying to avoid the camera. We reach the staircase and stand in a corner.

'This is a blind spot; there is no camera here. I need to talk quickly; Mohammed is starting to like you, to the displeasure of his right-hand men, so you need to be careful. He is impressed that you knew the man was wearing a bomb and tried to save his men. Hussain said things are moving fast; we need to find where the nuclear weapons are hidden. We will be sending more men to kill Mohammed; you need to show your skills and try to protect him better than others so he will make you his chief bodyguard.'

He runs down the stairs and I head back to my room.

As I approach my room, I see Moska sitting in front of my door.

'What are you doing here?' I ask.

I open the door and pull her into the toilet.

'I was told to come; the madam said you needed me. Ever since you requested me personally, I have not been given to any other men; thank you.'

'It would help if you did not repeat this to anyone else; everyone must believe that I'm a monster.'

I pull her by her hair as I drag her into the room in view of the camera. I then command her to get into bed. She does as directed, and I join her, pulling the cover over our heads.

'Sleep,' I whisper. 'We have another show to perform tomorrow.'

***

'I don't trust him,' Jamal says. 'How did he know that man was a suicide bomber? Maybe he has been sent to bring you down?'

'Come on!' Nader laughed. 'You have never liked him; you think he is a threat to your position. Why would he put himself in danger? He could have died trying to warn them.'

'I just don't trust him; he's very good with weapons, his instinct is on point, and someone else must have tried to recruit him, not just us.'

'I don't think he is a danger to us; I just think he wants to survive,' replies Omar, another right-hand man.

'That makes him dangerous; a desperate man will do anything to survive. I know there is war, but don't you think it is a bit convenient that his family just happened to all die at once when he is the best? I am not saying this because I am jealous; it is my job to protect you, Mohammed. I have been doing this for a long time now. Making him your chief bodyguard is too soon; some of your bodyguards have protected you for over five years without incident,' Jamal argues.

'The situation is becoming more volatile; citizens are becoming more rebellious, and we need to be more careful,' Nader adds.

'I think he is the best man for the job; he can be watched more closely when he's closer to us,' replies Omar.

'What do you think, Mohammed?' asks Jamal.

'People are trying to kill me because of that man, Hussain; they say he gives them hope. I need the best men around me, which means Ahmed; bring him to me tomorrow.'

Chapter Fifty-four: Sydney

Henry

I walk slowly up the stairs holding the wooden railing. I'm still trying to heal, but I need to talk to Carl; he refused to see me in the hospital. I've been home for a day, and I still haven't seen him. I knock on the door gently.

'Go away! I don't want to see anybody.'

'Carl, you need to open the door; we need to talk.'

'I said go away!'

'The police want to talk to you, but I told them no, they could decide to come at any time. I have to speak to you.'

'I don't care about the police; I'll tell them the truth that I stabbed you because I hate you so much.'

'Carl! Please let me in.'

I hear movement; the sound of the key. He opens the door, not moving any further. 'Say what you have to say and leave me alone.'

I look at my teenage son, he has lost so much weight, and he seems so angry.

'Oh God! Carl, are you OK? Are you eating? You don't look like yourself,' I say with a worried expression.

'Is that why you came to my door to ask after my health?'

'I hardly see you for months; and suddenly, you are back in the house pretending to care. I'm tired; If that's all you came to say, go back to your new home and leave me the hell alone.'

'Carl, I'm worried about you and so is your mum. I love you. God knows I've made many mistakes regarding my family, but I am trying; you have to try too.'

He closes the door in my face.

I raise my voice so he can hear me through the door, 'I don't know what is going on with you but, believe me, your mum and I love you so much. I would go to prison rather than you.' I walk away from the door slowly and then down the stairs with a heavy heart.

*****

Carl takes out his phone to chat with his only friend. 'My dad is sorry for all he did; he won't let the police interview me.'

'He is lying. He knows if the police should interview you, the truth will come out; his political career will be lost forever.'

'He says he would go to jail instead of me, and I believe him.'

'Baby! Like I told you before, I am the only one that truly loves you; everyone around you has a hidden agenda. You need to make him pay for all the years of neglect for playing second fiddle to his career.'

'I don't want to go to jail.'

'You will never go to jail; I won't allow that to happen to you because I love you. You need to trust me completely.'

'What do you want me to do?'

'Your father needs to be taught a big lesson; I'll let you know when the time is right, but for now, just don't believe anything he tells you, OK?

'OK,' says Carl as he ends the chat.

*****

'What is the next phase, sir? I already have the son in my pocket; he will do anything I tell him to do.'

'I am not convinced Mr Graham will completely work for us when he becomes prime minister; his loyalty needs to be tested. The House is debating on whether to allow the manufacture of nuclear weapons in the country. I want him to talk to the press, and convince the citizens, beyond reasonable doubt, that nuclear weapons are what is best for this country, using his current situation of being attacked in his home by an unknown assailant. His mother is a very powerful and influential woman; I want her on our side. What is her weakness?'

'Her son and grandson.'

'Use that against her.'

*****

My parents walk into the guest room. My mother looks around the room with dislike.

'Henry, why are you staying in the guest room? Why not come home to us.'

My father looks at my mum. 'Don't start, darling.'

'I'm not saying anything; I just don't like how she treats my son.'

'Mum, I'm fine. I deserve to be in the guest room.'

'No, you don't, but that aside, what happened? I didn't come to the hospital because I don't want to draw unnecessary attention; it's bad enough that the assailant has not been caught. I had a long discussion with the Deputy Commissioner.'

'Mum, it wasn't an unknown assailant, it was Carl.'

'What!' My parents say in unison. 'Where is Carl?'

'He is upstairs, he won't talk to me or his mother. He just stays in his room, and hardly comes out to even eat. Dad, please talk to him; maybe he will listen to you.'

He nods and stroll out of the room.

'Honey! Nobody must hear about this, do you understand? If this gets out, your political career is over. I'll take care of it,' my mum whispers.

'Right now, I'm exhausted. I don't care about my political career anymore; I've lost my wife and son to this.'

'Don't say that. You will get your wife and son back, but the most important is that you become the next prime minister. That is your legacy; I have trained you since birth for this position. You have worked harder than anyone I know, and you are about to reap the reward; this is not the time to back down. I'll get this case dismissed. I never really liked your wife, you fell in love with a woman below your status who never understood your ambition and her position to support you, but I can talk to her.'

'Mum, don't! You're going to make it worse. Stay out of it; I'll fix my marriage.'

'My dad enters the room looking bothered. 'There is something seriously wrong with my grandson, we have to do something, and we need to do it fast.'

'What happened?'

'He opened his door, I entered his room, and he started throwing a pocket knife against the wall. He wouldn't even talk to me, he is so angry.

I'm worried about his mental state, we need to get him hospitalised.'

'He won't agree.'

'We don't need his consent. They will come at night and take him away to be treated – before he kills everyone.'

Everything is a big mess, I think to myself.

Chapter Fifty-five: Rio de Janeiro

Ana

My hair has been washed, cut, and styled. I stare at myself in the mirror. Is this me? I have been brought to a luxurious boutique and fitted with the latest clothes, most notably for the gala happening soon. I'm tired; I just want to go home. I need to believe that it is just a nightmare, and when I wake up, my daughter and my husband will be with me.

'Do you like it?' the stylist asks.

'It's lovely, my brunette hair with blonde highlights.'

'You don't look excited.'

'I am excited; I just smile. Thank you!' I walk out of the building to a waiting chauffeured car ready to take me to my new apartment.

I sit in the back of the Bentley, tears in my eyes, and I quickly wipe them away. This is a life many people dream of having. I receive an alert on my phone that R$277,000 has been deposited into my account. I'm a simple woman; for many years, my husband and I have struggled to make ends meet; our salaries were never enough. Now, I am a woman with a brand-new car, luxurious home and clothes to match, yet I am so miserable.

The doorman opens the door to the building.

'Good evening, Mrs Santos. My name is Lucas; this is the key and the security code you enter for the elevator. Welcome to the building; I hope you enjoy living here.'

I have never seen such opulence in my life. A shiny marble floor leads to the elevator. I enter, type in the code 4324, and the elevator starts moving. The key has my apartment number written on it; 25. The elevator stops on the second floor and I get out and walk down the aisle to my new apartment. I open the door to a spacious apartment overlooking the bay. It is a three-bedroom apartment with a cream suite and a top-of-the-range kitchen. The fridge is stocked with food; but I have lost my appetite.

Gama automatically connects my phone to the house speaker.

'I can hear my sister's voice.'

'Ana, where are you? I am standing in front of your house.'

'I'm not at home.'

'What do you mean you are not at home? You are always home.'

'I'm at work; I have a lot I need to catch up on. I'll come and see you tomorrow; I'm sorry you didn't catch me at home.'

'That's OK. I just wanted to give you some exciting news; Pedro just got a new job in construction. You know how we struggle to make ends meet. The pay is good; we can stop worrying about money, courtesy of you.'

'I don't understand.'

'Pedro received a call to come for an interview this afternoon, and he was given the job; the person said he got the job because of you. I just want to say thank you for this. They said that after six months if Pedro is very dedicated to his job, he will be promoted and given a housing allowance. Can you imagine that?' she says excitedly.

'Congratulations, Maria! I know how difficult things are with you and the family.'

'We will be able to move out of our two-bedroom house to a better environment and bigger house, the kids are so happy. I'll talk to you tomorrow when I see you.'

The call is disconnected.

I have an instant headache. Who gave Pedro the job? My sister is on their radar, and she is being manipulated without her knowing; this is a warning to me.

There is knock on my door. It is Mr Montes; the CEO is at my apartment.

'Please come in,' I say quickly.

He enters the apartment and says,' Do you like your new home?'

'It is very nice, thank you.'

Ana, do you know why I am doing all this for you?'

I shake my head. 'No!' I reply.

'You are an excellent accountant, you could ask there are many accountants, why me? But why not you? You already work for my company, and you know what we are hiding.'

'I don't know anything.'

'But you do.'

A second man enters my apartment, pulls out a gun and points it at me.

'I am tired of pretending, so I will say this to you,' says Mr Montes. 'You determine the fate of your sister's family; if I were you, I'd enjoy this affluence.' He indicates with his hands. 'We will be getting new contracts with the government for more extraction of natural resources from the Amazon Rainforest, and you know what that entails. There is much protest about destruction of the Amazon and what that means to the world. That is not my business; I'm in the business of making money, the money that you are enjoying as well.'

'Please, Mr Montes, I haven't done anything.'

'That is the whole point; you better not be thinking of doing anything because I'll enjoy killing your sister and her family. You should be used to that by now; after all, you're an unfortunate woman, anyone close to you tends to die easily. You watched your husband die in front of you, then your only daughter as well. I'll start by killing your nieces and nephew before moving on to her husband and then your sister. The contract is with Brazilian billionaires; I need you to do a better job of manipulating the numbers for me; I need more profit.'

'Of course, sir, whatever you want,' I reply, terrified.

He laughs hysterically. 'Ana, you think I'm an evil man, but I'm one of the good ones. I am giving you the option of a good life, one that you have not experienced before, or the alternative that you will not like. I live in the penthouse of this building, so you know we'll be watching you. Be a good woman, and we won't have any problem.'

He leaves and the strange man with a gun follows him. I burst into tears as I close the door behind them. What kind of life is this? He's right; I held my husband in my arms as he took his last breath after fighting for years to beat colon cancer. We took out a loan against the house to pay for his private treatment, because the public health system was taking too long, only for my daughter to die a year later. My only relative is Maria; and they will take her away from me if I don't play along with their fraud. I don't care if I die, but I care if my sister dies because of me. What do I do now?

***

Antonio

I hold his father in my arms as he sobs bitterly. Through sweat and handwork, he built his automobile repair shop, and used the money to send us to school; now it's completely burnt down. The firefighters could not save the building, and people's cars were burnt along with it. He is in debt. I know all this happened because of me; this is just a warning from them. I need to fix this.

Chapter Fifty-six: Hong Kong

Huan

I enter my office after a long meeting with the CEO of Yamson Telecommunications. We are developing new technology that will allow a faster network to merge with Gamaplug software; this has never been done before. The Gamaplug software is pre-installed on all mobile phones, but now it will be given unlimited access to our network. I am not surprised. The government has never given singular entity access to all networks in China but Gamaplug.

That is the least of my problems right now. I need to find Feng, as the only person who could help me has been killed. I have contacted several private investigators, but they all refuse to work with me. There is an alert on my phone, and I open the text: 'Meet me at Sham Shui PO in the Kowloon district at 8.00 pm; come alone and don't tell anyone, Feng.'

What do I do now? Is this Feng, or am I being set up? I rise from my seat; I have a briefing meeting with my team on the new development integrating Gama software into our network. I'll deal with this later.

***

I look at my watch; it is 7.00 pm. I have been in the office for hours. I need to head out now if I am going to make the appointment. I have sent my chauffeur home and told Cheung that I would not need his services; he was not happy, insisting that I am putting my life in danger if I venture out by myself. I told him my life was already in danger, wherever I was.

I get into one of the company's old Toyota Corollas and drive through a congested area filled with people. I park and hope, when I return, I will find my car in one piece.

As I try to blend in with the crowd, I feel a hand tap me, and a voice whispers, 'Follow me.' I look around and see a man. I follow him, my heart pounding; what choice do I have? 'You need to walk faster; we need to ensure you are not being followed. Take off your jacket.' I do as he says and he takes it from me and gives it to a stranger.

'That's an expensive designer jacket,' I say.

'Keep quiet and follow me.'

We enter a building, and a man approaches me. 'Are you Chun's wife?' he asks.

'Yes.'

'I am Feng.' He casts his eyes around the dimly lit room.

'My husband gave me your number and told me to call you. Please tell me what is going on?'

'Your life is in danger. Even if I give you the document you are looking for, they will kill you and your husband. The only reason you are both alive is that they don't know how many people have this information.'

'What information?'

'Your husband was protecting Mr Xuē. You know him; he is one of the richest men in China. He owns the biggest e-commerce company. Chun worked for him for six months and discovered what he was not supposed to know. Some very powerful people manipulate others, and the only way out is death. He discovered that Mr Xuē is cheating many workers out of their money; it is bad enough that they are paid HK$34.5 per hour, but sometimes they are not paid for months. If any of his employees dare to complain, they will be fired, but if they make the mistake of going to the authorities, they will be killed.

'Your husband put together a spreadsheet showing how much Mr Xuē earns annually, how much he declares for tax and how much money he owes his workers. Unfortunately, it's not just Mr Xuē; I have a list of many successful people in China involved in many atrocities. Mr Lan Sòng, who owns the largest real estate development shares, killed his mistress, Ms Yang, whom they accused your husband of killing.'

I hear the sound of gunshot. Feng grabs me as we run through various rooms to get to an escape door on the opposite side of the building.

'What is going on?' I scream.

'You need to be quiet,' he says as a wooden trap door is pulled open by Feng. It leads outside of the building and we run through the streets until he pulls me into another house. We come to a stop, panting heavily, trying to regain our breath.

'Who are those people?' I say.

'I should be asking you; they followed you,' Feng replies.

'I didn't tell anyone, not even my bodyguard.'

'You have a bodyguard,' he says as we navigate our way through the shanty house in total darkness.

'Yes, he worked for my husband; you should know him, Cheung Wu.'

'You hired Cheung Wu? Your husband doesn't trust him; he gave me these documents to keep instead of him.'

'Are you telling me that my husband has been wrongfully accused? Why isn't he talking to the police or his lawyer?'

'These people are very powerful. Your husband would have been killed a long time ago; the only thing keeping him alive is the information he has.'

'What is the point of having this information if we can't go to the police? Who is going to help us?'

'You don't get it; these people don't care that you have the information. They just want to know those who are aware of this information so that they can eliminate them. Now that you know your life is no longer safe, we need to find out more about these people and how they became so powerful.'

'I'm not a detective; I just want my life back.'

Feng laughs bitterly. 'You can't have your life back. Don't you want your husband to be exonerated from all crimes levelled against him?'

'What can I do?'

'Your husband trusted me with this information and I have been on the run ever since. They killed my grandmother because she wouldn't tell them where to find me. About 50% of the people on the list given to me by your husband only became successful six months ago. Previously, they were broke. Suddenly, they are rolling in millions of dollars, joining the list of successful entrepreneurs in China.'

'I need to sit down; and I can't see a thing.'

'It is better to be in the dark; I think there is a seat somewhere; try to look for it with your hands.'

'I want to go home.'

'I don't think you can go home for now.'

'What! I have a deadline that I need to meet at work; what am I supposed to do now?'

'Go home, and you will be killed. The choice is yours.'

'Why did Chun get involved in this?'

'Your husband is a good man; he didn't tell you anything because he was trying to protect you, but he knew you were in danger. We need to find out what is going on; that is the only way to get your life back.'

I sighed heavily, allowing my tears to fall freely. No one can see me anyway.

Chapter Fifty-seven: London

Jude

I receive a call to say that I will be preparing the meal for an exquisite gala two days from now. I also receive an invitation, in a gold box, and a package containing a red cloak. The invitation clearly states that it is a secret gala and no one must know apart from the invitee.

My restaurant has been working overtime trying to get the menu in place. Money is no object, and it is the crème de la crème of society who will be attending. It is a four-course meal with 24-carat golden bun or golden steak; the options are limitless, and the best wines have been ordered from different vineyards across the world.

Roger

The doorbell rings at 7.00 am. I am at home in my two-bedroom house in Whitechapel. I get out of bed and pad barefoot to answer the door. A man, dressed in a tuxedo, hands me a gold box with my name boldly written on the front and an invitation card. The man gets into his black Audi without saying a word.

I look at the card; I've been invited to a gala this Friday at a place called 'Secret Cave', located in Kensington. I open the box; it contains a red cloak that the instructions say must be worn over a tuxedo, and no one else must know about the invitation.

What is this all about? I ask myself. I don't even own a tuxedo.

The doorbell rings again and I discover a man holding out, what looks like, a tuxedo in a long clothes carrier.

'Who told you to give me this?' I ask, but the man does not reply. As soon as I take the clothes carrier, he saunters over to another black Audi and drives away.

I carry the box and the tuxedo into my son's room and place them in his wardrobe. I don't want to answer any questions from my wife. I know who sent the invitation, and I have no choice but to attend the gala.

My life has changed dramatically in the past couple of days. When I returned to work, many of my colleagues raised an eyebrow when they saw me without my partner and, to make matters worse, I was promoted to inspector. My partner, Mike, accosted me in front of my house, questioning why I was allowed back to the police station, when he was still on a compulsory three-month suspension.

'Why are you attacking me? I don't know anything,' I told him. 'Why not ask the boss?'

'Are you now my boss? How did this happen?'

'I don't know. I just got a call that I should return to work.'

'I don't understand. You were the one who got us into this situation by investigating Jude Williams, yet you get off scot-free. I tried to speak to the chief inspector, but he won't even pick up my calls. Do you know what it means not to know your fate at work? I have a mortgage; I need my income,' he'd said as he stormed away.

Jude

Everything has been set up at the 'Secret Cave', and they assigned staff to come to my restaurant to pick up the food.

I look at myself in the full-length mirror in my bedroom, wearing a black tuxedo with

the red cloak over it. I pull the cape over my head, as per the instructions. The doorbell rings and, when I open the door, there is a man standing there. He tells me he has been assigned to take me to the location. I get into the back seat of the black Audi with trepidation. The back windows of the car are completely blacked out, and there is a partition between the driver and the passenger compartment.

'Where are we are going?' I ask, but there is no response.

The irony is that there is a cave in central London.

When we arrive at our destination, the chauffeur gives me a magnetic card, similar to the ones you scan on the Underground. I am shown into a room full of people wearing red cloaks. Everyone's head is slightly bowed, and you can't see their faces in the dimly lit room. No one is talking to one another. There are servers bringing round drinks, but they are wearing gold eye masks. There are hundreds of people standing anxiously, wondering what would happen next.

The next thing, I heard a voice I recognise very well, that sends shivers down my spine.

'I am glad you could attend this evening; this is a special gathering for the selected few. If you are here today, congratulations because you have been allowed to acquire power and fame. This is just the beginning; I have been assigned to the European Hub, and you're the selected few who will be given assignments to take over the world. We have chosen people from different walks of life, and you will dominate your section. For your loyalty, you will be given whatever your soul desires. If anyone crosses your path, don't hesitate to eliminate them; we take with force, not sparing anyone. Everyone will be given their assignments; we want world domination. Mingle, get to know one another. Today you register yourself as a member of Red Gama. The only way out is death; remember that.' We throw back our hoods to mingle with the other guests.

I breathe heavily, trying to steady my nerves. I watch as people started talking to one another. Is that the prime minister? It can't be. Is that the president of France? No! A woman walks up to me; and reveals her face. She doesn't need to introduce herself. She is the richest woman in Europe and owns the biggest beauty empire. She stretches out her hand. 'I am Susanne Waters.'

'Jude Williams,' I say, shaking her hand.

She smiles. 'This should be interesting. You look nervous, don't be! You are a chef, right?'

'Yes.'

'You could be the first billionaire chef by eliminating your competitors.' She looks around. 'It would be best if you meet others you will be working with.'

I follow her, and start talking to people; the founders and CEOs of automobile companies, construction and oil giants, the chairman of a bank, a police commissioner, judge, the list goes on. These are people I used to look up to. Now I'm not so sure.

I accidentally bump into someone. 'I'm sorry,' I say. It is Sergeant Smith.

'What are you doing here?' I whisper.

'I should be asking you the same thing.'

'I had no choice.'

'Me neither. We should meet up; we can't talk here.'

I watch him walk away into the crowd.

We are instructed to sit down and enjoy the four-course meal I had prepared. I look around and see people laughing, some smoking the best Cuban cigars brought in from Cuba. Classical music plays in the background. I have completely lost my appetite. These people don't care, they have money, and now they want power; and they don't mind bringing down their competitors.

A gold envelope is placed in front of everyone. I pick up the one in front of me and open it. It contains instructions to get to know the CEO of Bestfood, the largest food wholesaler in the UK. The goal is to increase the cost of food by increasing demand and reducing supply. There will be panic, and people will rush to buy what is in store and start hoarding food. The competitors will be eliminated, making Bestfood the sole distributor, and I will be his partner. I look for his seat number and move away from my seat; we meet halfway.

'This will be fun,' he says cheerfully. 'I can't wait to create a food crisis in the UK.'

Chapter Fifty-eight: New York

Martin

I carry my cardboard box to the dingy, roach-infested motel I am renting for the unforeseeable future. Is this my life now? Two weeks ago, I had a wonderful marriage, a job that I enjoyed, and I was well respected. Now I have been thrown out of the 14th Precinct like a thief. I know the only way out is to uncover the people pulling the strings my ex-partner and captain are dancing to. I can't do this alone. I need Edward's help; but he has warned me never to contact him again. He is the best hacker in the world; the FBI has been trying to arrest him for years.

'Gama, connect me to Edward.'

The phone goes straight to voicemail. I massage my forehead because I can feel a headache coming on. Has Edward changed his number? After all, he told me never to call him again.

My phone starts ringing. I see a very odd number: '22458'. Gama connects the call, and I hear Edward's voice.

'Why are you trying to call me? Didn't I warn you not to?'

'It went to voicemail; you wouldn't have called me back if you didn't want to help me.'

'Martin, whoever you went up against is tracking me; I've had to go underground to prevent them from finding me.'

'Edward, please, I am desperate. I have lost everything, my marriage has collapsed and I just lost my job, but I know the only way out is to trail Bobby and Captain Marcus. But I need your help. I have discovered they now hang out with Andrew Lawrence and the captain currently resides in Madison.'

'I don't know, I'm sorry for your predicament, but these people were able to get into my high-tech system. I know you have helped me in the past, but I have paid all my dues with interest.'

'I know! But you are my last hope. I need to know the connection between these three people, that's all.'

There is silence while he thinks. 'OK,' he says eventually. 'I'll do this last thing for you, for old time's sake, but you will not be able to reach me again after this.'

'Thank you. I appreciate it.'

The call disconnects.

I need to rest for now because tonight I'm going to follow Bobby and find out the truth. How can my partner turn against me? I haven't done anything to him. I lay down on the lumpy bed, trying desperately to sleep and take this weight off my shoulders.

***

It's 7.00 pm. I have been in my car for about an hour waiting for Bobby to arrive home. I've parked a few cars away from the front of his house to avoid being noticed.

He finally rolls up at 8.34 pm and I watch him enter his house.

I wait in my car for about two hours before I see a top-of-the-range black Bentley arrive and park in front of his house. A man gets out and presses the doorbell. I can't see much, but I think Bobby is dressed strangely. He gets into the back of the car. I don't think anything will surprise me anymore when it comes to my partner.

I follow the car cautiously, from a distance, until it drives into a building beside Central Park. There are security men everywhere. How can I get into this building? The security is so tight, I see men carrying semi-automatic pistols parading the building, talking into their earpieces.

My phone rings and Gama connects. 'Hello! Who is this?'

'I can't talk; you need to be careful. What I found out about your partner and your captain is not good. Did you know that your partner is a multimillionaire? He has about twenty-five million dollars in his account, not to talk of share options in the biggest companies, and the same goes for your captain. They have high profile people backing them. They are into many things; they are given licence to import and supply firearms to the police.'

'No way!'

'Yeah! I don't know why they are still working as police officers, but they don't need to.'

'My partner is about to enter a building beside Central Park. Can you get me in? He is wearing a strange red thing; I can't quite see.'

196

'Take a picture of the place and send it to me.'

'OK,' I say, still watching the security men. I need to lure one of them away to get in.

'I didn't know this building is still active. According to what I'm seeing in the government records,' says Edward, 'it has been abandoned for about five years. I don't know how you will get in, but I guess you need to use your police skills. All I can say is, be careful.'

After watching for another thirty minutes, I see one of the security guards moving away from the others to check the side of the building. This is my opportunity. I follow him and, when he is completely alone, touching his earpiece, saying, 'Clear!' I creep up behind him and put him in a headlock until he passes out. I drag him away, out of sight, and quickly change into his black clothes. They are a bit too tight for me, but I have no choice. I place the earpiece in my ear and tie the security guard to a tree. I can't risk going to the front of the building; they might notice and I can't take any chances. I move to the rear of the building and see staff bringing in food.

I call one of the men away; taser him, which knocks him out and take his clothes, putting on his gold eye mask. I tie him up and hide him also. I walk into the building and am given a tray of wine glasses, filled with different wines.

I enter the reception room and what I see shocks me. Bruce Cole, the richest man in the world, is talking to the governor of New York and the vice-president of America? I walk around, serving drinks. I could see their cloaks on the floor. I think every important person is here, from prominent film producers to the CEOs of tech companies, car dealerships, banks etc. Where am I? Then I hear a voice congratulating them on being chosen for the North America Hub. They will be called Blue Gama. The voice states it is time for them to take over the world and destroy their competitors; power and wealth are theirs.

I walk away, pretending to refill the tray, wondering why they would want to take over the world?

Chapter Fifty-nine: Lagos

Lola

I am sleeping on the floor of my room, laying on the large, fluffy, ecru rug. It is the only thing I know that hasn't been changed in my house. I must have been dreaming when the door to my room bursts open, and some people enter. I am struck across the face, which jolts me out of sleep. I scream as I am dragged across the floor. A female, wearing a balaclava showing only her eyes, asks, 'What is the name of the person helping you?'

I am shaking badly I can't get up. I am kicked in the stomach and I curl up in pain.

'I don't know what you're talking about.'

'How were you able to escape us twice?'

'I don't understand.'

'Get me her phone.'

My phone is given to her and she dials her number. My phone was locked. How is she able to open it?

'Who told you to change your number?'

'No one. I gave up on everything when I was told my friends and family would be killed because of me, but trouble still seems to find me constantly.'

I am forced up. 'Listen to me, if you don't want these people to break your arm, your leg, or use a blowtorch lighter to burn your beautiful body, you better start talking.'

Oh my God! I'm going to die! 'I'm begging you. I don't know anything,' I say, breathing hard. 'I wish I did and I could tell you.'

The woman pulls out her pistol and points it at me. 'I'll ask again, who has been helping you?'

I can't see through my tears. I drop to my knees. 'I swear I don't know anything; I just got back from Abuja today.'

'Thank your lucky stars that we have not been permitted to hurt you,' says one of the men in the room. All of their faces are covered. 'The next time we come here you might not be so lucky, remember that when you start acting stupid.'

I watch as they stroll out of the room. I remain on my knees, so afraid I vomit on the floor.

What have I got myself into? I told my 'helper' I was no longer interested. I don't think I am safe. I need to leave.

***

I observe the men storming into her house. I can't do anything this time because they suspect she is receiving help. I do hope she's OK.

I need her help, but I think her spirit is broken. I am determined to bring these people down; working in the shadows, putting her in the light, has helped me this far but has placed her life in danger. I am surprised she hasn't been killed already; they don't take kindly to interference.

I see them leave the house in the thick of the night, everywhere is completely dark. I follow them as they drive away. This is my opportunity to find out the truth. And Lola is going to help me if she is still alive, whether she likes it or not.

***

I look at my face in the bathroom mirror. My eyes are bloodshot from hours of crying. I can't I continue like this? I need to find a way out. These people don't believe I don't know him. I need to find out who this helper is? Why are they looking for him? I grab my purse and car keys; I'll book a hotel for the night. I can't stay in this house.

I haven't left the hotel room in two days. I need to plan what I'm going to do; I can't continue to hide here. There is a knock on the door. I look through the peephole but I don't see anyone. I place my back on the door, covering my mouth; I'm not going to open this door. I hear a voice I recognise as the helper. 'Open the door, Lola. I know you are in there.'

Reluctantly, I open the door. 'What do you want?'

He walks in, not covering his face this time, and smiles at me.

'Hello, Lola, it's nice to meet you.' He stretches out his hand for me to shake. 'My name is Segun.'

I ignore his outstretched hand. 'What do you want?' I repeat.

'I need your help.'

199

'You're getting no help from me,' I reply angrily.

'Lola, when will you understand? You can't escape this, they have you on their radar, and they are not going to stop. Either they destroy you, or you destroy them.'

'Thanks to you.'

'I was just trying to help when you were desperate about your friend. Anyway, I have great news.'

'What news?'

'Can we sit down? We have a lot to talk about.'

I nod and we sit down on the bed.

'I have been following those hoodlums that came to your house. Sorry, I couldn't help you this time.'

'You allowed me to be beaten? I honestly don't know why I'm not dead.'

'I'm surprised, too. Either you're important enough not to be killed, or they need you for something bigger.'

'I am tired; I have not slept in days. I'm sure my house is being monitored. They are probably somewhere in this hotel. I only order food; I haven't even allowed anyone to clean this room because I am afraid of being bugged.'

'Good! You should be afraid. What I discovered yesterday is mind-boggling. Strangely, I saw my father enter a house, on Banana Island, with a high fence and electric wire. I saw the men that came to your house, after following them for a day; they were all strangely dressed.

'I confronted my father when he arrived home. We had a big fight. He told me not to get involved; this was bigger than I could imagine. They want to take over the world and subdue it; anyone who doesn't accept will be eliminated. He told me we were going to be richer than we could imagine. I told him, at the cost of losing a son. He said that is the price we had to pay.

'They are the African Hub and Green Gama. My father looked me in the eye and told me that this was the biggest connection I could ever hope for. My brother died in a strange accident that I suspected was foul play; he doesn't care. He has just been awarded a licence to supply electrical power for Africa. He will not have any competitors, imagine that!'

'Who are you?'

'My father is Bankole Gerald.'

'Your father is the former governor of Lagos State; he is already wealthy; he was awarded a licence for oil and gas over five years ago.'

'Yes, but they want more wealth, more power. That is why I need your help?'

'But what can I do?'

'I intend to bring down my father and the others. Imagine one man supplying power for the whole of Africa, no one will be regulating the prices, people will be paying through their noses, they will become richer at the expense of others. I can never forgive him for my brother's death, even though he told me there was nothing he could have done to prevent it. They are manipulative and evil people. My father said almost all the wealthy and powerful people were there. Maybe your father also attended.'

'That's impossible, my father lives in Abuja, and he wouldn't come to Lagos without telling me.'

'I am not implying anything; a simple phone call will suffice.'

I picked up my phone angrily and call my mum. After greeting her, I ask after my dad, and she tells me he just got back this morning, having attended a business meeting in Lagos.

'He didn't want to disturb you, as you've only just gone back,' she adds.

I drop the phone and look at Segun.

What the hell is going on?

Chapter Sixty: Kabul

Ahmed

I enter Mohammed's office and he greets me enthusiastically.

'Ahmed! You are a very impressive man; you have proven to have impeccable skills in defence. How did you know the man was wearing an explosive device?'

'I could tell from his demeanour that he was agitated,' I reply. 'That made me suspicious.'

'Impressive! I am upgrading you to be my head bodyguard; the others will follow your instruction.'

'Thank you very much, sir.'

'I have not given up on my quest to capture Hussain, and I know you are the man for the job. This man has been a pain. I have found out from a reliable source that he lives in Kabul and operates here in the city. He has raised many followers that believe his continuous lies; he needs to be destroyed. The rate of attacks we have experienced has risen in the past month and people are becoming bolder; I know it is because of him.

'We have a meeting tonight. Everyone that works for me must be present; I'll table the agenda and set our goals for next year. Thank you, Ahmed.'

I leave his office and notice Latif close behind. I swing round. 'Why are you following me?'

'I was just told that I will now answer to you. I have worked tirelessly protecting Mohammed for three years without any incident, and now you come from nowhere and you're promoted ahead of me. You have been working here less than a month.'

I stand listening to him without saying a word. I can see him shaking with anger.

'Say something.' He looks me directly in the eye.

I remain silent. He tries to push me, but I move out of the way, and he nearly falls.

'I hate you,' he says. 'A lot of people don't like you. Your days here are numbered.'

He storms away and I walk to the bodyguard station. Some of them come up to congratulate me on my promotion.

'Mohammed will not be leaving the compound today; there's not much to do because his right-hand men surround him. I'm proud of the opportunity to meet and work with you. No matter what you think, I didn't come to take anyone's job. I just want to survive like anyone else.'

I approach Latif. 'In my eyes, you are still my boss. I admire your skills; I'll continue to learn from you because of your many years of experience.'

He looks at me; I can see he is struggling with how to act in front of his peers. 'Thank you, we'll see each other tonight.'

I enter my room and open the closet. The phone with the charger is wrapped in a piece of cloth taped behind my rail of clothes. I know this is dangerous, but I don't know where else to hide it. I know the men in the compound do not like me because everyone wants to be noticed by Mohammed and promoted accordingly.

I go into the bathroom to text Hussain that Mohammed knows he lives in Kabul. I get a reply telling me that the information was passed by one of his men to make Mohammed feel he is making progress. He also congratulates me on my new position, stating that this was now the time to seize the opportunity to know Mohammed better.

I enter the big hall in the compound. Most of the men that work for Mohammed are there, laughing; I think some of them are drunk. Young girls are dancing in the middle of the hall; there is food and drink everywhere. *What is this?* I ask myself.

Jamil sees me and walks over. 'Why are you not drinking?' he asks.

'I need to be alert all the time; that is the only way I can protect the boss.'

'Mohammed is with his people; no one would dare hurt him here, so you have no excuse for not joining in and drinking.'

I smile. 'Thank you, I'll get a drink soon.'

'Listen, Ahmed, you think I don't like you, but that is not true. I want what is best for Mohammed. I believe you're hiding something.'

At that moment, Mohammed walks to the top of the podium and sits on his throne and all the girls dancing are asked to leave the hall. He begins to address us, telling everyone how proud he is of instilling fear in the citizens' hearts.

'Afghanistan is a great nation,' he says, 'and it needs to get the global recognition it deserves. Our goal is to expand, take complete control of the country, and any rebels must be eliminated.'

People start clapping. He raises his hands, and there is silence. The next thing we hear is a voice I do not recognise. 'Congratulations, Mohammed, for a job well done. I will continue to sponsor your quest to rule Afghanistan with an iron fist. The nation has many natural resources that haven't been tapped yet. We need to exploit these resources to make ourselves richer than ever before. We will be working closely with the other Asia Hub; we will be called Asia_1 and Yellow Gama. Thank you all.'

Everyone starts clapping, whistling and shouting.

'Enjoy yourself,' Mohammed says, above the noise.

Who is that man talking on the speaker addressing us?

***

Hussain Atta disconnects the voice changer from the call and starts laughing hysterically.

Everyone thinks Mohammed Pir is the leader of Afghanistan, not knowing that he is just a pawn. I rule Afghanistan from the shadows. Very soon, the world will know. I'll kill everyone who stands in my way. They think I'm the good one, not knowing I needed someone to be my face while I gain the citizens' loyalty; they are willing to die for me, thinking I'll give them a better nation. Let the game begin!

Chapter Sixty-one: Sydney

'Hello, Mrs Graham, I admire your tenacity and the way you were able to mould your son Henry to be just like you.'

'Who is this?'

'The person who knows everything about you and your family. I know how much you love your son and grandson. It would be a shame for your grandson to go to jail and your son to lose his chance of becoming prime minister'.

'That's not going to happen?'

'It's not going to happen.' He chuckles. 'You think you have the connections, but I'll tell you that I can bring down your family with just a phone call. I know how you manipulated the election over twenty years ago, leaking documents that would incriminate your opponent.'

'That's just politics; it means nothing.'

'You have many sins, Mrs Graham. You are good at hiding them, exploiting the people of Sudan, and taking their natural resources with the promise to help develop their country, which you failed to do. I admire that about you; I can make you wealthier than you can ever imagine.'

'What do you want from me?'

'Your son! We are having a gala at a secret island off Sydney. The invitation card will be delivered to your doorstep now.'

The doorbell rings. 'Go and open the door, Mrs Graham. There is a man on your doorstop with two gold envelopes. You and your son are the only ones invited, convince him to come, and he will be able to meet his contemporaries; he will need them if he is going to be the next prime minister.'

The phone disconnects.

Henry

Carl struggles as he is carried out of the house into an ambulance, screaming at the top of his lungs,' I hate you.'

Mia is also shouting, 'Don't hurt him!'

I pull her back as she tries to get to him. 'He will be OK; he needs help, and you know that.'

The ambulance door closes as they drive Carl to Moreland Mental Hospital. He is going to be treated for a month. I pray that he gets better; he is getting worse.

Mia looks at me angrily. 'I want you out of this house. You agreed with your parents to take away our son without my consent.'

'What were you going to do? Keep wishing he will get better without doing anything,' I yell.

'That is not the point; you are supposed to talk to me before making that kind of decision. I know your mum doesn't like me. She merely tolerates me. I've taken so much from your arrogant family, but I'm done. Get out!'

'I'll leave, but remember I pay for this mansion and lifestyle you are accustomed to.'

'You're a bastard!' Mia yells after me.

I enter the guest room and start packing my things. How did I get here? I love my wife, but we don't see eye to eye on a lot of things. What was I supposed to do? My son stabbed me. If the police should get wind of this, we will be finished.

I wheel my suitcase out of the room. Mia is sitting in the living room, crying. I walk up to her. 'I'm sorry I hurt you. I know in my heart that Carl needs treatment.'

She continues to sob. I kneel down to try and hold her but she hits me with her fist.

'This is all your fault.' She keeps hitting me until she gets tired. 'I'm sorry,' I repeat.

'Is he going to be OK?' she asks.

'I'll make sure of it; you are allowed to visit him after two weeks. Mia, I love my son; I'd never put him in harm's way. The only reason I didn't tell you is that I was afraid you would say no. He is a danger to himself and others; to us.'

She wipes her eyes. 'I hate you most of the time.'

'I know, and I'm sorry for everything.'

'But why do your folks hate me?'

'They don't hate you.'

'Your mum finds it difficult to be nice to me, no matter how hard I try. Your dad is fair; he is not as bad as your mum. Is it because I come from a humble background and I'm not political royalty like your family?'

'Let's not talk about that now.'

'We should; I'm tired of keeping quiet. The worst part is that you never defend me against their subtle attacks.'

I shake my head sadly. 'You must believe me; I love you beyond words.'

'Just go!' she says.

I get up and wheel my suitcase out of the house.

***

'It's nice to have you back home; we don't get to see you enough, only during a crisis,' my mum says.

'Not now, Mum. I'm a very busy man.'

'I know! I know! And there is a business meeting I would like you to attend with me.'

'What kind of meeting?'

'One where you get to meet all your old friends and make new ones, but you need to dress formally.'

'I'm tired, Mum; a lot is happening to my family and me. I have not been to work in two days, I have so much to catch up on.'

'I don't ask much from you. You need people to back you and sponsor your campaigns; this is necessary. I am doing this for you and I am not taking no for an answer.'

***

I am wearing a beautiful black tuxedo. I enter the hall and see my mum elegantly dressed in an evening gown. 'Is Dad not coming?'

'No, he won't be able to attend. This is an excellent opportunity for you to network with the right people.'

'Where are we going?'

'You worry too much, just follow me.'

We are picked up by a man in a black Jaguar, who drives us to the seashore to get into a motorboat. From there, we are taken to an island and led up to a grand mansion. The entrance is laid with red carpet.

The security agents talk in their earpieces, and my face is scanned with a face scanner. I enter the house with my mum. It is full of elegantly dressed people, this is a black tie event. I recognise most people; these are people in my circle.

I turn to my mum. 'How come I didn't know about this?'

'You were going through a lot, and, to be frank, you're homeless,' she says, laughing, and tapping the back of my hand. 'You ask too many questions.'

I walk up to the prime minister who is talking to the opposition leader. Jackson Paul acknowledges me and smiles. 'I wondered whether you would be able to attend,' he says. 'How are you feeling?'

'I am fine, thank you.'

What kind of business meeting is this? I ask myself. These are the wealthiest people in Australia, why are they all in the same room?

I stay close to my mum, as we dine and mingle with the rich. It seems no expense has been spared on the lavish evening.

Later, a voice addresses the room, although I can't see anyone speaking. We are instructed to be quiet.

'Welcome to the Australia Hub of White Gama. I want you to know each other better because we are about to take over the continent. We have been tasked to dominate every sector in Australia, if possible, the world. You will be tasked with goals that you need to meet, giving you an opportunity for immeasurable wealth and power. We don't take kindly to disloyalty; that will lead to death. This is a party; enjoy yourselves. Before you leave; everyone will be given an envelope. You must perform the task you will find inside. You must not show, or talk about, your task to anyone else.'

***

I am about to leave with my mum when I was given a gold envelope. I open it, and read the instruction: 'Have your wife killed in the next twenty-four hours'.

The envelope drops from my hand. What is the hell is this?

Chapter Sixty-two: Rio de Janeiro

Ana

I didn't know how long I have been sitting on the new cream sofa in the living room. It's a beautiful apartment, but I hate everything. I love my two-bedroom house with the old furniture we had for over eight years. It has sentimental value. I stand up and move to the bedroom. I didn't know what is next for me, but I can't live like this anymore.

Antonio

I am tied to a chair and slapped across the face. Carlos takes out his folding knife and places it on my face.

'Antonio! Mr Montes sends his greetings.' I cry out as the blade pierces my skin. 'What design should I sketch?' sings Carlos.

'Please, please!' I scream.

'You were given a simple job; you failed miserably. You looked me in the face and lied to me. I found out you told her everything, so we decided to take the bull by the horns and confront Ana, not giving her any choice. You are of no use to us anymore.'

'Please! No!' I cry, as he pulls the knife down my face.

Ana

I am going through the new figures for the contract extension when my newly appointed personal assistant, Márcia, informs me that Mr Ribeiro wants to see me in conference room 4.

Carlos is sitting down waiting for me.

'Good afternoon, Carlos, you wanted to see me?'

'Yes, Ana. Antonio will no longer be working for this company; I'll serve as a liaison between you and Mr Montes from now on. He would like to see the new figures for the contract extension in the general meeting with the shareholders and directors today. Thank you, that will be all.'

What happened to Antonio, I wonder.

***

Pedro is sitting in the canteen, taking a break from work, excited that he has secured a job after being jobless for two years, depending on his wife, Maria, and the help of others.

He hears the intercom telling him to go to the manager's office.

He is filled with fear. Did I celebrate too soon? I just started this job today, he thinks, entering the manager's office.

'Hello Pedro, as I told you yesterday, your job depends on your sister-in-law, Ana; we need her to be committed to us. That way, you will become richer than you can ever imagine.'

'What do you want from me?'

'Do whatever you can to compel her to obey us. You are invited to a gala today to get a chance to meet the wealthiest people in South America; imagine that could be your future eating and dining with the rich.'

'I'll do whatever it takes.'

'Good! All information will be provided for you; it's strictly by invitation; see you tonight.'

Ana

I sit in the designated chair assigned to me in the conference room. Mr Montes is seated at the head of the conference table, surrounded by people I don't know. I am introduced to the group, which consists of nine men and five women. 'This is the lady I told you about. She is a genius when it comes to numbers.'

One of the men speaks. 'Mrs Santos, it is a pleasure to meet you. Everyone here is a shareholder in this company and several other companies. I also own a waste disposal company; among others, we have a standing contract with the government to help with the waste affecting our country, but we all know that is impossible to fix. We get paid billions of dollars to collect trash from other countries; we use Brazil as the dumping ground. Who is going to question us? Everyone gets paid,' he says, laughing. 'We invited you here because we are told you are the best and we want only the best.'

One of the other shareholders introduces himself. 'My name is Rafael

Lima; you must have heard of me; I own Brazilian City Bank, the largest bank in the country. I would like you to work for me from time to time, I have asked your boss and he doesn't seem to mind. Of course, you will be paid handsomely; you will join the league of millionaires in dollars.'

I nod, and try to clear my throat, before asking, 'What will I be doing, sir?'

'It's nothing new, just numbers. The interest rate of loans is at an all-time high; it's about 40%, making it impossible for people to pay back; we can take away the collateral used for the loans, and the rich will become richer.'

***

I am grateful that today is Saturday, and I don't have to face those monsters; all these people care about is money. They have no compassion for the masses, only to exploit and use them for their benefit.

The doorbell rings, but there is no one there, only a big envelope on the floor facing my door. I open it in my room, wondering what could be inside. It contains surveillance pictures of the most influential people laughing at, what looks like, a party. To my surprise, I see my brother-in-law, talking to the director-general of police. What is he doing there? I pull out all the pictures from the envelope, and I see a voice recorder. I switch it on and hear Antonio's voice.

'I have gone into hiding. It seems Mr Montes never forgives failure, even though I have worked for him for five years. I lost my father last night from heart failure after losing everything in a fire. I got these pictures and information from one of the security guards working for Mr Montes. I had to bribe him R$10000, but he needed the money desperately.

'You need to go through the images carefully; everyone in these pictures is part of something called Purple Gama. I don't know precisely what they do, but they are very powerful and influential.'

I look again at the pictures and recognise a few of the people in them; I met some of these monsters yesterday in the meeting. That is the least of my problems. I need to call my sister; what was her husband doing at that party?

'Hello, Maria, how are you? Is Pedro around? Can I talk to him quickly?'

'He's here! He just got back from a fancy party he attended yesterday; he said our lives are going to change for the better, can you believe that?'

'Yes, I can, now please give him the phone. Pedro, how are you? I was told you went to a party yesterday and you had a great time.'

'That's right; thank you for getting me that job, it is a stepping-stone to a greater height.'

'I'm calling to warn you to be careful.'

'Hold on!' he says. I hear him moving away from his family; we need privacy. 'Ana, you don't think I know what you are up to? I was told you moved out of your old house into a swanky new apartment, and have a flashy car and promotion. Don't you want that for us? Would you prefer we beg for money constantly?'

'No, of course not. That is not my intention.'

'Keep your intentions to yourself; I'll do whatever it takes to care for my family. And if I were you, I'd do what they tell you.' The phone disconnects.

***

Pedro holds his wife's face in his hands.

'I don't want you talking to your sister anymore. Can you imagine she just told me to quit my new job? She likes us being poor. I'm sure she hasn't told you about her new apartment and promotion. She is a selfish woman after everything we have done for her.'

I'll need to use her sister against her for her to comply, Pedro thinks. It's the only way.

Chapter Sixty-three: Hong Kong

Huan

'What are we supposed to do? Hide here and hope they don't find us?'

'Do you have a better suggestion?' Feng asks. 'Where is your phone? I hope you switched it off?'

'I'm sorry, everything was happening so fast I forgot about that, oh no!'

'They will find us soon, switch off your phone immediately. We need to find another place to hide.'

We open the wooden window and jump out to search for another abandoned house before they find us.

'Have you switched off your phone?' he asks again.

'Yes! I did it as soon as you told me.'

I am out of breath when we finally find an empty, rundown building.

'What do we do now?' I ask.

'Wait! We need to hide till morning to be safe.'

'Who is chasing us?'

'I don't know, but I know they are getting desperate; they will do anything to eliminate us.'

I am sitting on the floor in the dark, when my phone suddenly lights up. I drop it in shock.

'I told you to switch off the phone,' Feng hisses.

'I did; I swear, I don't know how it came back on.'

I pick up the phone and see that a video has just been sent to me. My hands are shaking badly as I open the video to see my beaten husband with a rope around his neck; standing on a chair.

One of the men standing behind him says the chair will be removed; if I don't surrender and give up Feng. I have thirty minutes to return to where I parked my car.

I look at Feng. 'Tell me what to do. I can't allow him to die; I'll never forgive myself.'

'If you go back to your car, you will die. It's your life or his; everything Chun did is to protect you from these malicious people. Don't let them win.'

'If I don't go, I'll continue to live like a fugitive; everything I've worked for, I'll have to give it up. I'm not ready to do that.'

'You have to be alive to enjoy what you've worked for; don't you get it?'

'I'll go; we are not safe here. I'm sure they know where we are; you need to disappear now! Go!'

Feng runs to the back of the room and jumps out of the window into the street below.

I attempt to navigate my way out of room in the dark. When I open the door, Cheung is standing there.

He laughs, 'You can run, but you can't hide.'

They have Feng.

'What are you going to do to him? I had nothing to do with this,' I yell as I am dragged away into a waiting car and pushed into the back seat. 'What do you want from us?'

Sitting beside me, with a gun in her hand, is Chyou. Cheung gets into the front seat with the driver.

'Hello, boss,' Chyou says to me sarcastically.

'What do you want from us? My husband was kind to you; he doesn't deserve this.'

'Speak for yourself. Your husband is a fool. The boss wants to see you. That is the only reason you are still alive.'

I am driven away and taken to an unknown address. I am yanked out of the car and taken inside, where I am put in front of a man in his sixties and told to kneel in front of him.

'Do you know who I am? You must have seen me on many media platforms. I am Lan Sòng. I own the largest shares in real estate development for Liquid Holdings. You are only alive today because you are of great use to us; you have achieved so much despite your background, which is impressive. But, first of all, I need to know what Feng told you?'

'I didn't understand what he was talking about; he said some rich people are cheating the poor.'

'Did you say that the rich are cheating the poor?' Lan asks. I can hear laughter, but I am too afraid to look round.

'We have interrogated Feng, found out where he was keeping those documents, burnt them, and eliminated all interested parties.'

A phone is placed in front of me and I watch as Feng is shot in the head. I start to cry. 'Please, don't kill me.'

'Now, back to the issue at hand. Yamson Telecommunication has the largest number of subscribers in the whole of China. I have had a long conversation with your CEO and it seems the government have agreed that they need to give Gama more access to the network, which you are aware of and working on. This will allow us access to financial details, personal conversations, passwords, subscribers and other endless possibilities.

'You know how reluctant the Chinese government is to give such access to a company, but it is going to serve everyone well. We would like you to join us; we are a group of people who want the same thing; to take over the world. That is not too much to ask?

'Like I said before, I don't want to kill you; I want you to join us. We are Asia_2 and Yellow Gama. If you agree to join us, your husband will be released from jail and all charges dropped. You are presently the CTO. I know you have small shares in the company, but we can make you more prosperous and powerful than you can ever imagine. I know you are ambitious, and this is your chance to win more accolades.

'We are reasonable people; we give choices. The alternative is you watch us kill your husband, making it look like suicide. Oh! How he loved you, everything he did was to protect you from us, but he failed. I heard you slapped him once, thinking he cheated on you and had kids with another woman. Why would you get angry? You know full well that you are barren.' He chuckles. 'That was my mistress. She was getting too big for her boots. She needed to be put in place. So, what do you say?'

Chapter Sixty-four: London

Some time later…

Jude

I walk into my empty restaurant; people are no longer queuing to eat, reservations are no longer being made and, with great remorse, I have been forced to let go of my employees. Some of them have been working for me from the beginning. I watched with sadness as

a few of them begged to be retained, willing to have their salaries slashed by half to have a job in this challenging situation, knowing that they might never find another. The rate of unemployment has increased drastically. I know the problem will get worse; the false news is that farmers are complaining of soil erosion affecting the farm crops, hence the scarcity of food all over Europe.

I walk into my office with the world's weight on my shoulders, constantly asking myself, *What am I doing here?* I no longer own a restaurant. I now work with John Bennett member of Red Gama, and we are the cause of all these problems, the food scarcity, the supermarkets, the local market and restaurants being closed.

I go out into the street and see people sleeping in front of supermarkets. The queues are long as they wait for the shops to be opened so that they can be the first to buy whatever is in stock. I am faced with people begging for food as soon as I leave the house. I have so much food that I can feed many people, but the rules prevent me from helping anyone. I brought my mum over to stay with me after the death of her boyfriend, and she's constantly asking me where I got so much food when there is such scarcity everywhere.

I have all this wealth, yet I am not safe. I arrived home yesterday, and was trying to open my door when I felt a knife on my back.

'Give me all your money.'

'Mister, take it easy; what do you need money for? The supermarket shelves are empty.'

'Just give me your money,' a man said, looking around agitated.

I elbowed him in the eye and he dropped to the ground, screaming,

'My eye! My eye!'

I have a meeting with the big boss today; we need to update him on our progress with our biggest competitor, Sam Wholesale, who just went into administration, with thousands losing their jobs. The number of CVs being dropped into my closed restaurant, on a daily basis, is alarming. I can't continue like this; I have sleepless nights. I place my head on my desk and sigh heavily. The question that haunts me daily is: *How do they always know everything?* Joining Red Gama was the biggest mistake of my life.

***

We gather at a secret location, somewhere in central London, as the leader of the European Hub has requested an urgent meeting. Every task has to be clearly defined, and the deadline must be met. Failure to meet those deadlines means certain death for you and your family.

I find it difficult to drink the expensive alcohol being passed around by the waiters, watching as powerful men and women laugh and talk to one another with no care. They feel no remorse for what is happening all over Europe, and this is just the beginning.

The big boss walks in, and there is complete silence. He looks around, and I hear my name being called, 'Jude Williams and John Bennett'. We are asked to step forward and provide an update on the assignment given to us.

John Bennett smiles broadly. 'As you already know, our greatest competitor, Sam Philips, the founder and CEO of Sam Wholesale, has just been arrested for the death of ten people from food poisoning. He is going away for a very long time,' laughs John Bennett. 'It is such a pleasing feeling to see him being publicly humiliated, leaving his house in Knightsbridge in handcuffs.'

Wine glasses are lifted as the members hail us.

The big boss looks at us sternly. 'I know the company has gone into administration. He has a daughter called Sarah Philips. They have just announced that she is taking over the company; I don't want the company revived. Jude, I need you to get closer to her, she might be helpful to us, but if you encounter any resistance from her, I want her taken out of the way. I don't want any hindrance to our plans. Do you understand?'

'Yes, sir,' I say.

'Presently, all food is stored in different warehouses all over Europe, and it is not being distributed yet. We are going to hoard the food for one more week. There will be severe panic and desperation. I can already see long queues outside the shops, local markets and even restaurants. Next week the lines will be longer, and people will become more desperate, and they will do anything to survive.

'Then we release a few food items to be distributed in the shops, local markets, and restaurants. The demand will be higher than supply; this will allow us to drive up food prices to over 200%, which means more money in our pockets. Then we can sit back and watch them turn on themselves to survive. That will be fun.' Everyone laughs.

'A Platinum Card has already been given to every member here, which allows you access to those warehouses. You take as much food as you need, but remember this is only for you and your immediate family; we are not a charity organisation. Anyone who disobeys this order already knows what will happen. Don't forget; we know everything.

'Every Friday, we will reconvene; I need constant updates on your progress. There is no rest until Europe becomes ours.'

Chapter Sixty-five: New York

Martin

I sit in the motel watching the news. There are mass protests in all states, and roads and bridges are blocked. People have come out in droves, young and old alike, all for the common goal of a safe environment for themselves. Thousands have lost their lives through water contamination due to accidental oil spill from tankers that happened two weeks ago. President Thomas Green has addressed the nation, requesting calm and patience, stating that the government is working very hard to fix this problem. There are cops everywhere arresting and detaining people. Bottled water has sold out across the whole country. The government has declared a state of emergency.

I receive a visit from the motel manager.

'What do you want?' I ask.

'I'm sorry, Mr Hills. I have to ask you to leave this motel now. This has come from head office.'

'I don't understand. I paid for a month, and I've only been here for two and a half weeks.'

'We'll refund the balance, but you have an hour to pack your bags and come to the reception for your refund.'

He walks away, shaking his head. What the hell is going on?

I pack my few clothes into my suitcase. I never removed the boxes from my car, so I placed the suitcase in my vehicle and go to reception.

The manager refuses to meet my eyes.

'Tell me why head office is interested in me enough to throw me out of this unhygienic motel?'

'I'm afraid I can't answer that question, sir. Here is your refund. Thank you for your stay here,' he says walking away to the staff office.

***

I watch the president return to the Oval Office after addressing the public on the oil spillage. The big boss has given me limited time to eliminate him; he is a hindrance to the North America Hub; as soon as he dies, I will assume presidential powers and duties.

President Thomas looks at me. 'Dan, how can this have happened?'

'It happens! It's an accident; we just have to find a way to fix it quickly, and we have the right people on it.'

'You are my trusted friend. I had known you for over thirteen years before the party agreed for you to be my vice-president. I don't think it was an oil spill; I think chemical waste is being disposed into the rivers and seas.'

'We sent our men there; the report we got is an oil spill; you need to rest. You have lost so much weight and have been ill for over a week. The White House doctor is waiting for you. Everything will be taken care of; the most important thing to me is your health right now.'

'Thank you, Dan,' he says as the nurse assigned to him helps him out of the office.

He has less than six hours to live. The Tiallon poison has been given to him in small doses for the past week by the White House doctor. It is slowly killing him; it's colourless, tasteless and odourless. It will not be detected in his body even when a test is done; it will look like he had a heart attack.

I stand outside the door to the president's room with the Chief of Staff, special advisers and White House staff, waiting for an update. So many doctors are running in and out of the president's room, trying but failing to revive him. 'How can this happen?' I ask. 'He had a twenty-four-hour medical team around him.'

The White House doctor emerges, looking downcast. 'I am sorry to report that we have lost the president; he died in his sleep.'

Everyone turns and looks at me. 'Sir, you are now the president of the United States. President Dan Campbell, you need to address the citizens.'

*****

I walk into the building, and everyone is clapping and shouting. The big boss walks up to me, congratulating me on a job well done. 'But we still have a lot that needs to be done,' he says.

'Yes, sir!'

'Your predecessor was an idiot who refused to work with us; we have tons of chemical waste that still needs to be disposed of.

'We had to stop pumping it into the rivers and seas because the president suspected foul play even during his illness.

'Now that you have been declared the new president and have decided to work with us, unlike your predecessor, we have a common goal. I need you to dispose of the remaining chemical waste in the central water system; more people will die of all sorts of illnesses, but that is not our problem.'

The members of Blue Gama all come up to me, congratulating me on being the new president; I feel on top of the world.

The big boss has given me so many tasks that need to be done. The citizens of North America haven't seen anything yet; this is just the beginning of their nightmare.

Chapter Sixty-six: Lagos

Lola

Why do I feel like I am being followed? *Not again!* I say to myself. The situation in the country has got worse; people are now being kidnapped from their homes. The rate of killing has increased astronomically since the free market forces, supported by the government, have resulted in soaring inflation, rising prices and growing unemployment. Even the wealthy cannot enjoy their money because hoodlums target them.

A car moves in front of me and blocks my way. Two men carrying guns get out of the car and approach my vehicle. They tap the driver's side window with the end of their guns. I start to tremble.

'Madam, open your door and get out if you value your life.'

I raise my hands, shaking my head furiously. 'Are you going to kill me?'

'No one will hurt you; we just want your Range Rover.'

I open my door and I am told to lay down on the road. Other cars are reversing and trying to escape the scene, but no one was tries to help me.

One of the men gets into my car and they all drive off.

I sit on the road, tears falling down my face. Eventually, a car stops to help me. I don't hear what is being said to me; I can only think about what has just happened. I hate my life.

I am dropped in front of my house by a good Samaritan, telling me how dangerous it is to drive expensive cars in the city. People are hungry, they will do anything to survive; I'm lucky I wasn't killed.

I am so frustrated. I have just spoken to my dad, and he told me the perpetrators would be caught and dealt with. I have lost transmission, Gamaplug cannot communicate with my Range Rover. The economy has deteriorated so badly that the only way people can survive is to steal. You are afraid to leave your house because you might be killed. You stay in your home, and you can still be murdered.

My father told me not to worry about the car and just concentrate on my job as a new director for Bankyemo Oil & Gas Limited as he has just been awarded an exploration licence for oil and gas. I need to find out whether my father is a part of the group of people responsible for all that is happening in this country. I hope not, but I have a nagging feeling that Segun might be right; it is too coincidental.

***

In a secret building on Banana Island, the wealthy have gathered to congratulate themselves on the fear and confusion spreading across the continent. Citizens know never to trust the police, so whom would they call when they are in trouble – no one! They laugh hysterically as wine flows and food is served. The big boss appears and talks to those assembled, one by one, about the targets that need to be met.

'There has already been a hike in insecurity in the country, and people are terrified to leave their houses,' he tells them. 'I want the situation to be worse; supply the hoodlums with guns, allowing them the liberty to kill and kidnap. The continent will be in complete chaos and, when people are living in fear, we can coerce them into doing anything. Happy and secure people can't be easily manipulated, but desperate people will do anything to survive; they will turn against family and friends. The election is coming. We need this to happen fast.'

He turns to Mr Adeyemo. 'I heard that your daughter's car was stolen today; that should never happen to a member of Green Gama. Our families should be safe even when the world around us is crumbling. The stupid people who dared to touch your daughter have been caught and were executed immediately as they left the scene of the robbery. Your daughter's car is now parked in her compound. She will find the keys on the floor by her entrance door when she leaves the house.'

'Thank you very much, sir.'

'Understand this, everyone, we take care of our people, but we do not spare those who disobey us. The only reason your daughter is alive today is because of you, and that; I'll not spare her next time she tries anything stupid. Forewarned is forearmed.'

'Yes, sir! She'll not do anything foolish; she is traumatised about what happened today. She will be working for us, I promise you.'

'She better do, or you can bury your daughter, your choice. Enjoy yourself today. There is much to do, we will take over Africa, and no one can stop us.'

223

Lola

I wake up in the middle of the night. I am so emotionally drained; in just over a month, I have lost my building, my house was vandalised, and I have survived many attacks on my life. I am a walking target of bad luck; what are the odds of all the cars driving on the road that mine was the one targeted?

I need to switch on the security light in my compound; I have refused to hire another security guard. What help was the last one I hired? He couldn't protect me. But now I am beginning to rethink. At least if I die, someone will be able to tell my parents. I open the front door only to see my car keys on the floor. I don't understand; how did they get there? I walk outside and see my car parked on my compound. I look around. My gate is still locked; someone drove my car into my compound and left. How? Not again, I'm too tired!

Chapter Sixty-seven: Kabul

Ahmed

I stand behind Mohammed in the conference room, waiting for the few men and women allowed into the compound to plead their case to him. He sits on a specially made chair, higher than any other chair around him, behind bulletproof glass. This allows him to see the people, but they cannot come near him.

I watch as about twenty adults, some with their children, are told to kneel for Mohammed and not get up from the ground.

An elderly woman pleads her case to Mohammed. She states that the country is facing severe drought, animals and crops are dying, and she hasn't eaten in two weeks. She pushes her feeble daughter to kneel in front of her saying she is willing to sell her to him since she can't take care of her anymore. I watch the daughter, as tears roll down her cheeks. She can't be more than sixteen years old. Mohammed's right-hand men snigger as Jamil walks up to the girl.

'Stand up,' he says, 'and turn around.'

The girl struggles to stand up; I know she hasn't eaten in days; and timidly turns around as instructed.

'We can manage her,' Jamil says. 'How much do you want for your daughter? We can only afford five thousand Afghani.'

The woman bows her head to the floor in gratitude as the money is thrown on the floor. The little girl is pulled forcefully away from her mother as she tries to hold on tight to her.

'Take her to the madam,' instructs Mohammed. 'She will entertain me tonight.'

The woman takes the money without lifting her head and leaves the room.

I watch with great sadness as different people try to sell themselves, their daughters or their sons to Mohammed.

Some daughters are rejected, stating they are ugly and had lost too much weight. They look like boys. Some of them were bought to be cleaners and to wash clothes for their men. Those rejected were driven out without compassion; some were pleading for leftovers they were willing to collect food from the dustbin.

'Get them out of here,' says Mohammed, standing up. 'I hate to look at poverty-stricken people for too long.' I follow him and stand behind his door as he enters his office and closes the door.

Allah! I hate this man; I have to find a way to bring him down. I notice he wears a chain that he never takes off, with a pendant that looks like a key; I wonder what it opens?

I hear a loud sound in his office, and I rush to open the door, but it is locked. I bang on the door with my fist. 'Sir! Sir! Are you OK?'

The office door opens, and I see that Mohammed has pushed everything on his desk to the floor, including his laptop. I fall on both knees, picking things up off the ground, and I can see him pacing in his office angrily.

Omar enters the office and sees the mess on the floor. 'What happened?'

'Don't worry about it, leave my office now and close the door,' Mohammed says.

I catch fleeting resentment in Omar's face before it disappears, and he walks out of the office.

'I want him killed,' Mohammed says, looking at me. 'He has been trying to get my position for too long. I want him dead tonight; I'll use him as a scapegoat for the others vying for my position.'

He bangs his fist on the desk as I put everything back on it.

'Why did they stop the transfer of ten million dollars from entering my bank? They promised me that money to inflict dreadful carnage in the country,' he repeats to himself.

I follow behind as he enters the meeting room. All of his right-hand men are seated; Mohammed looks at me and nods. I walk over to Omar and pull him into the middle of the room. 'Get on the floor,' I say, placing my gun on his head.

'What is the meaning of this? How dare you!' screams Omar.

The meeting room door is blocked by Mohammed's bodyguards when some of the right-hand men try to walk away.

Sit down, all of you,' says Mohammed.

He addresses Omar, in a stern voice. 'I know that you want my position, and you are trying to kill me.'

'I would never do that,' pleads Omar. 'I have been with you for years;

why would you believe such lies.'

'You had a secret meeting with some of your men who are loyal to you.' The door of the meeting room is opened, and five men with bruised and cut faces are dragged into the room. 'Do you know how hard I worked to get to this position? Do you think you can eliminate me just like that? I have known for a while what your plans were, so I placed a mole in your midst to catch you red-handed.' One of the men stands up and brings out a recording of the meeting.

'Please! Please! I made a mistake; forgive me, remember our years together.'

Mohammed nods, I pull the trigger, and Omar slumps on the floor. The other four men are dragged outside to be killed. I point the gun at another of the right-hand men.

'Let this be a warning to you all; I will not hesitate to kill you if you mess with me,' says Mohammed. He then storms out of the room; and I follow closely behind.

***

Hussain Atta is in his office.

I have just spoken to Mohammed; the only way he is getting more money is if he can prove to me that he can make money from this crumbling economy. I have twenty-four other countries I am running. He has promised me he will increase taxes; if people can't pay, we take away whatever they own that is of value; if they don't have anything, then forced labour will be employed. Allah has given me these countries, and I take them with force.

Chapter Sixty-eight: Sydney

Henry

I switch on the television to relisten to the prime minister addressing the nation on fear of terrorism and national security.

'…that is why the House has approved the building of a nuclear plant in the country. This will mean our country does not have to depend on any other country for protection; the world is changing, and we have to make the protection of our citizens our number one priority. We live in constant fear of being attacked for no reason by people who hate us. We have relaxed the law for gun possession, and citizens are now allowed to buy guns for self-defence.'

I shake my head as the prime minister utters these words; things are already changing. Medicare was scrapped last week, and people are now forced to pay for medical care. I have never seen so much violence in the streets of Australia, police cars have been set on fire, homes vandalised and mass protests carried out in front of Government House. Now you want to give them guns so that can start killing each other?

I am sick of this group that I have been forced to join; they control the whole continent, they make all the political decisions. The prime minister is just the mouthpiece for the big boss. Many people have laboured for years and have now retired; but we are forced to announce that the government can no longer take care of them in spite of the many years they worked and paid taxes. They are forced to pay for their medical care at exorbitant prices run by White Gama. Their frustration is displayed in the continuous protests that have been going on non-stop for seven days now.

I switched off the television. Sadly, I was one of the ministers answering questions by the press about our decision on nuclear plants and health. To make matters worse, I can't find Mia, she disappeared into thin air two weeks ago. The police have closed my case telling me, my wife left me. I place my head on my pillow as I remember that horrible day when I opened the envelope after the party.

I didn't bother picking up the envelope as I stormed away, although I could hear my mum calling my name. Who the hell are these people to tell me to kill my wife? What has she done apart from the fact that she married me? I stood by the sea waiting for the motorboat to take me to the other side, seething with anger. I could never do this. My mum came and stood by my side. She had the envelope that I dropped in her hands. She rubbed my back. 'Honey, I know how you feel, but what choice do you have?'

I turned and looked her directly in the face. 'Who invited you to this godforsaken party, Mum?'

'The same people threatening you, I would do anything to protect you and my grandson.'

I laughed sarcastically. 'But that doesn't include Mia; why do you hate her so much? She hasn't done anything to you.'

'I don't hate her, but if they tell me to choose between you and her, I'll choose you always; that is what mothers do. The boat is here; let's talk when we get home.'

We were dropped at the shore where a black Jaguar was waiting to pick us up. I didn't speak to my mum throughout the journey. I just didn't get her. You should never wish death on anyone, especially your daughter-in-law, but she never liked Mia; I honestly think she was relieved when we separated. I entered the house and walked up to my old room, my mum following behind. 'Why are you so angry?' she asked. 'I wasn't the one that told you to kill her?'

'The problem is that you don't seem to think it matters if she dies.'

'Honey, these people are dangerous; they gave you twenty-four hours to kill your wife. The time starts now; I saw the driver press a stopwatch the minute you got out of the car. I don't want to lose you; if you don't do it, you will be killed instead.'

'I don't want my wife to die,' I told her.

'Then you have to think of something, and fast, but I don't want to lose you, so think wisely,' she said, as she walked out of the room.

I needed to do something; but what? I looked at the time. It was 5.00 am in the morning.

'Gama, connect me to Rob.'

'Hello, sir.'

'Rob, I need you to check up on my wife and make sure that she is safe, and I need you to do it now! When you get there give me a call,

OK?'

I went to take a shower, planning to sleep after.

My mobile connected as soon as Rob called.

'Sir,' I heard panic in his voice, 'I can't find your wife.'

'What do you mean you "can't find my wife"?' I rushed to get dressed as I had just got out of the bathroom.

'I went to your house as you instructed, but the front door was already open. I walked in. I didn't find anyone, the house was empty.'

'I don't understand. Has the house been vandalised? Were there any sign of struggle?'

'No, sir, it's as if she just disappeared without a trace.'

'Wait for me; I will be there shortly,' I said, as I raced to my car.

I walked into my house; the alarm was down, and there was no sign of forced entry. I checked my wife's room and I saw that some of her clothes had gone from the closet. Did she decide to just up and leave without Carl? It seemed impossible.

I called my mum to tell her about Mia's disappearance and she seemed genuinely shocked, because she was my number one suspect. The police came to investigate. I insisted that my wife would not just disappear, but I don't think they believed me, they thought she had left me.

***

Mrs Graham is in her study.

'Have you taken care of Mia, my son's wife?'

'Yes, Ma'am?'

'Good!'

The phone disconnects.

My son may think I am flawed but I would do anything to protect him; he is weak. That woman made him vulnerable, he needs a strong woman with the same focus as him by his side, not a sentimental weakling crying wolf all the time.

He doesn't understand that the big boss will not hesitate to kill him if he doesn't obey his instructions. I will help carry his burden so he doesn't have to feel the guilt of eliminating his wife himself.

Chapter Sixty-nine: Rio de Janeiro

Ana

I have hardly slept for two weeks as I go through the pictures sent to me by Antonio. The most powerful and successful people are in these pictures, but to what end?

The president has allowed more mining and agriculture in the Amazon Rainforest, stating that the country needs these natural resources to develop the nation; why should we let our people suffer while other nations take advantage of their natural resources and we don't?

My boss signed an agreement with the government that 40% of the profit generated would be given to the country, but, going through the figures, I see they are making more profit than what they have declared and the Rainforest is gradually being destroyed. This agreement is supposed to provide more jobs for the locals and improve the country's infrastructure, but none of that is being done. The poor are getting poorer, and the rich are getting richer. The margin is growing wider and wider by the day.

In the bid to survive, some are going into the oldest business, prostitution. To make matters worse, my sister is refusing to talk to me. I know Pedro is behind this. I'll talk to him today. He thinks he can use my sister to manipulate me, but I have been through hell and came out the other side.

I knocked on Mr Montes's door, I was told he wanted to see me.

'Come in!'

I enter the room and see Carlos and the lady I saw in Brazilian City Bank waiting for me alongside Mr Montes.

'Good, you are here, have a seat.'

I sat down timidly, as they smile at me.

'You have been doing an excellent job for us, but now you will be given higher responsibilities; you will not only be working for me but for the other board members as well. We have made money, we need the money to move from bank to bank worldwide discreetly, and I know you are the woman for the job,' says Mr Montes.

'We have been able to make billions of dollars in various businesses from mining, banking, and agriculture, the list goes on, and the necessary authorities have turned a blind eye to our various activities. Now we need this money distributed to seven different hubs, and we will also be receiving money from other designated accounts and banks.'

A laptop is placed in front of me. I am looking at more zeros than I have ever seen in my life.

'Each amount is broken down for various hubs and how much they will be receiving. Your job is to calculate, look carefully at the figures, make sure there are no discrepancies. When that is done, send the figures to Carlos. He knows what to do next.

'Let me introduce you to Fernanda; she said she met you at the bank, she is a bank manager, and she told me you have not been running the account you opened.'

She stands up and we shake hands. 'I don't need the money for anything,' I say.

'Anyway, you have done an excellent job so your salary will be increased, you'll be handsomely rewarded for any extra work. We have transferred a million dollars into your bank account. Make sure you run the account and enjoy your new life as a millionaire.'

I hear congratulations around me, but my head is spinning. 'Thank you,' is all I can say.

***

I knock on the door of my sister's house at 7.30 pm. I know her deadbeat husband will be home; I am not surprised when he opens the door.

'Your sister doesn't want to see you,' he says.

'I came to see you.'

I don't have anything to say to you.'

I laugh. 'You don't have to say anything, just listen. I know it was you who has manipulated my sister into not talking to me. Do you know that this new job, promotion and money can be taken away from you by just a phone call from me?'

'Then I am right. You don't wish us well; you are the only one that deserves a lavish lifestyle,' he responds angrily.

'You have not allowed me to see my sister and your children for two weeks. If you want to keep your job, fix what you broke because otherwise by tomorrow, I will make sure you are fired.'

I storm away, getting into my Mercedes Benz G-Wagon.

***

I settle down in the apartment to look at the spreadsheet given to me. It is the most complicated spreadsheet I have ever seen; these people are making money from so many businesses in South America, both legal and illegal; they even dabble in prostitution and human smuggling. I need to find a way out of this mess I have got myself into. How do they know so much about me? Every day I feel like I am digging my own grave. I look at the lavish apartment I live in, the car I drive, I am now a multimillionaire in Brazilian reals. I cover their crime by manipulating the figures; how am I different from them?

Gama connects a call and I hear my sister's voice.

'I heard that you threatened Pedro that if I don't talk to you, you will get him fired; why would you do that, knowing everything that we have been through?'

'Maria, you are my sister; you are all I have. Why would he tell you not to talk to me, and you agreed?'

'He wasn't the one who told me not to talk to you. I was just angry with you for keeping things from me; why didn't you tell me about all the good things that are happening to you? Do you now think you are better than us now?'

'Never, I can't think that. I was going to tell you, but you found out before I had the opportunity.'

'Whatever, I am only calling to tell you that if you ever want me to talk to you again, Pedro must not lose his job.'

The call disconnects.

That manipulative bastard!

Chapter Seventy: Hong Kong

Huan

I am surprised when the charges against my husband are dropped. No further investigation will be made into the case. How powerful are these people that a man with overwhelming evidence against him for the murder of three people can have his case dismissed and no one questions why? Agreeing to work with them is one of the biggest mistakes of my life, but what choice do I have? Either I agree or I die.

I welcome Chun home. He has a broken arm that happened recently and a bruised face. I tell him, 'You need to rest, then you will explain to me how you could place our lives in danger.'

I will never forget the fear I felt watching them kill Feng. I honestly thought I would be next. That was two weeks ago. There has been much death recently; billionaires dying from natural causes like a stroke, or heart attack, the numbers are too high to be just a coincidence. People on the list Feng showed me have now taken over the businesses of dead billionaires. This has led to much disruption to the economy; the manufacturing of goods that China is known for has stalled. The worst part is that no one is allowed to raise their voice and complain. This action of the government will affect the world as a whole; they have refused to export steel and coal for the next couple of months.

I have been kept alive only because of the 100% access given to Gama by all networks in Asia. We have been instructed to work with other network providers to provide them with unlimited access. They already have access to conversations and texts being made by the callers, but now they will be able to sync with all the applications on the phone to access people's bank statements, medical records and personal information; the possibilities are endless. If you go to the toilet, they will know. I have been working non-stop to make this a possibility.

I haven't tried to convince the CEO that it is not advisable for any company to have such power because this is bigger than him. Instructions do not come only from the CEO but the president of the nation as well, and I am certain that my boss is part of Asia 2. What that means I don't know.

***

I wake my husband up when I get back from work. I am informed by my temporary maid that he has been resting all day. I desperately need to know who Ms Yang is, I know she is not his mistress but those pictures I found on my bed raise a lot of questions.

'Chun, you need to explain to me what is going on? These people are becoming more and more powerful, they determine the economic growth of the country.'

'I'm sorry I got you involved in my mess, I just wanted to save that woman and her children.'

'Why would you say they are the only family you ever wanted?' I take out the pictures and throw them at him showing his familiarity with this woman and her kids.

He looks at the pictures. 'Don't believe what you see; I am not that close to her. She came to my security agency to buy protection for herself and her kids stating that their lives were in danger. I was hired by Lan Sòng about six months ago; I have seen her with him, so I know she was his mistress. I realised my life was in danger when I found out about those people taking over China. I knew my days were numbered. I didn't tell you anything because I was trying to protect you; I didn't know they would come after you to get to me.'

'Listen Chun, we are now a member of some group called Yellow Gama Asia 2. I know that the people on your list are members; they are taking over Asia. The only way to protect ourselves is to join; they have access to everything in people's lives. Things will go from bad to worse in the next couple of months.

'The death of those billionaires is all over the news; I am sure they were behind it. They have everyone's medical records, and it is easy to eliminate someone when you know everything about them. The money was siphoned from their accounts, and when the children of the deceased questioned the banks about their parents' money disappearing, they were told it was out of their hands. People think they killed themselves because they couldn't handle the shame of being broke.'

'I am sorry for getting you into this, but we need to find a way out

235

together.'

'The only way out is death; that is the option they gave me,' I say.

'We need to play along and discover as much as we possibly can; until we can find a way to bring them down.'

I sigh heavily. 'Have you eaten?'

'Yes, I just need to rest some more; I have not slept well in over a month, and I always keep an eye open for fear of my life.'

'Sleep then, we can talk later again when you have fully recovered, and maybe find a way out of this mess.'

***

Lan Sòng is standing in front of the big boss, giving his report on his assignment.

'We were able to stall the manufacturing company from producing anything for the next month, and our natural resources will not be exported for the next couple of months. This will cause a problem all over the world because they depend on us the most. I know many people's lives will be affected negatively in this country, but who will they complain to if they die. It doesn't bother us; the most important thing is that it is for our good. Companies will become desperate, but we only sell to our members in various part of the world, they will control those whom they will sell to. We will monopolise the world market.

'We have become more powerful than ever. We have approval from governments all over the world to give you full access to their mobile network; making it easy to destroy someone; all we have to do is change their medical records, and the doctors will mistakenly diagnose something that will lead to their death. The possibilities are endless.

'We will rule the world; there is no stopping us now!'

The End

Fred Demson

I put my feet up, smoking my cigar in my state-of-the-art penthouse overlooking Central Park. My personal assistant is standing in front of me.

'I need you to set up a meeting with the head of each hub, and I need them in New York in two days. We need to discuss the way forward.'

'It will be done right away, sir,' he said, walking away.

I need to move to the next level of my plan. My deputies have recruited some highly powerful personnel, but we need more. Everybody has a price; we just need to find it. I chuckled, opening my 'Domaine Leroy' wine to drink.

'My greatest desire is to take over the world. Very soon, the world will feel more pain!'

WATCH OUT FOR VOLUME 2 – *POWERA!*

Character/Place List

<table>
<tr><td>

A
Ademola Adetokunbo Street (Lagos)
Ahmed Nazar (Kabul)
Aisha, Ahmed's wife (Kabul)
Ahedan, militants (Kabul)
Abdul, Ahmed's son (Kabul)
Ana Santos, accountant, widow (Rio de Janeiro) works at Platoon PLC
Antonio Gomes (Lagos)
Abdul-Ali, part of Ahedan (Kabul)
Paul Appleby, Secretary of State for the Environment, Food and Rural Affairs (London)
Asokoro, where Lola's parents live (Lagos)
Ampropaim, antidepressant drug
Angela, police office and her partner, Steve (Sydney)
Andrew Lawrence, CEO of Largas Corporation, the biggest broadcasting network in North America
Asia_1 and Yellow Gama
Asia_2 and Yellow Gama
Australia Hub of White Gama

</td></tr>
<tr><td>

B
Bobby, a New York cop, and Martin's partner
Principal Baker, NY
Brenda, PR (London)
Bruce Cole, the richest man in the world
Bankole Gerald, former governor of Lagos State
Blue Gama, North America Hub
Bestfood, the largest food wholesaler in the UK
Banana Island (Lagos)
Bankyemo Oil & Gas Limited, Lola's new job (Lagos)

</td></tr>
<tr><td>

C
Chidi, son of the woman in the flood (Lagos)

</td></tr>
</table>

Carl, Henry's son (Sydney)
Chioma, Lola's murdered friend (Lagos)
Carlos Ribeiro, the head personal assistant to Mr Montes
Chun, Huan's husband
Charles, PI, employed by Jude
Charlotte, Martin's daughter (NY) Leila & Charlotte
Cheung Wu, trusted friend and employee of Chun (HK)
Chyou, female bodyguard (HK)
Captain Marcus (NY)
Canberra, Prime Minister's Office (Australia)

D
Ms Dias; the temporary accountant during Ana's absence (Rio)
Demalon, drug (London)
Domaine Leroy, expensive wine
President Dan Campbell, president of the US (when the president is poisoned)

E
Ella, Jude's ex, London
Emeka, Chioma's fiancé (Lagos)
Emilia, Martin's daughter (NY)
Ebute Meta (Lagos)
Edward, Martin's friend and hacker (NY)

F
Fred Demson, founder of Gama
Francisca Dias, murdered accountant (Lagos)
Frank, Lola's contact in IT (Lagos)
Feng (HK)
Feng Zhao, Chun's colleague/employee (HK)
Fernanda, bank manager (Rio)

G
Gama Labs
Gamaplug
Gamaplug N24 postnanometer

George, restaurant manager (Jude)
George and William, restaurant workers (Jude, London)
Ghani, head of security, Ahedan Group
Green Gama, African Hub

H
Harper, Bobby's girlfriend
Henry Graham. Minister for Defence (Sydney)
Huan Li (Hong Kong) Chief Technical Officer of Yamson Telecommunications company, the biggest in Asia.
Hussain Atta, Yusuf's boss (Kabul)
Hoi, Huan's chauffeur (HK)

I
Ikoyi, a posh neighbourhood in Lagos / where Lola lives
Ibrahim, the owner of Afghan TV (Kabul)

J
Jane Brown, Fred Demson's wife (the Browns are a monied family)
Jason Atkinson Jnr. opposition leader (Sydney)
Jaiora, 1953 vintage wine
Jude Williams (London), successful chef
Jackson Paul, the prime minister (Sydney)
Juliana (Lagos)
Ju Liáng, Fujian Chun's call history shows call to her (HK)
Jabar, Hussain's contact in the compound (Lagos)
JPH publishing company (Lagos)
Jamil (Kabul)
John Bennett (London), Jude's business partner and member of Red Gama

K
Kandahar (Kabul)
Kirribilli Harbour (Sydney)
Khost (Afghanistan)
Kung Group (HK)

Katy, Jude's illegitimate daughter

Khan, one of Mohammed's right-hand men (Kabul)

L

Lola Adeyemo, a journalist (Lagos) / also owns a beauty range called Moshébì Cosmetics.

Laila, Ahmed's daughter (Kabul)

Liam, assistant of the mayor, New York

Leah, Martin's wife (NY)

Lily, the mayor's daughter (NY)

Ling, Huan's personal assistant (HK)

Lucy; Carl's 'friend.'

Latif, the head bodyguard (Kabul)

Lucas, security at Ana's new apartment

Mr Lan Sòng; owns the largest shares in real estate development for Liquid Holdings (HK)

M

Martin Hills, New York, a cop (has a wife and two daughters)

'Martin Osborne Hills' and 'Mary Ashley Cox' Martin and fake wife

Mr Matthew Cleborne (mayor) New York

Mia, Henry's wife (Sydney)

Marcus, the name of the man Ella cheated on Jude with

Martha, Bobby's wife (NY)

Mohammad Pir, Ahedan Group leader

Hon. Matthew Cornwell (Sydney)

Maria, Ana's sister (Rio)

Mr Montes, CEO of Ana's company (Rio)

Mike, Roger Smith's partner

Musa, Lola's security man at her address (Lagos)

Michele, Roger's ex (London)

Martha, Bobby's ex-wife (NY)

Márcia, Ana's new personal assistant (Rio)

Moska, a prostitute given to Ahmed

N

Judge Noah Clark (London)

Nader, one of Mohammed's henchmen
NBS News (Lagos)

O

Obedian, an opposition group to the militants (Kabul)
Omar, one of Mohammed's henchmen (Kabul)

P

Parliament House (Sydney)
Pedro, Ana's husband (Rio)
Purple Gama, Rio (South America)

Q

Qiang Lin, the private investigator (HK)

R

Rafael Lima; owner of Brazilian City Bank, the largest bank in the country (Rio)
Rob. Henry's assistant, Sydney
Mr Robinson, Head of Australian intelligence (Sydney)
Roger Smith, sergeant, London
Rocinha on the favela hill (Rio)
Red-gate School, Lily's school, (NY)
Mr Ribeiro - Carlos (Rio)
Robert, Jude's mum's boyfriend (London)
Red Gama, European Hub

S

Stella Cleborne, mayor's wife, New York
Stephanie, mayor's assistant, New York
Shawn, Evelyn and Jason, are suspects in cyber hacking (Sydney)
Sade, Lola's friend (Lagos)
Stanley (HK)
Susanne Waters, the richest woman in Europe and owns the biggest beauty empire.
Segun, Lola's helper (Lagos)
Sham Shui PO in the Kowloon district (HK)

Sam Philips the founder and CEO of Sam Wholesale
Sam Wholesale, a competitor in the food chain (London)
Sarah Phillips, daughter of the above

T
Tiallon, odourless, tasteless, colourless poison
Tör Ghar mountain (Kabul)
Top Hong Kong Detectives (HK)
President Thomas Green USA; USA President
Tom, Mrs Graham's security man (Sydney)

V
Vanessa Allen (woman impersonating someone having an
affair with Martin) NY

W
William, a waiter at Jude's restaurant (London)
White Gama, Australia hub

X
Xiuying, Qiang's business partner
Mr Xuē, one of the richest men in China (HK)

Y
Yichen, delivery team leader at Yamsen (Hong Kong)
Yusuf, Ahmed's friend (Kabul)
Ms Yang & kids, murder victims/mistress (Hong Kong)
Mr Young, Carl's science teacher, (Sydney)

Z
Zhao, lawyer, Huan (HK)

About the Author

Josephine Ronk lives in England with her husband and children.

Her life is mostly spent multitasking, writing her books and raising her kids. She developed her passion for writing at a young age. She loves to create powerful characters that are mysterious and allow you to unlock your imagination to infinite possibilities, though she did not start writing until later in life after being encouraged by her loved ones to just start.

Once she started, she became hooked. When not writing in her favourite library, she spends most of her time reading, cooking, and travelling the world with her family.

Make sure to follow Josephine Ronk on Amazon, Facebook, Twitter, and Instagram. Sign up for her newsletter to get all the information about upcoming releases.

Website: http://www.josephineronkauthor.com